Dust, Grit, and Vengeance
Drew Baker

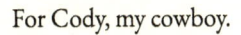

For Cody, my cowboy.

Prologue

An arrow of dust shot across the desert with a lone rider at its tip. In the dark cold of desert dusk, the man's breath steamed thick as locomotive smoke and his horse's bloomed the same. It was the heavy breathing of a man on a mission; assertive yet steady. He galloped toward the city of Graben, which lay before him ripe and ready to be plucked; a darling sprout in an otherwise barren landscape. The West would soon be his, for he was advancement, he was industry, and Graben was just another section of track to lay along his path.

Sunset was fresh along the horizon then, and a long shadow fell upon Graben. The man, Casey Calhoun, saw that it looked like a grasping hand laying its weight over the city.

Fitting, he thought, and rode on.

In the distance, hanging high above the plateaus that surrounded the Graben Valley, a swollen storm cloud flickered hot with blue lightning. *Heat* lightning, Casey thought with a smile.

Dry lightning.

A thunderclap ricocheted across the valley, agitating a visible wave of dust from the earth as it passed. Carrion birds squalled, settled. The ground before Casey obscured itself under a haze of fine desert dust. Behind him, it kicked up into an angry yet focused beam, aimed directly at Graben.

"Good," Casey said to the desert, then threw his right arm free from his coat. He leaned over, straddling his galloping Arabian, and held an open palm below the sea of free-floating dust. It parted like ruddered water.

Casey's fingers tingled beneath the dust, and he felt a hot power surge through his body. Strength, dominion, and the Grit of Man. The dust changed course, ever-so-slightly at first, pulled by the wake of his power. Casey lifted his hand and pointed his palm toward Graben.

He *pushed;* not physically, but with the Grit contained within him. The dust and sand rushed forward, building pressure, building speed, until it became a great wave bearing down the valley. Casey Calhoun had brewed a sandstorm, and drove it right through the streets of Graben.

With the obfuscating dust as a cover, Casey strode into town, unbothered and unrecognized. That was good, for he had grown a reputation in Arizona. None with half a mind dared cross him, but it was nice to be invisible for a night of slaughter. They might suspect his responsibility for what was to come, but none that might see his face would live to tell.

Casey crossed a street corner, where several horses were tied to a hitching post, ducking their faces away from the blowing sand. He got close, squinted hard, and recognized the horses. They belonged to Cassidy Reeve and a few other members of Casey's crew.

He turned down an alley and came upon a large manor with a grand courtyard, though the sand in the air made it exceedingly difficult to see. Still, he knew the yard would be empty. Above, sweet music leaked from an open window and the muffled chatter of a fancy ball whispered faintly into the night. A dark figure was lurking on the steps before the manor's front doors, barely visible in the haze.

"The staff?" Casey asked, approaching the figure.

"Dispatched," Cassidy's voice replied, hard and smooth like old wax. Under the cover of the sandstorm, Casey could make out none of the woman's striking features. That was fine, for he already knew her face well.

Casey held his wrist up to Cassidy's face, letting her read the time on his golden wristwatch. It was half past midnight. "Give me ten minutes," he said to the woman. "The others?"

"Making clear the surrounding street," Cassidy said. "Guns blazing?"

"Of course." Casey smiled.

While he could manipulate sand with his Grit, Casey Calhoun still preferred the feeling of a gun in his hand. Men were more easily persuaded when staring down a barrel of iron.

Cassidy opened the door and ushered Casey through. She remained outside. *Ten minutes.*

Blue cigar smoke and sultry parlor music swirled sweetly through the air inside the manor. The foyer—currently vacant—was grand indeed. Expensive red tapestries hung from the walls, draping over exotic wood molding. Golden sconces provided warm lamp light. Gold *plated*, Casey noted.

Gold was coveted above all. It was strength and power, not to be wasted on lighting fixtures. Casey believed gold was meant to be *used*. Most people assumed gold to be precious from its rarity alone, but Casey thought differently. It was his gold that gave him power, one way or another. His wristwatch. His bracelets. His necklace. His pendants. All those things made him a man in the most fundamental way. He *owned*. He controlled. And people were smart to recognize that.

Casey came to a set of swinging doors. Beyond, the grand ballroom waited. His hand fell to his hip, and he rubbed his thumb up and down the grip of his Colt.31 revolver. He traced the argyle pattern carved into the walnut with his nail. Of his many tics, this one pleased him the most. It was that familiar pattern in his hand that gave him his other power. The power over life itself.

He entered the ballroom.

Now, bathed in golden light and through clean air, the attendants could see well enough the man that had come to end the party. Casey Calhoun was tall and handsome, with a jawline that could cut oak and stubble to sand it smooth. His black hair was neatly greased back like crude oil over a field of alfalfa. He ran his palm up his forehead, making sure the perfect hair was still in place. He smiled at the crowd.

Casey could see a pit as black as his hair sink into all their hearts. They knew him, and in that moment wished they didn't. Worried eyes watched as he crossed the ballroom.

On a bench near a window, Sarah Dallas and Emma West had been having a deep conversation. Makeup smeared down Sarah's face. She had been crying. Emma rubbed Sarah's knee, consoling her. The window behind them stood tall and loomed with indifference. Casey nodded to the women as he passed.

He also noticed Homer Dallas—Sarah's husband—standing before a grand fireplace, teetering drunkenly like an inverted pendulum. Homer tipped a glass back and poured a large gulp of liquor down his throat. The man burped, liquor dancing in his stomach, threatening to come back up. Absently, he stared out into the ballroom, clearly oblivious of Casey's passing—likely the only one. He would be dead in minutes, with fresh whiskey draining from the bullet holes in his belly.

Near the center of the ballroom, at a small round table, sat Thomas and Harriet Abernathy and Edgar Lawrence. Casey had been looking for Thomas Abernathy for quite some time now, and a festering anger returned to him when he saw the pissant of a man. Edgar Lawrence sat across from Harriet, and Casey noticed the woman's foot buried deep in Edgar's lap. She held her arms folded and distinguished above the table, showing no signs of the dirty game she played with her husband's business partner below. *What might Thomas think of that?* Casey wondered with a sly smile.

The men grew silent as Casey approached their table. He heard Harriet's heel click back to the marble floor and imagined Edgar's erection shrinking away in fear.

"Mr. Calhoun, what a pleasant surprise," Thomas said as he stood and held out a hand. "Had I known you were coming, I would have brought you a—" His eyes shifted uncomfortably. "Well, I hope you'll settle for a drink instead." His hand remained extended, waiting for Casey to shake it.

Casey only stared back. He couldn't bring himself to shake hands with the coward. Thomas finally withdrew his hand and returned to his seat. Casey took an empty seat across the table.

"Please, continue your earlier conversations," Casey said, gesturing to Edgar Lawrence.

"We were just—" Edgar started.

Casey interrupted immediately. "Enough. I don't care after all." He turned to Thomas again. "You've made me angry," he said plainly.

"Mr. Calhoun," Thomas said, "I would never do anything to upset you. You know that! I can assure you—"

"Shut up." Casey snapped. "I didn't come here for *who-did-what*s. You owe me, and I've had a rather difficult time of finding you. It would seem that you've been avoiding me."

The smell of urine rose from Thomas's lap. "O-okay, Casey. I'm really sorry. Whatever I can do to make this right, I will. I just need a little more—"

Casey held a hand up and shushed, then sighed as if the conversation was nothing more than a minor annoyance. In reality, this was a big deal to Casey, but he wasn't about to let Thomas know that. "Do you think I would be where I am today if I let every other asshole off that easy?" he asked casually, then laid his pistol on the table in front of him.

Thomas's eyes grew wide and he started to sputter. "I—I—Oh God, Casey, please. Not here. Not in front of my wife." Sweat burst from the pores on his forehead and joined the tears that had begun coursing down his cheeks. He took a sip of whiskey, the ice in the glass rattling with his shaking grip.

The double doors to the ballroom swung open just then, and Casey's crew of gunslingers entered with their weapons drawn. A Black woman stepped forward, holding a shotgun in each hand. She parted the dreadlocks hanging over her face with the barrel of one of her shotguns, revealing a constellation of freckles on her cheekbones. The crowd gasped, for they knew her too. Some began praying. Others chugged their drinks, hoping to black out before they found themselves on the other end of Cassidy's barrels.

She shouted over the crowd. "The first person to try anything smart is gonna lose their brains! My fingers are feeling restless, so keep your own off your hips unless you think you're quicker!"

Casey smiled, proud of his woman and satisfied with the smell of piss wafting up from Thomas's side of the table. "Thank you, Cassidy," Casey said, then raised his own gun at Thomas's head. "The thing is, Tom, I ain't gonna kill you tonight. You owe me, and you're useless dead."

"Sir—"

"So, what do you say? You think I can count on you going forward?"

Thomas, stupidly, started to protest. "Well, I'm sure this is not the—"

KA-BLAM!

Edgar's head burst open, spraying blood and brain across the table. Smoke drifted from the end of Casey's revolver, whose face had become a wicked mask of blood and viscera. A unanimous scream filled the room.

"Nobody move!" Cassidy shouted, raising her shotguns at the crowd. They screamed again as her guns scanned their faces.

Harriet threw up into her lap, clearing the bits of brain and skull that had found their way into her mouth. Casey aimed at her head, then, and stood.

"Do you think I can count on you, Tom?" Casey shouted. His greasy black hair had fallen out of place and now hung before his eyes.

"Yes! Yes, whatever you want!" Thomas cried, snot spewing from his nose.

Somewhere a woman cried out and fainted, her body crashing into a table full of fine china and glassware.

"Great," Casey said with a smile. "That wasn't so hard, now was it?"

Harriet wiped the mess from her chin, then stood and pointed a finger at Casey. "You'll hang fo—"

KA-BLAM!

Harriet's head blew out the back.

Another round of screaming.

Thomas choked back a scream of his own, instead only letting out a pitiful gargle of bile.

Casey pulled a handkerchief from his pocket and began wiping the fresh blood off his watch and pistol. Then he said, calmly, "'If a man commits adultery with the wife of his neighbor, they shall both be put to death.' Leviticus, I believe. I did you a favor, Tom." Casey groaned, pretending as if this caused him awful grief. "Now you owe me twice."

"You're a monster." Thomas sobbed.

A squabble broke out on the far side of the ballroom. Someone tried for their weapon, and one of Casey's men dashed his head before he could cause too much of an issue. Nobody else tried anything more.

Casey pulled Thomas up from the table by his arm, then asked, "How is that young boy of yours? Gary is his name, isn't it? I'm sure you will raise him to be quite the man someday, won't you, if given the opportunity?"

Thomas scowled and spat a glob of blood and snot onto the floor. "You won't be around to find out." He threatened.

Casey laughed. "Save the attitude for after you do your job."

"I seriously don't know where—"

"Shush." Casey cooed, almost kindly. "Let's go for a walk, just the two of us."

Casey pulled Thomas out of the ballroom through the swinging doors. Once in the foyer, Casey put his arm around Thomas's shoulder and spoke calmly. "All I need is an address. I think you could have managed at least that."

"I'm sorry, sir. As I've told you before, I know he lives in Bluff's Reach, but that's all!" Thomas began to heave, the sobs growing in his throat.

"Hush, hush. We will get this matter settled, don't you worry."

Casey led the man out into the night, where the sandstorm was now settling into a low blanketing haze like cold morning fog. He ran his hand through his hair, fixing the stray locks back in place. "Oh, and Thomas, let's keep this business to ourselves, shall we?"

The manor's grand doors swung shut behind the two men, and a barrage of muffled gunfire snuck out into the night.

***

Thomas Abernathy's body was found four days later, bloated and purple, floating down the Colorado River. Nips of flesh were missing from his belly and back, having been picked at by crayfish and carrion birds. The body was mutilated in other ways as well, and the authorities were glad they didn't have to explain *that* to his wife. She, and a dozen other people, had been found massacred in a Graben banker's manor the morning after an unexpected sandstorm.

Nothing had been stolen from the manor. It appeared to the authorities that this was a business deal gone horribly wrong. And Thomas Abernathy had apparently been on the wrong side of that deal. With whom, they didn't know for certain. But the scatter of shotgun shells found among the ballroom massacre gave them a pretty good idea.

PART ONE

GRIT

1

The desert sun baked down on Luke Morgan as he rode along the edge of a tall plateau—his lips drying to tack. He bore east toward a massive bluff that overshadowed Lake Powell, where the town of Bluff's Reach perched magnificently. Luke had left his home in Bluff's Reach the previous day, spent the night on the road, and returned again in the morning, though not as himself. That day, the young man rode in as Sam Clangour, outlaw.

His ride galloped steadily, unaware or uncaring about its purpose.

Sam looked to the right, where the cliffs sloped down into a valley of tiered escarpments. It looked like the staircase of giants. At the bottom, the Colorado River meandered its way southwest. Sam wondered how long the battle between river and land had waged on; he figured it may well have been forever. Downstream from Lake Powell, the grand city of Graben grew from the sands like an orchard of brick and steel. Rusty smokestacks rose above the town, spewing black soot into the dry air. Hundreds of bustling carriages swarmed the city—a colony of ants in the distance—and a web of railroad tracks converged along the city's western edge. A single track ran southwest along the Colorado toward California.

Graben was the fastest growing city in Arizona, and its connection to California made the city's owning class extremely wealthy. The wealthiest among them had built the town of Bluff's Reach on the tip of the Powell Bluff. There, they lived together in opulence and watched down over their precious possession: Graben itself. As such, both places were ripe for thievery. Corruption poisoned Graben, and though Bluff's Reach had thus far stayed peaceful, its riches proved to be a major temptation.

Leaning forward, Sam stroked his ride's muscular neck. "How you doing, gal?" he asked the creature. Though it did not reply, he knew it was fine. The horse was Sam's—not Luke's—and was made for riding hard. Skinny, wiry muscles propelled the animal. A stranger looking at the mount would have no doubts about its purpose: to flee. When pushed hard, it ran like a thunderclap. Not like Luke's horse—now stashed in a private little barn halfway to Graben—which was bulky and lumbering. *His* was a casual ride, bred to bring a man from town to town with little urgency, and nothing more. Sam kicked at his horse's sides and it ran harder.

Guilt picked at Sam as he make his way across the plateau. More accurately, it picked at Luke. Sam was not a man that had guilts. He was an outlaw, and felt no remorse for his actions. That was what his persona was *supposed* to feel, anyway. But Luke felt the crushing weight of his crimes as heavily as a landslide. He often wondered about the fairness of his situation. He had a gorgeous home in Bluff's Reach, something most people could only dream of having. And though his friends and family saw Luke Morgan as a successful businessman, Sam Clangour and his *business associates* knew the harsh truth. He was a thief and a liar, though the latter seemed more shameful than the former.

Yet, beats of justification always managed to thrum through the man's heart. The people of Bluff's Reach were not so innocent themselves. They were businessmen of Graben, and almost certainly operated with less than noble business practices. Some may have even killed to gain the power and influence they now held. Sam was only stealing from these people. He had never killed, *would* never kill. Sure, he had roughed guys up before, but nothing more than that.

A soft wind picked up, driving lines of light dust across the plateau like ocean currents. *How easy it might be*, Luke thought, *if he could control the sands.* But unlike his boss, Luke had no Grit. He wasn't as rough a man as Casey Calhoun, though Sam Clangour put on an almost believable show.

No matter how much he bargained with himself, Luke Morgan would always feel shame and guilt about his profession. That would never change. The lie itself was harrowing enough. *What would my husband think*, Luke wondered, *if he knew the truth*? Like everyone else, Kootala believed that Luke was a traveling businessman. The money Luke brought in paid for their house and kept Kootala comfortable—and more importantly, safe. To Luke, that's all that really mattered.

To know these things would crush Kootala. *That* tore Luke up more than anything. But Luke Morgan's feelings didn't pay back Sam Clangour's debt, so he rode on.

Sam soon approached Bluff's Reach, then briefly stopped a good distance away. The town sat in silence, waiting for him to come and violate it. He hesitated. It would be the first time he robbed his own town. His neighbors and friends. *Luke's* neighbors and friends.

The road was empty, still early in the day, and Sam would be easily spotted if anyone was watching. Before going any closer, he pulled a long white horsetail wig over his head, tucked the untempered strands behind his ears, and fixed it in place with his wide-brimmed hat. He ran his thumb across his upper lip, tracing the gnarly slash scar that Casey had given him years ago. Sam would often stroke his scar before a job, hoping it might miraculously be gone. Yet it always remained; a reminder of his past and his debt.

Sam pulled a black bandanna up over his nose—concealing the last of Luke Morgan—and rode into Bluff's Reach.

***

Kootala Morgan hammered a nail through a poster, attaching it firmly against a wall outside the sheriff's office. He stood back—hammer hung from his hip and a bucket of nails in his hand—reading the poster.

Wanted: Information Leading to the Arrest of the Outlaw Known as Cassidy Reeve.

The poster displayed a rough sketch of the woman, including a brief description; freckles under her eyes, a beehive of dreadlocks, usually seen with two shotguns. The reward: four hundred dollars. Her last known location was Graben. There was no reason to believe she would come to Bluff's Reach, but the poster cautioned anyway.

Remain alert to her presence. Contact local authorities, and do not engage the woman.

Kootala felt a seething hatred for the woman on the poster. His blood steamed at the mere glance of the crude illustration. The way she lived, the barbarism of it, was antithetical to Kootala's way of being. He was a man of peace and justice; she was a woman of brutality for the sake of greed. It was a poison, Kootala thought, a deep evil that had no place in his world. *Tama take her.*

You've never been so angry as to fight? Luke had once asked Kootala, not believing.

I've found anger often, Kootala had responded. *But only once to fight.*

As a boy, Kootala had lived the streets with his mother, long before Luke had taken him in. It hadn't been easy, and there were many times when that life had tempted anger. Once, Kootala had thrown rocks at another boy who had stolen their food. His mother scolded him for the action.

But we are hungry, Kootala had argued.

Is he not, as well? she responded. *And were not the first people hungry, when Kongwuti fed them mud? All creatures deserve compassion, Kootala. Even the wretches.*

A mother's scolding—and the disappointment in her eyes—hurt Kootala more than the loss of the day's food. Since then, he had never shown violence, never acted on anger, no matter how inflamed his heart might be. Now, with his mother gone, that virtue was more important than ever.

With the wanted poster in place, Kootala retired inside the sheriff's office. He placed the tools and nail bucket inside a metal locker near the door.

"Thanks for that, kid," Sheriff Abner Brooks said while sitting at his desk, penciling something into a ledger. He bookmarked the page and closed it with a heavy thump. "If you're for it, I was thinking we take a walk to the bakery and have a chat with Sue Barlow."

"Why so?" Kootala asked, leaning over the desk on his elbows.

Abner smiled pleasantly, wrinkling his eyes and wiggling the squirrel tails he wore for eyebrows. On his lip sat a large mustache to match. "Mrs. Barlow's about twelve dollars short on her taxes. I figure we'd let her know, and maybe I'll buy something while there. Etta's been dying for fresh rolls lately." The sheriff took a coffee tin from his desk drawer and pulled out a wad of cash. "I think fifteen aught to cover the rolls and a few loaves of bread, don't you say?" He gave Kootala a playful smile. "Unless, course, you're too busy."

Kootala agreed to go. "Sir, of course I'm not busy."

As sheriff and clerk in Bluff's Reach, the two were rarely busy, if ever. Brooks handled the occasional drunken disturbance, and as sheriff, he acted as a mediator between domestic disputes. Other than some minor misbehavior, the jail cells always remained empty.

The residents of Bluff's Reach kept trouble *outside* their little paradise town as best they could. On the bluff, they dealt behind closed doors and outsourced their violence to Graben. The town of Bluff's Reach was, in its entirety, their home. They owned it, and they made sure to keep it nice.

For Kootala, sheriff's clerk was the perfect job. It was safe, easy, and for the most part enjoyable. He did not need the money; Luke made enough for the both of them. Yet Ron Barker didn't need to doctor. The Lybucks didn't need the money from the general store. And Bill Williams didn't need to run the saloon. But they all worked anyway, because in Arizona, 1872, you had to do something lest you lose your mind from boredom. When your partner was constantly away on business, that was more true than ever.

The only resident who seemed tight on cash was Sue Barlow. Something about her husband and the war... she never got into details. Yet the townsfolk never let her fall too far behind. She was the kindest of them, and they always returned the favor.

Sheriff Brooks and Kootala walked down Main Street toward the bakery. Someone had dumped a trough of water into the street. The water had saturated the mudcracks and made the street steam like baking bread. It was a sweltering day, like most on the plateau—no matter how close they were to Lake Powell. Sometimes, the heat made Kootala want to dive off the edge of the bluff into that cool blue water.

Brooks removed his hat and wiped the sweat off his forehead with a handkerchief. He was balding, and always wore his hat to keep from burning the dome of his head. He kept a single live bullet tucked into the hat band, which now glinted sunlight into Kootala's eyes.

Kootala had wondered about that bullet often, but never asked about it. The men of Bluff's Reach—as well as Graben, and even greater Arizona—kept strange rituals. Superstitions, tics, whatever they were, it was best you never mentioned them.

The bakery had a whimsical porch, painted with light pinks and blues, with a swinging bench and a potted bunion cactus near the steps.

The men entered the establishment, and Sue Barlow greeted them with a friendly smile. The sweet aroma of blooming yeast filled the air. It reminded Kootala of the baker in Tucson who used to give him day-old loaves for a penny each.

"Can I get you boys some coffee?" Mrs. Barlow asked, setting the men at a small table.

"That'd be good, Sue," Abner said warmly.

"None for me," Kootala said. "But I could use a glass of cold water if you have any."

"You're in luck," said Sue as she took a fistful of her dress's ruffles and went behind the counter. She put on a fresh pot of coffee, strong and smelling like earth and char. "What are you two up to today, anyway?"

Kootala replied first. "Just making our rounds, ma'am."

Sue Barlow rolled her eyes. "About that Cassidy Reeve..." She trailed off.

Abner cleared his throat. "You've heard?"

"Oh, yes, of course. Absolutely awful." She set the men's drinks at their table. "You really think *she* did all that? She must have had help. And *why*? What could she *possibly*—"

The sheriff coughed. "I ain't supposed to talk about the details. Try to keep the rumors at a minimum, aye?"

"Yes, my bad," Sue said. "I try to remain skeptical about the things I hear, especially coming from Bill Williams' mouth. But anyway..." She trailed off.

"Anyway," Abner said. "We came for another reason. Your taxes are behind, Sue."

"Right, right," she said, huffy. "I mean to get that to you, but, well—"

"It's twelve dollars. Get it to us when you can," Abner said, then pulled the wad of cash from his coat pocket, handing it to the woman. "A pan of sweet rolls and three loaves of bread, please."

"Oh, but that's too much, please!" Sue held the money out, trying to give it back. "A loaf of bread is only—"

Abner pushed Sue's hand back. "For the bread, the coffee, and your hospitality. But don't forget your taxes, please."

Sue Barlow's face dawned with realization, and she seemed to do the math in her head. She blushed, then curtsied ever so slightly. "My thanks. You really are too kind. The both of you!"

Kootala remembered when just ten dollars seemed like an unimaginable amount of money. Before Luke took him in, he was lucky to find more than a few pennies a day. A nickel was good luck, a dime was a godsend. Kootala's mother hated the idea of money, but it kept them fed as they worked their way north. 'Twas the life of a nomad, though they never did make it to Hoki territory. Kootala's mother had died in Graben.

The bakery remained empty of other patrons, so the men stayed and chatted with Sue for a time.

"When did Luke last leave?" Sue asked of Kootala.

"Just yesterday, and he isn't due back until tomorrow evening at the earliest," Kootala said. *It was a routine trip*, Luke had told him. *Meet with a few mining investors, have a fancy dinner with them, that kind of thing.*

"Oh, well I hope nothing happens in Graben like last week. So terrible." She shook her head in feigned grief, as if she knew everyone that had been lost in the massacre. *Perhaps she had*, Kootala thought.

"Yes," Kootala said. "I worry for him every day."

The crime in Graben was growing, and Kootala worried every time Luke traveled down there for work. They had the money to retire and settle down at home, and Kootala wished they would. Yet there he was, working, too. The irony was hard to ignore.

2

Sam Clangour rode casually though the northern outskirts of Bluff's Reach, where the roads had been empty, and none had seen him ride in. *Good,* he thought. *Better to attract no attention.* Escape would be easy enough—his ride was plenty fast—but to fail his task would be trouble on its own. One did not screw up Casey Calhoun's plans.

The homes north of town were larger than the rest (which were impressive in their own right), and clad with decorative brick and ornate fixtures. It was a pageantry of wealth, and although Sam felt remorse for stealing from them, he figured they wouldn't hurt all that much. What's one gold watch to a man with a hundred? About a month of work, if that. They'd recover.

He passed the estate of a Graben bank owner, where the home's shadow loomed out over the street and onto the opposite lot. As Sam crossed the shadow, he wondered about the predatory mortgages that likely funded the estate. Who had he screwed over to acquire so much himself? All things considered, some petty theft seemed almost moral in comparison. It took a full minute of riding to pass through the entire shadow.

Sam continued riding until he came upon a large brick manor, distinguished by a white wraparound porch and a grand, three-story window that looked out over the plateau. He tied his horse to a long hitching post. "Hold steady, girl," Sam said, brushing the animal's neck. "Shouldn't take long, but be ready."

The horse whinnied quietly, almost as if it knew better.

Casually, Sam strolled up to the front door. If someone *was* home, he would play it off. He had a story prepared, both to deflect suspicion and potentially coerce the owner to leave. But after several swings of their horseshoe-shaped door knocker and no answer, Sam decided the home was empty.

He found the door locked. To the left, an open window invited Sam in. A simple oversight, but who would expect a robbery, at midday, in Bluff's Reach?

Sam crawled through the open window and found himself in a smoking parlor. A wide chaise with obnoxious upholstery sat in the middle of the room, flanked on either side by two hardwood tables. An ashtray on one of the tables let off a thin stream of smoke from a recently discarded cigarette. That was another good sign. The owner had recently left, and Sam assumed it would be a time before they returned.

He crossed the room, through the foyer, and into a study that was furnished with wall-high bookshelves and a massive mahogany desk opposite the door. *It should be here*, he thought. *I've got time, but I should still be quick if I can.* He began rummaging through the shelves.

Sam had been in the business of stealing for a long while, and had developed a rather keen sense of where people kept their things. Men often believed themselves clever, but Sam Clangour knew men almost always kept the same hiding places. Combinations and keys to safes were kept in hollowed-out books and old coffee tins. Safes were hidden behind unassuming paintings or in the floor under a rug. If you didn't trust the banks, you kept your money buried under the dirt in your hay barn. It was a uniquely clever idea, most men thought, to keep your cash dry and in a place nobody *else* would think to look. And most men *wouldn't* look there, since they thought themselves the only one with such a clever idea. Yet they would still find their hay barns upturned and their money gone, Sam having sniffed it out like a truffle pig.

Thinking these things, Sam noticed a slight curl at the corner of the study's central rug. He flipped it up with the toe of his boot, revealing a combination safe built into the floor boards. It was a Brigg's and Son, and Sam knew he could crack it in under five minutes if lucky, ten if not.

"Bingo," he said with a grin.

Sam bent down and put his ear to the dial. He began twisting, listening to the gears click and tick into place. Then he froze. Something caught his eye.

From the low angle near the floor, Sam noticed a small latch on the underside of the desk, right where a knee would sit when working.

"Double bingo."

He went to the desk and pulled the latch. Some internal mechanism clicked, and a secret door along the desk's side popped open. Inside, a single key sat, lonely and covered with a thin layer of dust. Sam snatched the key and dropped it into his pocket.

He heard another click, then the creak of a heavy door slowly being opened.

The front door.

Shit. Sam cursed under his breath as bootsteps tiptoed into the house.

Silently, Sam dropped to the floor and rolled under the desk. His hand fell to the butt of his gun. *Don't you dare*, he thought to himself. *You will* not *shoot someone over a damn key.*

Boots squeaked as they moved through the foyer, rubber against marble. Then Sam heard one more click, louder than the others, and certainly more dreadful; the sound of a gun's hammer being pulled into place.

"Who the fuck is in my house?" a man's voice asked, harsh and angry, but unable to conceal the quiver of fear. "Your horse is tied to my hitch, so I know you're still here. Show yourself, and I won't make this too big an issue."

Sam crouched, frozen, breathing slowly, steadily. *No need to worry,* he thought. *He'll look into the room, see nothing, and move on. I can run out when he goes to check upstairs. Don't worry about—*

The rug was still curled back, the safe exposed.

Shit, Sam cursed.

"Shit," the man shouted, then dashed into his study and dropped over the safe. His back was turned to Sam, furiously turning the dial with his free hand.

"Ah, come on. Come on!" The man struggled, then finally managed to unlock the dial and pulled the safe open. He grunted, clearly confused that nothing was missing.

Sweat broke from Sam's head.

The man froze, his shoulders tensed, and Sam saw realization in that posture. *The thief was not here for his safe.*

He turned, facing Sam with a scowl, and raised his pistol.

Sam pounced, driving his shoulder hard into the man's chest.

They tumbled over the open safe door and the man's pistol flew from his hand, clattering to the floor. A single shot whizzed through the study. A spray of shredded books blew off a shelf.

"Sorry!" Sam cried and ran from the room. He burst out the front door and quickly mounted his horse. "Yah! Let's go!" He yelled and kicked his heels hard into the horse's side. They took off down the street.

KA-ZING!

A bullet whizzed past Sam's head. He felt its wake through the air. Dread caught in his chest, anticipating the next shot to connect with its target.

Instead, the man fired three reports up into the air.

BAM! BAM! BAM-ZING!

The last shot seemed to echo in frustration.

"Hey, someone stop that asshole!" the man yelled. His voice grew distant. Sam couldn't tell if he was shouting to someone specific, but he dared not turn around to find out.

***

Kootala Morgan, Abner Brooks, and Sue Barlow were chatting over coffee and sweet breakfast bread when they heard gunfire echo through the air. Sue jumped at the sound, splashing hot coffee onto the table. Brooks remained calm, sipping his mug as if nothing had happened.

"Oh! What in God's name?" Sue said, frustrated at the mess the noise had caused. She grabbed a crusty rag from a nearby washbasin and began to mop up the spill.

"I'm sure it's nothing to concern about," the sheriff said, standing. "It's probably just McCready shooting bottles again. How many times I have to tell him to practice *outside* of town, I don't know."

"He doesn't much care," Kootala said. "You can fine him all you want, but to him, that's just a cost of having fun."

Brooks returned his hat to his head—he had respectfully removed it during their breakfast. He sighed heavily. "Well, we had better go have a chat with him again. Thank you for the coffee, Sue. Was mighty kind of you."

"Mighty kind of *you*, sir," she said, throwing the rag back into the wash. "Enjoy your bread, boys. And Kootala, tell Luke I said hello."

Kootala smiled. "Will do."

Sue turned and muttered to herself. "Handsome feller."

Brooks and Kootala left the bakery with a sack of bread in each hand. They walked back to their office with little urgency, stashed the bread, then carefully saddled and mounted their rides. Abner's mule nipped at his shin as he climbed up, and he kicked the thing's head with his bootheel. "Got-damn swayback ol' nag." He yelped. The mule snorted back.

Kootala's brown quarter horse made no protests, happy to be worked.

Together, the men strolled lackadaisically down Main Street. They carried little concern.

They rode quietly for a short time, then Brooks spoke suddenly, startling Kootala. "You know, kid, I think I aught to let you do some of this work on your own. Let loose your reins, so to say."

Kootala hesitated at the thought. "You would be terribly bored, if so. Already we have little to do. I think Mrs. Barlow might get sick of you after a while, and Etta might end up getting jealous."

Brooks blew a raspberry. "Ah, phew! Ain't no woman could make Etta jealous, that's for damn sure. I know her, and she knows me. Besides, I'm too old for those kind of games."

"Well, my point still stands. You'd have nothing to do if I took on more work," Kootala said. "Besides, you could never convince me to wear a gun on my hip, and sometimes I think that alone makes you more convincing."

"Ain't a whole lot of convincing need to be done round here," the sheriff said. "Even McCready is harmless. The lack of shattered bottles in his yard proves *that*!" He laughed.

It was true, Kootala supposed. Nothing much happened in Bluff's Reach. The biggest problem they seemed to have was the discomfort of heat. Sometimes, your pants would stick to your sweaty legs and you'd have to peel them off like spud skins. When it was exceptionally hot, your hair would dry to a stinking crust that would jab the back of your neck when you looked up at the sky. Still, those minor inconveniences were worth the peace and tranquility.

The pair rounded Jointer Street, which divided Garrison's Hotel and Bill Williams' Saloon on either side. Bill Williams himself stood leaning over the banister in front of his saloon, smoking a thick cigar. Kootala tipped his hat kindly, causing a lock of his long black hair to drop in front of his face. He tucked it back, and—

—a man on a galloping gray flew past, nearly crashing into Kootala. They both yelped at the near accident. Brooks' mule bucked and let out a surprised squeal that tapered off into an angry *hee-haw!* Abner held fast and managed to calm the stupid beast.

Someone yelled from the opposite end of Jointer Street. "Hey! Stop that skunk!" He was running in their direction, flailing his arms frantically above his head.

Brooks pulled hard on the reins, turning his mule. He shouted. "Kootala, go see if that man, or anyone else, is hurt down there. Write down everything they tell you, all the details. I'll go after that hellion. Probably some no good troublemaker kid!" He began to take chase, then called back. "Wait for me back at the office."

They separated, and Kootala raced down Jointer Street with fear creeping into his chest. *Probably just a troublemaker.* Brooks' words echoed in his head. But that fear remained. Their illusion of tranquility had finally shattered.

"Thief! Thief!" The man at the end of Jointer cried.

Kootala had only caught a glimpse of the thief.; he had been more focused on not crashing his ride. The perpetrator was a man, that much Kootala noticed, with long hair as white as salt. A bandanna had covered most of his face.

The victim stopped running, then keeled over, hands on knees to catch his breath. He did not seem to be injured, and there was no blood.

Kootala stopped to calm the man and take his statement.

3

Sam raced out of town with sweat dripping into his eyes, burning worse than sand. His horse galloped a perfect gait with each stride landing in sync with its breath like a well-timed melody. He was a great mount, bred and trained for racing across the desert. For that, Sam was grateful.

He looked back to see Abner Brooks following. The sheriff's mule was the total opposite of Sam's horse. It had grown fat and lazy after years of loafing around the boring town. They followed far behind, the mule lumbering out of tune. For that, Sam was *more* grateful.

After a time, it was clear that the sheriff would never catch up. Sam slowed, though not much. He would ride hard, but would not push his horse to its limit if unnecessary. Already it had snot flying from its nostrils and sweat slicked its neck. The well-broke animal would run until it collapsed if commanded, but it was best practice to save the energy when possible.

Sam turned again and saw Brooks and his mule come to a stop. Brooks would know full well that the chase was over. A glint of light indicated that the sheriff had raised his gun, and six reports—a full cylinder—followed. Not one bullet came close to hitting its target.

Soon, the sheriff turned and began a slow ride back to town. Sam smiled at the sight, though he couldn't say he was happy about the situation.

After a time, the sheriff and his mule shrank from view, and the town of Bluff's Reach soon after. By then, Sam's excitement had faded and his heart slowed to a normal rhythm. Shame took adrenaline's place, grew fat, and settled sour in Sam's stomach. He had tackled a man that morning, nearly crashed into his own husband, and had caused two episodes of gunfire.

Yet, Sam was fortunate that was all that had happened. The man he tackled wouldn't even develop a bruise. The town was physically unscathed, and that was good. How they were doing emotionally, Sam was less sure of. How Kootala might be doing, he dared not even consider.

***

Kootala wrung out a wet rag, which rained nearly clear water into a wash tub; he had wiped down almost every surface inside the sheriff's office. When nervous, Kootala cleaned, and by the time Sheriff Brooks returned from his pursuit, the cells were spotless. In one corner, Kootala had swept up a small pile of sand and dust.

The office door slammed open, and the sheriff came stomping in. He hung his hat on a hook near the door, then dropped to his desk with a heavy sigh.

Kootala did not need to ask. The criminal had gotten away.

"You took a report?" Brooks asked.

"Yes, sir." Kootala dug a small note pad from his pocket and handed it to the sheriff. "Nobody was seriously injured, though there is some property damage and a stolen key. Nothing else besides that. Seems to me like a simple enough theft. Some kid saw an open window and a fancy house, and found an opportunity."

Brooks discarded Kootala's notepad, tossing it carelessly onto the desk. "Thanks, but I've had enough for the day. Take an early off. We can work on this tomorrow." He stood again, opened a nearby cabinet, and pulled down a bottle of brandy. "Ugh!" He cringed, clutching his right wrist.

"Are you alright?" Kootala asked.

"Oh, just swell." Brooks tipped the bottle and took a deep swig of the liquor. "Damn mule twisted my wrist when he bucked. As if I wasn't sore enough already."

"Hell," Kootala said, reaching for Brooks' hand. "Let me see."

Brooks pulled back, hesitated, then finally gave Kootala his wrist. "If Etta ever saw me like this, kid..." He trailed off.

Kootala pinched the wrist, causing the sheriff to yelp in pain. "Right," Kootala said, then dropped the arm. "Hold on." He went to the corner of the room, where he had previously swept the pile of sand and dust. Kootala scooped a handful of the sweepings, took them back to the desk, and rubbed a generous amount on the sheriff's wrist.

Brooks cringed. It hurt, for a moment.

Kootala took a deep breath, felt a calm sensation wash over his body, then pushed it out through his hands. The dust on the sheriff's wrist warmed, then he relaxed and signed with relief; his pain subdued.

"Thank you," Brooks said, and pulled his wrist to his chest.

It was always a pleasure, Kootala thought, to use his Dust to help others. Though Dust could not *reverse* injuries—at least, as far as Kootala knew—it could speed up healing and relieve pain.

Dust soothed. Dust cared.

Kootala turned his palms upward. Some fine dust still clung to his skin. He channeled that calming force again, and the dust on his palms dissipated into a smoke that smelled like fresh rain and cinnamon. The smell filled their noses, and the two men grew calm as it washed away their tensions.

"Now don't go making a big deal about that," Kootala said with a smile.

"Right, right." Brooks returned his brandy to the cabinet.

While Kootala was fond of his Dust, it was not something to be outwardly *proud* of—especially not in a town like Bluff's Reach, and certainly not in the rough city of Graben. For Dust was a soothing art, and was often seen as *feminine*. In the west, men were expected to be strong. They were supposed to be tough, powerful, full of Grit. For a man to display use of Dust was seen as abnormal, something to be looked down upon. If it was well known that the sheriff let another man use Dust on him, just imagine what people might think.

"Hey," said Kootala. "You said we would work on that report tomorrow, but Luke is supposed to be back then. I was hoping to spend the time with him, if that's alright."

"Sure," the sheriff said. "We can work on it another time. That snake won't show his face around here for a while anyway. He was quick, but I think we scared him good."

"Thanks." Kootala headed for the door.

"You know," Brooks said, interrupting Kootala's withdrawal. "I took this post because I'm old and worn out. I figured being sheriff of Bluff's Reach would let me have my peace." He sighed deeply. "If this isn't a one-off thing, I'm a fool as well."

"I wouldn't worry too much, sir," Kootala said. "I'd bet you a dollar that the guy gets picked up in Graben within the week."

"Others, though." Brooks' hand strayed to a pile of fliers that had not yet been distributed. *Wanted: Cassidy Reeve.* "There's a lot more than a couple dollars to bet this town on. He'll be back, if not someone else. It may be only a matter of time, I'm afraid. See, there's a poison in that stinking city down in the valley. Let's hope it doesn't spread up here to us."

"Let's hope." Kootala agreed. "Otherwise, I'd have a lot more paperwork to do."

"Right," Brooks said. "Have a nice day with Luke tomorrow. See you in a few, kid."

Kootala nodded, then left.

***

After a few hours of riding, Sam had reached the western side of the plateau. He slowed, turned south, and began descending the meandering switchbacks into the valley. Another couple hours' ride, nestled halfway along the only route between Bluff's Reach and Graben, stood the Lonely Outpost.

Lonely wasn't much. Basically a glorified rest stop, the outpost was run by a single man, all on his lonesome. Hence the name. The man, Howard, had a small home with a crumbling roof, a musty hotel of two rooms with three bunks each, and a stable just large enough for half a dozen horses. There, one could find cold water, a hot meal, and a half decent sleep. Sam had spent many a night in Lonely's decrepit hotel, and he had come to think of the place as a second home.

He had seen the outpost from a good distance away, many switchbacks up, though it had appeared only as a shimmering blur until he was closer. As Sam rode up, Howard came out to greet him. He was slightly older than Sam, but still young enough to grow a strong black mustache that curled at the ends like the horns of a mountain ram.

"Afternoon, Sam." Howard called out.

"Howard," Sam said, tipping his hat. "Good day, huh?"

"Sure seems to be."

Sam took a wide look at the outpost. Seeing the place always seemed to calm his nerves. He found Lonely welcoming, regardless of its somewhat lousy accommodations. In fact, most travelers welcomed the quick stop, though they always moved on when they could. Howard often mentioned people's offers to spruce the place up, and he had always rejected them. *Strange*, people would claim. Plenty passed through the outpost, and certainly the money was coming in, so why not fix the place up somewhat?

Sam knew why. Lonely's appearance was by design. See, Lonely was inconspicuous. It was easy to pass through, and just as easy to forget. All the better that way, for it was also in Lonely where *another* route diverged. A secret route, running west through a crack in the plateau and beyond the scattered mesas. West, where the route met up with an offshoot of the Colorado River. There, was Devil's Gulch, hideout for Casey Calhoun and his gang of outlaws. Unnecessary as it was, Devil's Gulch was well hidden and impenetrable. The only way into the gulch was a treacherous ride down the roiling river from the north, or through Lonely.

And of course, the only man in Lonely worked for Casey Calhoun (though how willingly, Sam wasn't certain).

Positioned as it was, Casey's control over Lonely proved invaluable. He knew of every horse, coach, and caravan traveling to and from Bluff's Reach. Between the city of Graben, the town of Bluff's Reach, and the little Lonely Outpost, Casey seemed to know all.

Sam stopped near Howard's house, dismounting his horse as Howard grabbed the reins. "What's for supper?" Sam asked. "I haven't had a bite of food since I left here, hours ago. My stomach is part-near ready to eat itself."

"I've got a stew on," Howard said as he began leading Sam's horse. "Go on in and help yourself. I'll stow this and come join you in a few."

Sam's stomach growled enthusiastically. A hearty bowl of stew was his favorite, and just the thought made him ravenous. Kootala's stews were the best, but Howard's were a close second.

Sam gasped, suddenly remembering the key. "Oh, Howard, hold up!" He pulled the key from his pocket and turned it over in his hand. *Marble Springs Safe Deposit Box #116* was etched into its face. He tossed the key to Howard. "There's a pocket on the inside wall of the left saddle bag. Put it in there, and let them know when they make the swap."

"Thanks," Howard said, leading the horse to the stable.

Sam went inside and filled his belly with hot broth and fatty chunks of beef. When Howard returned from the stable, they chatted for a while, mainly about mundane things like local news and the weather. They rarely talked *business* unless pertinent to their current job, per Casey's request. It was an order they were more than happy to follow. They were happier talking about positive things, or about the doings that they were not involved in. Sam had a feeling that they *both* harbored guilt, though they had never once brought it up.

When the sun finally set and the sky grew dark, Sam went off to bed. By morning, his horse and score would be gone, replaced by Luke's brown and black appaloosa, his personal belongings, and a wad of cash. Then, Luke would return to Bluff's Reach before the next night as himself once more.

Luke woke a few times, uncomfortable upon Lonely's creaky bunks. He stared out a nearby window where the silhouette of the massive plateau severed the sky in two; twinkling stars above, slate black nothing below.

Howard's stew had filled Luke's belly, but a deep hollow still echoed in his chest. He felt as if he had been banished to the outpost, reflective of his inner ache. Lonely.

He rolled over onto his back and stared at the bunk above.

This is for you, Kootala, he thought.

4

"Howdy, cowgirl," Kootala said, taking a stool next to his good friend Missy as she nursed a tumbler of amber liquid.

Missy tucked a thick curl of red hair behind her ear and flashed Kootala a flirtatious wink. "Hello, handsome. Here to buy me a drink?"

"You seem to being doing alright in that regard," Kootala said, nodding to Missy's half-empty glass.

They both laughed.

"How are you doing?" Missy asked earnestly. "I heard about yesterday."

"Oh, fine, I suppose." Kootala rasped his knuckles on the bar top, calling Bill Williams' attention. "Word spread, huh?"

"Oh yeah, like the plague! I heard about it last night, as did the rest of town. We all slept on it, and now it's all anyone can talk about. Listen." Missy gestured to a table nearby.

Vanessa Deetman and LeAnn Cheek were gossiping loudly enough to hear. "I guess nobody wants to work for a fair day's pay anymore," Vanessa was saying.

LeAnn groaned. "We moved up here to get away from that kind of stuff."

Vanessa turned up her nose. "Indeed! Those people down in Graben are total filth. Such a shame."

"To think," LeAnn said, "we have to depend on that sheriff to keep us safe from those miscreants."

"Hmm." Vanessa scoffed. "And think of the children! They must be terrified."

Missy pointed opposite the bar, said, "And there."

Ron Barker—the town doctor—was standing at the end of the bar, chatting with McCready. "...and make sure you find a good place to hide your valuables. Can't expect *the law* to protect our stuff," he said, glancing at Kootala.

"They're seriously blaming Sheriff Brooks?" Kootala asked.

Missy shrugged. "They're blaming you both."

"Kootala," Bill Williams said, sliding forward a glass of clear tequila. He corked the bottle, then stashed it back below the bar. Behind him, the wall was stacked high with crystal bottles of expensive spirits. The cheap stuff he kept hidden below, where its presence could cause no offense. Though Luke and Kootala could afford the nicer drink, they hadn't yet developed a high-end taste. However, they always tipped Bill the difference.

Kootala thanked him for the drink with a pair of quarters, then Bill moved to the end of the bar to polish steins and nod apathetically as Todd Lybuck and Jim McCready told him the same story again and again.

"When is Luke supposed to be back?" Missy asked.

"Some time today, probably afternoon," Kootala said. "Would have spent the night in Lonely on his way back, so I'm expecting him for supper."

"I wonder if he crossed paths with that guy from yesterday?" Missy gaped. "He'd almost have to! They'd both be in Lonely around the same time."

A chill ran up Kootala's back. "I'll ask Luke when he gets home. I sure hope they managed to steer clear of each other."

"They're saying the guy goes by Sam Clangour. Someone saw him in Graben not long ago. Long white hair and a bandanna. I'm guessing it's a wig. What young guy's got white hair?"

"I wouldn't doubt that. Hell, I certainly wouldn't want to be seen. Though that Cassidy Reeve sure seems to like her picture on the wall." Kootala's stomach tightened at the thought. He bet that Cassidy found joy in seeing her wanted poster all over the state. She was sour, all the way through.

"Well, maybe Luke caught the guy and is bringing him back in a hogtie!" Missy laughed. "Wouldn't that be a sight? Little ol' Lukey capturing a big bad outlaw."

Kootala rolled his eyes. "I sure hope not. We stay out of that kind of business."

"Man, you work for the damn sheriff. That *is* your business!"

"I just do the paperwork, you know that," Kootala said.

Bill Williams slid the duo another round of drinks.

"Yeah, Mr. Peaceful." Missy jabbed Kootala with a playful elbow. "You're always making it known how much better you are than the rest of us."

Her comment was all in fun, but Kootala couldn't help feeling irritated. "I wish you wouldn't joke about the way I choose to live my life, Missy. The Hopi teach peace and unity with all things."

"Well I just think some people need a good whack every so often. It's the only thing most men understand."

"Maybe you just need to keep better company," Kootala said, rubbing the spot where she had elbowed him.

Missy's hair had fallen in front of her face, and she tucked it back again. "Even bad men have certain needs that only a woman like me can provide. But don't you worry your little heart about that. They aren't all that tough once you got their pecker in your hand."

They burst out laughing and Kootala's irritation fell away as quickly as it had come. He whooped until his belly ached and the drink threatened to come up. Once they had caught their breath, Missy waved Bill Williams over again.

"Hey, how 'bout a round of your not-so-secret shine?" Missy asked.

"So early in the day?" Bill teased. He left to a back room, then returned soon after with two inches of clear liquid.

"Kinda easy pours, eh?" Missy asked.

Bill set the drinks on the bar. "Evaporated on the walk over."

"Twenty feet?" Kootala asked.

Bill just shrugged, as if that was all it took.

Kootala and Missy downed the moonshine, which burned Kootala's throat and warmed his belly.

"Hey," Missy said, pointing out an open window to a man walking down the street. "Eddy out there..."

"Yeah?"

"Can't get it up unless you hit him first."

Kootala gagged. "No horseshit?"

"None," Missy said. "I swear!"

Just then, the desert's hot breath blew in through the window, filling the saloon with a swirl of dust.

Missy sighed and tipped her glass upside down on the bar top, then said, "I suppose I'd better pay for these drinks." She gave Kootala a playful smirk, then got up and made her way over to McCready.

The dust followed her in a barely visible current that only Kootala seemed to notice.

With a twirl of her hand, Missy sent the beam spiraling around McCready's head. The dust dissipated soon after, leaving the smell of dried roses in its absence. McCready turned to Missy, looked her up and down, then smiled a large set of fake teeth.

Kootala stood from the bar, feeling woozy. Bill's moonshine worked quickly. "I'd better get home before Luke does," he said, though not really to anyone in particular.

"See you both tomorrow night?" Missy called as Kootala lumbered across the saloon.

"Surely!" Kootala hiccuped.

He stumbled home, dragging the toes of his boots through the dirt as he went. By the time he climbed his porch steps, he had somewhat sobered and splitting headache took over instead.

5

Etta Brooks stood near her kitchen window, watching the sky grow a dark bruised purple as Abner sauntered home on his mule. They rode slowly, for which the animal was likely relieved. The air outside was growing thick with humidity, and everything seemed to slow within it like molasses. Rain was on the way.

Abner came in and kissed Etta on the lips, then sat down at the table with a heavy sigh. She could taste liquor on his breath, but said nothing of it. With a deep wooden ladle, she filled two china plates with a steaming mound of potato mash and creamed corn. Etta slid a plate to her husband, took a plate for herself, and found a seat opposite the table.

Abner removed his hat and set it aside, where lamplight shimmered lightly across the brass casing tucked into the band. His few strands of white hair remained in place, slicked back and hardened with the grease and sweat of the day. "How was your day, hun?" he asked of Etta.

"Oh fine. Nothing much happened around here," she said pleasantly, took a bite of the spuds, and continued. "I added a few squares to the quilt I've been working on. Went and had coffee with Gayle. Read some of my book."

"What are you reading?" Abner asked while rubbing the bridge of his nose between his thumb and middle finger.

"Do you honestly care to ask?"

Etta's husband produced a small and subtle smile that said, *No, but it's nice to ask, anyway*. It was funny, Etta thought, how easily they could communicate without any words at all. It was a skill that came with the years, and she wouldn't have it any other way.

"Well, since you asked." She smiled back, playfully teasing. "*Against Nature*, by Huysmans. Quite a boring read, truth be told, but I find it a very interesting comparison to the people in our town. I—" She stopped. She had noticed Abner was favoring his wrist. "Damnation, Abe!" Etta cried. "Why didn't you tell me you hurt yourself? This from the other day?" She made to stand, but one stern look from her husband kept her seated.

"It's alright," Abner said. "Just that jackass nearly bucked me off. It'll be fine in a week or so. Besides, it ain't my pistol hand."

"You expect to use your pistol anytime soon?" Etta asked. She was growing nervous. Abner hadn't told her much about the episode the other day, but Gayle had provided plenty of hot air over coffee. Etta had assumed Gayle's recollection of events was more far-fetched than reasonable, but Etta knew her husband well, and the look in his eyes was telling. "Did you have trouble today?" she asked.

"None at all. Paperwork, mostly. I can say, that hurts my wrist more than any damn riding will." Abner took a heaping spoonful of corn, ate it slowly, and said, finally, "You ask if I had a rough day. In honesty, no. But I can feel rough days to come. It's a feeling that reminds me of the old days, back when the frontier was as wild as *we* were." He smiled with decades of love on his lips. "I got comfortable. And old."

"You can't protect yourself from getting old, Abe. Lord knows I'm not the pretty young woman you married." She laughed. "But every wrinkle on our faces is a year that we have loved each other. That's worth the cost of getting wore out, I think."

Abner blushed. "That's the one thing that gets better with time. You're like a smooth whiskey."

"Beg pardon, Sheriff!" Etta feigned offense. "But I like to think of myself as a fine wine. Sweet, refined, but with a little bite." She giggled, and suddenly she felt like a kid again. Kids giggle. She hadn't done that in a very long time.

"You always know how to cheer me up," Abner said. "But..." He trailed off, staring out beyond Etta's shoulder.

"But?"

"But I still worry. About this town. About you." He sighed, pushed his plate forward. He had lost his appetite. "And that kid, Kootala. He's a good man, pure to the core, and that can be a problem out here."

Etta frowned. It wasn't like Abner to get in such a sorry state. Sometimes he would come home grumpy or exhausted from a long day, but a full belly and a warm kiss usually took care of it. This was different, Etta thought. Whatever the old man was thinking, it laid heavy on him. Etta put her elbows to the table and held her chin between her fists. She gazed deeply at her husband, wishing to take his pain away. But a man's pain is his own—something her mother had once said—and all you can do is let him work it out in time. That, and give him a soft bosom on which to lay his head now and again.

Abner fiddled with his hat, rubbing his knuckles across the felt.

"Do you remember," Etta asked, "the day you put that bullet there?" She gestured to the single round tucked into his hat band.

"Yuh." Abner sucked at his teeth. "It was the morning after Lincoln was shot. Well, when we heard the news, anyway."

"We could hardly believe it. And you had such a fear that the war wasn't quite *over* after all. You worried, same as you are now." Etta shook her head. "Yet when Missy came in, the last thing on your mind was Lincoln."

Abner nodded silently.

Their daughter had crashed through the front door that morning. Etta remembered clearly: Missy's hair was tangled and hung over the left side of her face. She had tried to march past her parents, but Etta had jumped up and stopped her, placing a grip on the girl's shoulder.

"What gives you reason to storm in here like that?" Abner had asked.

Etta pushed Missy's hair back behind her ear, revealing her left eye, swollen shut, with a thin line of blood scratched through her eyebrow.

"Oh, my baby!" Etta had cried and cleaned the injury with a wet rag.

Abner, younger then, stood tall and dangerous. "What the hell happened? Who did this to you?"

"Nobody. I fell from my horse." Missy had lied.

"Don't." Etta said. "We know you better than you know yourself. Be honest, girl."

Abner's fists had grown white. "Where were you last night? Were you with someone? A man. Did he..." He trailed off, unable to find the words to his question.

"No, he didn't do *that*," Missy said. "I had some drinks with Jesse. We kissed, but that's all. He wanted more. He hit me, tried to... Well, I didn't let him, see?" She held out her hands, showing dried blood under her nails.

Abner's face turned purple. "I'll kill that boy! I'll... I'll..."

"Father, stop. It's already taken care of. The next girl he looks at will be through one eye only."

Abner returned to the table with a sigh. "Fine. But I'm going to be keeping a tighter watch on you from now forward."

Missy pushed free of her mother. "I'm practically a grown woman. I don't need you to treat me like a child anymore. I can take care of myself, seems I already have. I certainly don't need *one* man to keep me safe from another!"

"You worry me, Missy. You keep finding yourself in these situations, and I want to believe it's all by coincidence. But it's not coincidence. You're becoming wild, untamed, and you are constantly putting yourself in danger's path."

"That is *my* problem, Father. Not yours. I'm my own person, and I'll do what I want. You're my parents. Be that for me, help me when I ask for it, and let *me* be *me* the rest of the time."

Etta had laughed at that. "You are certainly your father's daughter! That's all you, Abe. Stubborn as a mule and tough as iron."

"Yeah," Abner agreed. "And I was young once, too. I know the trouble that kind of attitude will get you."

"Yet here you are," Missy said with her hands on her hips. "Turning gray, with more years on you than scars."

"You want to be covered in scars when you're old?"

"I wouldn't mind a few." Missy laughed, and Abner scowled. "Seriously, you need to quit worrying about me so often."

That was when Abner had gone to the front door and removed his gun and holster from its hook. He ejected the chamber and removed one bullet. "Fine. I'll keep out of your business as much as I can," he said. "But if any man hurts you again, or even threatens as much, this bullet is going through his head." He tucked the cartridge into the band, where it remained for years. Rumor must have spread, or perhaps the girl held her own, for no man ever laid a heavy hand on her again.

Missy had rolled her eyes at her father's gesture. "Has he always been so melodramatic, Mother?" she asked.

"Since we were kids," Etta had said then. She said it again now, some fifteen years later, as if no time had passed at all.

"I remember clearly," Abner now said. "Why bring that up?"

"Because you're a worrier. Just like you worried about our daughter, you now worry about Kootala. Missy is fine, and the boy will be, too."

"You really think so?" Abner asked. His eyes revealed genuine curiosity, as if he would believe whatever Etta next said without question.

"Yes," she said plainly. "Kootala keeps you in check. He keeps you thinking fresh. But you needn't worry. That kid is the nicest man west of the Mississippi, and he's got God on his side. I'm sure of it."

"Right as always, darling." Abner pulled his plate back to his chest and began eating once again, his appetite returned. That was the end of the conversation. As much as the man's head rolled with uncertainly, he could always count on Etta to set him right.

That, she thought, *came with the years, too.*

6

Luke Morgan chewed a thick cube of beef steak, grinding the meat thoroughly to buy himself time to think.

"You crossed paths with nobody on the way?" Kootala had asked.

They were sat at their small dinner table, plates piled high with steak, beans, and fresh bread from Sue Barlow's bakery.

Luke swallowed, cleared his throat, and answered. "None that fit your description, anyway." The lie choked down his throat like a tough chew of sinew.

Kootala picked at his plate, leaving much of his food uneaten. He had smelled of alcohol when Luke arrived, though he figured it wasn't a sour stomach that had ruined his husband's appetite. He had tasted moonshine on Kootala's breath, but only barely.

"I hope you weren't drinking because you were worried for me," Luke said.

"Missy and I were just having a good time."

"And running your mouth about others?"

Kootala flinched, as if he had been struck.

"I'm sorry," Luke said. "I didn't mean that to sound so harsh. Just, you two enjoy talking town, and I figured there was much talk about what happened yesterday."

"You're off today, Lucas." Kootala accused.

Luke sighed. "I'd be lying to say I wasn't irritable today."

"Business?"

"No," Luke lied. "Business is fine. Some big investors from California wanted to purchase the entire operation. They're looking to move into Arizona, and wanted to buy an existing business instead of starting from nothing. If they go through with the deal, I won't need to keep traveling anymore. I can stay up here with you."

That last part wasn't a total lie. Yes, the business deal was fabricated, but *Sam* had nearly cleared his debt with Casey Calhoun. He had been in his employment for years now, and the money he had accumulated would be enough to live on for quite a while. Luke figured he only had a few more jobs to do until his debt was paid. He could leave that life behind, and Kootala would never be the wiser.

Kootala scooped another helping of beans onto Luke's plate. "That would be wonderful! Being honest, I get nervous every time you leave for Graben. Though now, after what happened yesterday..." He trailed off.

"You really shouldn't be so concerned for me," Luke said. "As for the events yesterday, it sounds like no more than petty burglary. Nobody was hurt. I'm sure that's the extent of things around here."

"Nobody got hurt *yet*." Kootala corrected.

Luke refrained from rolling his eyes. Kootala always seemed to have something more to say about any topic. He always got the final word.

Kootala continued. "There was that massacre recently, and that Cassidy Reeve had been seen around Graben, and now they're saying this *Sam Clangour* guy is associated. Rumor is it was Sam who came through yesterday. It's just, well..." He struggled with his thoughts for a moment. "I don't know," he said finally. "I just have a bad feeling about the future of this town is all. So does everybody else."

"Well..." Luke paused. Knowing *his* actions had caused so much turmoil inside his husband made Luke ache terribly. "Perhaps you should quit working for the sheriff, then." He silently hoped Kootala might consider the option. "If you're worried about crime, then you're in the wrong industry."

Kootala shook his head, then looked out the window at the town's sunset silhouette. "I can't. I enjoy the work. Honest! I like helping around town, even though I can't be much help apprehending criminals. Being sheriff is so much more than *that*, and being the clerk is very rewarding."

"Alright." Luke pushed his plate forward; his own appetite now expired. "But if it *does* get bad around here, please just keep yourself safe. You are under no obligation to danger yourself for anyone else's sake."

Kootala was silent for a time, clearly struggling with his thoughts. This was not a topic he enjoyed thinking about. "Can we not talk about this any further?" he asked bluntly. "You just got home. The least we could do is enjoy the evening."

"You're absolutely right!" Luke agreed. "We should be enjoying ourselves." He gave Kootala a wink. "Rather, we should be enjoying one another."

Kootala pondered this, as if it was a terribly difficult thing to decide. Finally, and with a devilish grin, he said, "If you insist."

There was a knock on the front door.

Kootala startled. "Who—"

Luke stood with a sigh. "I'll go see who that is. You stay here and look handsome until I get back."

"I'll see if I can manage that." Kootala laughed.

"Who in their right mind?" Luke muttered to himself as he went to the door. "Come bother us this evening. Don't they know…"

Then a thought came to him, and he had an idea who it might be. He held the doorknob, cool and smooth in his hand, then took a deep breath and stepped out into the desert evening.

Cassidy Reeve waited outside. She tipped her hat to Luke, causing her dreadlocks to fall over her face. She swept them back and fixed them in place again with her hat. In the dim light, Luke could barely make out the splatter of freckles on the Black woman's cheeks. Behind her, the light of a distant storm flashed, and for a silent minute the two stared at each other until the air filled with a rolling, echoing thunderclap.

"Casey is satisfied with that last job," Cassidy said, simply. She had never been a woman of many words, but the words she *did* say meant much.

"What the hell are you doing here? Your face is all over town! Are you *trying* to get caught?" Luke said, trying to keep his voice low. "This couldn't wait until next week?"

"We don't have a week. He wants us on another job in two days' time, here in town again."

"Is he damn stupid? They're all on edge around here. My husband is inside, and he is going all goofy about *the future of this town.* God knows what else is rolling around in his head. All that, and all I did was steal a single key." Luke folded his arms. "Tell Casey no. We can do whatever job another time. I just got done causing a scene around here, and I doubt the people are gonna be looking down for some time. Now I'd really enjoy it if I could spend some time alone with my husband."

Cassidy leaned back on one of the porch posts, lit a cigarette, and puffed a rolling cloud into the night. "Do you want to make some serious money or not?" she asked.

"No." Luke's voice grew threatening. "I want you to get the hell away from my home."

"Well," Cassidy said, flicking cigarette ash into the sand. "Too bad. You still have a debt to pay, and you know what happens when Casey's debts go *unpaid*."

Luke boiled, nearly ready to explode. Then he calmed, and said, "Dammit, fine. What's the job?"

Cassidy smiled. "The bank."

Luke was silent for a moment, trying to decide if he had heard her correctly. Cassidy's face was hard as stone, and Luke knew she was serious. If there was one thing he knew about Cassidy Reeve, it was that she did not kid, and she did not lie. "Oh, hell no," Luke said. "No way! Casey is out of his damn mind."

Cassidy sighed, as if providing an explanation was a horrible chore. "A couple fellas made a rather significant deposit recently. The bank is going to—"

"What does Casey need with stolen cash? Isn't our whole purpose to do things *other* than steal money from banks? Why, robberies like that are only stories in the print!"

"We aren't stealing *money*, you donkey." Cassidy was growing annoyed, as well. "They're moving ledgers, contracts, bonds, stuff like that. In two days, a caravan is moving the stuff to Graben. We certainly aren't stupid enough to steal from a Graben bank, so we need to do it while it's here."

"Oh, yes, because stealing from a bank *here* is so much less *stupid*." Luke huffed. "Can't we just pick them up as they pass through Lonely?"

"Last thing Casey needs is the authorities snooping around *there*."

Luke pulled Cassidy away from his house, a dozen feet or so into the shadows. "Then rob them on the trail. I'm *not* robbing the fucking bank in my own town!" He was putting in serious effort to not yell at the woman.

"You want me to tell Casey that you refused to do what he asked?" Cassidy said. She pulled at her hair, twisting the locks behind her head. The normally unreadable woman was growing uncomfortable, possibly even worried.

Luke would get no justification, then. He wondered about Casey's reasoning; in fact, Luke couldn't see a reason *not* to take the caravan while on the road. Something else was going on, but damn if he'd ever find out the truth.

He kicked hard at the dirt. "Dammit, fine." He conceded. "What are the details?"

"Meet me outside of town in two days. I'll have Sam's stuff waiting for you. You won't even need to leave town with me after the job. I can take it all back, you go home, and nobody will suspect a thing."

"Whatever," Luke said. "Get the hell away from my house."

He went back inside, leaving Cassidy in the dark without any pleasantries. The door he closed with a heavy hand, but refrained from slamming it with all his strength.

"What was that?" Kootala asked, going to stand.

Luke put a hand on his husband's shoulder, making him sit. He thought up a quick lie. "That was one of my business associates. They are requesting a meeting at the Newports' place in two days."

"Is this about the investors?"

"Yes. The deal might go through after all, faster than we had anticipated."

"You should have invited them in. I'd very much like to meet the people you work with."

"Perhaps another time. For now, I wanted to get back to you," Luke said. "Alone."

"Oh!" Kootala smiled. "Well then, come get me."

7

No rain fell that night, yet the morning air remained hot and humid and the sky was overcast with deep gray clouds. *Perhaps it would pour this next night*, Luke thought, watching from a kitchen window.

Hot pig fat sputtered out of the cast iron pan that Luke was attending. He jerked his arm back in pain, swearing, then reached back in and removed the blackened bacon. Carefully, then, he cracked four speckled eggs into the grease and waited for the whites to crisp around the edges, just how Kootala liked them. He flipped the eggs, busting the yolks, then swore again and threw the spatula across the kitchen.

"Hey, calm yourself," Kootala said, hugging Luke from behind. "It's just breakfast. I don't like my yolks runny, anyway."

"I'm sorry," Luke said. He always felt bad being irritable around Kootala. "I must not have gotten much sleep last night."

Kootala turned Luke around by his shoulders, then kissed him deeply. It relaxed Luke, but not much.

"Here," Kootala said. He reached over to the window and swiped a finger-full of settled dust from the sill. This he smeared across Luke's forehead. Luke felt an ease push through his skull, filling him with relaxation. He dropped his shoulders and took a deep breath of warm cinnamon air.

"Thank you," Luke said, loosing himself in Kootala's arms.

They broke, and Kootala poured Luke a hot mug of coffee.

"Would you go into town with me today?" Kootala asked. "I'm in need of some supplies, figured I'd stop by Todd's."

"Alright."

They ate their breakfast, and it was quite fine after all. Luke hadn't ruined anything, and he felt a shadow of shame about his outburst. Kootala sucked the eggs down hungrily.

They did their chores after breakfast. All the while, Luke noticed a sense of tension between Kootala and himself. Something was off. Was Kootala nervous, perhaps thinking about Luke's fake business meeting? Was he picking up Luke's own apprehensions? Though Kootala's Dust had made Luke less irritable, he still dreaded the upcoming robbery. In all honestly, he was afraid, though not for himself. He thought of others, the safety of the townsfolk with Cassidy milling about. And he thought of Kootala, and what it would do to him if he were to ever discover Luke's secret identity.

Around noon, they saddled their horses for the trip downtown. Neither man had spoken in some time, until finally, while cinching his saddle's girth, Kootala asked, "Are you alright?"

"What?" Luke asked, surprised.

"You've been strange today."

Luke blushed. "I could say the same for you."

Kootala looked away, ashamed. Perhaps he felt equally as paranoid as Luke did. Perhaps their strangeness was mutual that day.

Kootala reached down to scoop up a handful of dirt. "I could—"

"No." Luke interrupted. "That can't be your solution to every sour emotion. Some things must be processed alone."

Kootala dropped the sand. "I... You've never said something like this before. What's going on with you?"

"We can discuss this later." Luke said. Without another word, he mounted his horse.

Kootala wiped his hand on his shirt, then hopped on his horse as well.

Luke's lie was eating away at him. He had always been ashamed to lie to Kootala, but never so strongly as this. *How much longer can I keep this up?* he asked himself.

Kootala took the lead silently. They walked through the north side of town, passing the house that *Sam* had robbed. Soon after, they turned and passed down Main Street.

Townsfolk greeted them as they passed, flashing grand smiles and friendly waves. Sue Barlow called out from her window. "Welcome home, Luke! You missed the commotion the other day."

Luke tipped his hat to her in acknowledgment.

Kootala stopped outside the sheriff's office and Abner Brooks came out to meet them. His eyes were tided and slow, but he spoke in as friendly a manner as he could muster. "Mornin' boys, you come in for lunch?"

"Wasn't planning on it," Kootala said. "We're in for chores, but if you want to grab a bite with us, you're more than welcome."

"I'll have to decline, I'm afraid. I'm wore out from the other day yet, and I was gonna go home early to have a calm day with Etta."

Luke averted his gaze, avoiding eye contact with the sheriff out of shame. He stared at the hot, curdled water of a nearby horse trough instead. His sorrowed reflection stared back.

"It's good to have you back, Luke," Brooks said. "Any trouble on the road?"

Luke searched the sheriff's tone for any hint of perception, but found none. He said, "No, sir. I passed a few travelers on the way, but all were well and friendly."

"Good, good." Brooks tipped his hat at them, and the bullet in his hat glistened. "Well, I'd best close up and get home to the old lady. Enjoy your day, you two. Kootala, I'll see you in the morning."

They continued down Main, then stopped again at the general store, tied their horses, and went inside.

Todd Lybuck greeted them from behind the counter. A border of cabinets wrapped around the walls, and a single exposed shelf hung above them, sagging under the weight it held. All the items were neatly displayed and organized by category. Todd mainly sold tools and horse tack, but he could get just about anything if you requested it.

The general store was flanked on either side by two doors. The left led into the butcher shop, operated by Todd's daughter Katie. The door opposite entered the gun shop, run by his son Tucker.

Todd's face lit up with a massive grin when Luke and Kootala walked up. His fat cheeks bloomed like rising dough balls, red with rosacea. "Kootala, Luke, good to see you both!" he exclaimed.

"Happy to see you as well," Kootala said. "Did you ever get that shipment I asked for?"

"Oh, right," Todd said, rummaging through the crates behind the counter. He looked up. "Two boxes of hardware and a roll of cowhide, right?"

"That's it," Kootala said.

"What's this?" Luke asked, puzzled.

"I took up leatherwork since you've been out. I was hoping to make you something before you got home, but the post was slow."

"Ah, here it is," Todd said, placing a box on the counter. "Anything else?"

Luke leaned over and began digging through the container. He saw scraps of leather, chunks of hide, and various metal grommets, rivets, and other unknown pieces of hardware. "Can you make me a new bridle?" he asked Kootala.

"I can sure try." Then, to Todd. "That's all, thanks much."

A jarring crash took Luke's attention as the door to the butcher shop swung open and crashed against the shiplap walls. Glass jars rattled on a nearby shelf. A young woman came through, and Luke noted that her cheeks were more jolly than her father's.

She saw Luke, and her eyes burned at him with a passion. "Hello, Lucas." She swooned, fluttering her lashes. She leaned against the door frame and puffed out her chest.

"Hi, Katie," Luke said dismissively. He had hopped she wouldn't have noticed his presence, but it was as if she could smell him from afar, like some keen bird of prey. Luke had told Katie on several occasions that he was not interested in her advances, but that only seemed to make her try even harder.

Katie Lybuck pouted her lips, which were dry and cracked with bits of blood. "Would you be interested in something big and juicy from my shop?" she asked.

"Ease up, Kate," Todd said. Luke could feel the heat of embarrassment radiating from the man's face.

"No, thank you," Kootala said pleasantly, answering for the both of them.

"Well, if you change your minds, you know where to find me," Katie said with a wink and returned to her shop. She closed the door softly behind her this time.

"I really must apologize for her," Todd said. "I swear I raised that girl better."

"It's not my fault I'm irresistible," Luke said.

They all laughed.

Kootala gathered his items, and Todd helped load their horses

"Thanks again," Luke said to Todd, before they took off once again.

***

After some time in town, Kootala had completed all his chores. Their horses' bags sagged heavily with fresh food and materials for the week. It was early afternoon when they made their way home, and the sun beat down on them furiously. It was still humid, and hot sweat poured down Kootala's face, slicking his hair and sticking his shirt to his chest. The streets shimmered in the heat, and fence posts danced the mirage waltz.

"It's a miserable one," Luke said absently.

"Hold on a minute," Kootala said.

They stopped, and Kootala drove his horse in a tight circle. A light cloud of dust kicked up.

Luke pulled back, watching with great interest. "Dust, Kootala? What could that help? Do you think you can... block the feeling of heat?"

"No," Kootala said. "Though I suppose that could be done, in theory."

"Then what—"

"Just let me work."

Kootala focused on the cloud of dust, not as one might focus a punch, but instead as if he were studying the veins of a flower. Delicately. Deliberately. He felt the nature of the dust, could sense the weight of each particle, sticky with humidity. Then he imagined the dust rising over their heads and clumping tightly to itself. He took a breath, holding steady, then pushed the image out of his head. He shoved it away—hard—that sense of *imagining* the world to be a certain way. In doing so, he let the world take shape on its own.

Above them, a shadow coalesced and hung alone in the air. The beating sun filtered through the artificial screen, and Kootala felt the cool absence of heat wash over him.

Luke was dumbfounded. "Kootala, did you just... control the sand? You have *Grit*?"

"Of course not," Kootala said. He had never possessed Grit, no matter how hard he tried. No matter how hard he willed the sand to take shape. It never happened. Grit was for strong men. Men of power and control. "This is no different than any other time I've used Dust, though perhaps more visible. Honestly, I didn't think it would work."

"I don't understand," Luke said. "You can't *see* Dust work. You smell it. Cinnamon and tobacco. Making *things* takes Grit."

Kootala thought on that for just a moment, then said, "I didn't make any-*thing*. Think of it as an illusion, of sorts. Grit forces *things* against their nature. I only saw the nature of the Dust, and guided it into a new configuration, though one that is harmonious."

Luke chuckled. "I don't understand you, my love. Whatever you did, however you did it, I'm grateful for the shade."

They continued on and the shadow followed above, keeping the two men out of direct sun.

"You could capitalize on this, you know," Luke said. "People would hire you to follow them around and make shade. Imagine what else you could make! Honestly, this needs to be explored."

"Always the businessman," Kootala said with a smile. "But I'm afraid my nature is not for sale."

"That's a shame." Luke gazed forward into the desert. "I'll cherish it for myself, then."

That reminded Kootala of Katie Lybuck, and he tried not to gag on laughter. "You know, Luke." He stifled a giggle. "I give you permission to go with that Lybuck girl."

Luke snapped his head and grimaced. "You..." He stopped, seeing the smirk on Kootala's face, then smiled back. "What if I find that I fancied *her* more than *you*?"

"That would be a miracle, by God, and I'd have to start going to church, I suppose!" Kootala couldn't hold it any longer. He started laughing wildly, gasping for air and trying not to fall off his horse.

Luke laughed too. "Hey, she's a nice gal. I just think she needs someone *else* to give her the time of day."

"I guess. I don't blame the other men in town. Who in their right mind would dare test Todd's patience by going with his daughter?"

"Also," Luke said. "I think Katie could whoop any man's ass in town. Tough girl, she is."

They both laughed again, and continued joking until they got home. After tying their horses, they carried the day's shopping into the house. Three armfuls each. Finally, they were done with the day's chores, and Luke pulled Kootala to their porch. He turned somber, and that feeling of wrongness washed over Kootala once again.

A rocking bench on their porch begged for their seat. The men took to it with a heavy sigh, and the bench's hinges squealed in summer agony.

"Let's talk," Luke said quietly.

Kootala's heart sank into his gut. His mind raced with dozens of unwanted scenarios. Was Luke going to tell him he didn't love him anymore? Did he find someone better in Graben? Or perhaps, forbid, he wasn't joking about Katie after all. Kootala scanned Luke's sorrowful eyes. "Tell me," he said, simply.

"I'm worried for you," Luke said. "Your safety, I mean. Things are changing around here, and I'm not always around to protect you."

"I don't need you to protect me. Anyway, you aren't so big and tough yourself," Kootala said, trying to lighten the mood.

"I know, but I'm afraid that if you were to find yourself in danger, that you wouldn't *do* anything about it." Luke looked away. "Do you know what I mean?"

"Oh. Yeah." Kootala sighed. He always worried that it would come to this.

"It's just... I think you need to buck up and realize that *sometimes* violence is justified. You aren't going to get out of every situation by being nice or by doing neat tricks with Dust. There are people that would kill you to take what they want. They don't know peace, and they can't be taught, either."

Kootala was reminded of the boy that had stolen his food, and the feel of a heavy rock in his hand. *Never again*, he thought. Earnestly, he said, "I value peace more than any possession, Lucas."

"More than me?" Luke asked with tears welling in his eyes.

Kootala opened his mouth to speak, but closed it again with nothing to say. How could he possibly answer such a question? What was Luke expecting from this conversation, other than pain? Finally, Kootala spoke. "I guess I don't know. Would you abandon all your values and morals for my sake?"

Although Luke said nothing, his face contorted, and seemed to speak on its own. *I already have*, that look said.

What to make of that? Kootala wondered.

They sat in silence for a while.

The bench hinges groaned, and the desert wind whispered faintly of mysteries and secrets.

Kootala finally spoke again. "When I was young, when my mother and I slept on the streets of Tucson or on the vast desert floor, I would often lie awake in fear. To help me sleep, my mother would tell me old Hoki stories. My favorite was that of our creation, the creation of this world, in fact. May I tell it to you?"

"Please do," Luke said, leaning his head on Kootala's shoulder.

Kootala cleared the desert dust from his throat and began.

***

In the beginning—long before men roamed the world, before even the world itself or the space in which it hung—there were only two things. The first, and greatest, was Tama, the Sun God. The other was the untamed energy of the universe. For ages unknown, Tama lived alone, in silence, and in utter dark. Their only company was the pure energy of the cosmos. Eventually, Tama grew lonely in their empty void, and so they decided to create something with which to share the universe.

Drawing upon all the energy of the cosmos, Tama molded a world of mud and slime. Then, Tama created Kongwuti, the Spider Grandmother, and shared with her the power of creation. Tama instructed Kongwuti to weave together a form of life to inhabit their world. She did so, fashioning insect-like creatures out of the clay of the earth.

For a time, the Sun God and the Spider Grandmother watched their world go about its course, but they soon saw their creation's flaw. The first creatures were miserable, horrid wretches that wallowed in the dank filth of their world. They fought, scratched, ate one another. The first world was infested with fleas, and all upon it was abomination. Life deserved better than that, and so Tama and Kongwuti decided to try again. With Tama's instruction, Kongwuti led only the least wretched of the creatures into an anthill and sealed them inside with tar. Kongwuti moved aside, and Tama destroyed the first world with fire, then blew away the smoke and ash to reveal a new, second world.

Spider Grandmother unsealed the anthill, and all the creatures emerged, now transformed into animals with four legs and fur, reminiscent of today's bears and wolves. These creatures were smarter and happier than their ancestors, and the second world was more comfortable, with oceans of water and planes of thick grass. The creatures were thankful, and worshipped Tama for creating this world, and Kongwuti for being their guide.

Ages passed, and the creatures began to forget their Sun God and their Spider Grandmother. The gifts they had been given faded from memory. Their peaceful land was not enough. Some of the animals became unhappy, for reasons unknown even to Tama, and fighting grew more common. The animals learned violence. They became vicious. Evil had sowed its seed throughout the second world, and so Tama decided to try again.

Kongwuti guided only the peaceful and happy animals into caves, and sealed them in with massive rocks. Tama, in turn, froze the world in a layer of ice, then shattered it away. The third world emerged from the snow, and Kongwuti opened the caves. The animals stepped out as apes. They were smarter, kinder, could learn, and most importantly, remember.

The third world was a paradise, with tropical jungles and plenty of food to go around. The apes were happy and lived peacefully with nature. They bellies were always full, and they worshipped Tama for providing such a wonderful world. Over time, the apes multiplied and covered the world.

Time passed again, and the ape population grew out of control, uninhibited by starvation or sickness. They became crowded. And they became jealous. Intelligent as they were, they found perfection unfavorable. Stagnation was a prison for thinking creatures, and so even paradise proved flawed. Wars broke out over personal and cultural disagreements, and infinite resources only led to more weapons. Tama, rightfully, was furious. The outcome of their paradise world was the biggest disaster of all, and so decided to try yet again. But this time, Tama would be careful. Another step was necessary.

To prevent the evils of the previous worlds from leeching into the next, Tama created a gatekeeper: Waasam, the Skeleton Grandfather. Tama tasked Waasam with the judgment of the apes as they sought entrance to the fourth world. For him, Kongwuti crafted two masks to wear before his gate. To the wretched and evil, Waasam wore a hideous and fearsome mask. Those apes fled in fear of Waasam, to stay in the third world until its destruction. To the pure of heart, Waasam wore a mask that was handsome and welcoming, dripping in jewels. The kindly Waasam ushered the good apes onward.

With Waasam's guidance, Kongwuti sealed only the most worthy of apes inside swamp reeds, and Tama flooded the world and washed away all evil. When the waters dried, Kongwuti opened the reeds, and humans emerged into this world. We are the direct ancestors of those people.

Now, we can see that this world is a combination of the previous three, with deserts and oceans and plains and jungles. The people of this world have to struggle in life, but they were given gifts so that they could survive and remember their heritage. The gods gave kindnesses, so that the people could keep their peace forever.

First, Spider Grandmother wove a web across the sky, and dew drops on the web formed the stars. Kongwuti retired to the sky and became the Moon. With her gift, we can look up and remember our creation and the journey our ancestors took to get to the forth world.

Next, Skeleton Grandfather gave the gift of knowledge and steward-ship over the land. He taught us to cultivate and hunt. He taught us how to live in peace with the world, so that we might sustain it forever. Then, Waasam created an eternal gate and retired to the underworld, where he judges the dead and grants passage to those that deserve it. With his gift, we have purpose, and we remember to live in peace and harmony with nature.

Finally, the Sun God gave us Grit and Dust. With this gift, we earned power to alter the world; for the better, it was intended. With Grit, we can protect. We can fend off evils, and we can form tools to restore nature. We heal with Dust, ease tensions, and treat sickness. With Tama's gift, we have responsibility, and we remember the need for stewardship.

Yet even with Tama's precautions, and with the gifts from the gods, the evils of the old worlds persist. Today, people kill for selfish purposes. We reap the land, abandoning our stewardship of nature. Instead, we violate Tama's creations, believing ourselves to be superior. There are those that wield Grit for their own greed. And so Tama came, finally, to a new conclusion; that evil comes not from the people, but as an undeniable force of the universe itself. Evil cannot be burned, frozen, or washed away. Yet there was good in this world, and Tama believed the good would always prevail, for our gifts guide us along the right path.

Thus, Tama created a fifth world, the gift yet to come, and retired to it alone, and in wait. For it is said that some day, Pamaha, the Lost Brother, will come from the east with blazing gold fires and burn away all of creation. Only those in the underworld, the people who lived in peace with nature, will find new residence in the fifth world, to live in harmony with Tama, Kongwuti, and Waasam for eternity.

So, though the evils of this world persist, true children of Tama re-member our past, and our purpose. To live in peace is the greatest virtue, and the only path to eternal life is one through harmony with nature.

***

When Kootala finished his story, he sighed and leaned back, letting the story's message take hold. The bench hinges squealed again, like some final hymn to an epic anthem.

"Thank you for sharing that with me," Luke said. "Though the ending was a bit confusing. It contradicts itself. If evil cannot be burned away, then why would Pamaha—"

"It is an imperfect tale." Kootala interrupted. "Stories passed down from mother to son, to grandson, to great-granddaughter, and so on. Details are bound to change. These days, most Hoki see these stories as myth, mere metaphor, rather than historical records. Personally, I can't say one way or the other."

Luke kept silent, then. He wished he had more to say, but couldn't find the words in that moment.

Kootala continued. "These stories are all I have left of my mother. They *may* only be stories, yet to my mother, their values were as certain as the setting of the sun. She lived by those values, no matter how difficult, no matter our circumstance. Often we found ourselves in situations where fighting would have seemed appropriate, but she always refrained. Did she believe she would greet Waasam in the end? I don't know. But I *do* know that she thought her ways were right, no matter the reason.

"She died with the belief that peace is the most important value of all. I *must* carry that part of her with me. If I should fail her in that regard, there will be nothing left of her." Kootala took Luke's hand in his own. "Do you understand?"

"I understand," Luke said. He was reminded of his own mother, who had abandoned him without hesitation. Luke's experience couldn't have been more different. "I will respect that part of you, I suppose. But I can't say I share your sentiment."

"Thank you," Kootala said.

"And what of your job?" Luke asked. "What would you do, should danger ever threaten this town or yourself?"

"I can't say for certain, but I will do everything I can to foster peace. How, exactly, will depend on the circumstance."

That was not the answer Luke had hoped for, but he knew nothing he said could change Kootala's mind. Some things ran so deep that no rationale could carve them out. Such was Kootala's staunch position of anti-violence, or Luke's love for Kootala in return. Neither would ever break, not even at the end of the world.

"I will not kill to protect the value of this town," Kootala said, perhaps thinking he needed to reiterate.

Luke sighed. "Then let's hope it never comes to that."

Kootala nodded, but said nothing in return.

They sat there for a while, holding each other in silence. Soon, a soft wind kicked up and blew in cool air. The pressure dropped—Luke could feel it in his lungs—and he was certain that it *would* rain that night. The desert could only hold moisture away for so long.

Luke found that change in the air to be dreadful. Tomorrow was the day that he and Cassidy would rob the bank. There was sure to be mischief, and danger, and Luke feared for Kootala more than he ever had before. What would the Hoki man do when faced with dire conflict? Luke could only wish for such a circumstance to remain hypothetical. Yet he didn't think they would be so lucky.

The two men rocked on the bench, its squeaky hinges singing a sharp cry of impending doom.

And distant thunder rolled.

8

That night a torrential downpour crashed from the sky in waves. Rain was rare, but when it finally came, it was quick and full. The earth drank greedily, not knowing when it might get another sip. Floods carved rills through the loose sand. The desert mice and insects were washed down gullies and into the valley. Lightning scattered the land, turning the sand to shards of green glass where it struck. And all the while, the Colorado River swelled and raging waves crashed over the docks of Graben.

Luke slept restlessly. Thunder manifested as gunfire in his nightmares. Kootala held him tight, Luke trembling in his arms.

In the morning, they had a breakfast of leftover potatoes and some eggs, after which they rode their horses into town. The streets boiled sweat from the heat of the morning sun, and the air was thick and humid. Luke kissed Kootala goodbye, lingering longer than usual, then they separated for work. Luke rode to the Newports' house, paused to make sure he was not being watched, then continued past the estate. He turned north and rode briskly out of town. His horse's hooves left a trail of freshly exposed soil that steamed in the sweltering sun.

The desert vegetation was already coming back to life after the refreshing rain. Chaparral shrubs had begun to unfurl their leaves, and the pampas grass stood nearly upright and would be rigid by noon. By noon the day following, Graben Valley would be speckled with vibrant green. In a week, all would dry, reverting to dormant gray and brown once again.

Luke approached an outcropping of rocks, behind which he found Cassidy Reeve waiting with her horse—Sam's horse was not with her—and a covered wagon with something bulky underneath the canvas.

"Are you fully committed today?" Cassidy asked. "I want this to go smoothly."

"I'm ready," he said, dismounting his horse. "And believe me, I want this to be as uneventful as you do. More so."

Cassidy rolled her eyes.

They stowed Luke's horse behind the rocks, and Cassidy handed over Sam Clangour's disguise. He stripped to his britches, then folded his clothes and placed them inside his horse's saddlebag. He stepped into a pair of stiff blue jeans, pulled a white undershirt over his head, and a leather vest over that. Then, he covered his head with his white wig and hat, and tied a bandanna around his neck.

Cassidy mounted her horse, then pulled Sam up to sit behind her. They started off, pulling the wagon behind them, its wheels leaving a trail of parallel channels through the sand. *Let's hope nobody inspects those*, Sam thought.

Sitting bareback behind Cassidy was quite uncomfortable, and Sam knew his legs would surely be sore at the end of the day. He adjusted his seat, but it was no use, and he dared not close the gap between his and Cassidy's hips. Instead, he leaned back, resting his elbows on the horse's rear.

"Be still," Cassidy said.

They rode on in silence.

Sam Clangour and Cassidy Reeve had worked together for many years, but had rarely ever talked about anything other than business. In their line of work, you kept to yourself. They didn't need to know about you, and you didn't need to know about them. It was safer that way. Smarter. If they died, you wouldn't care quite so much. Yet after so many years together, most people couldn't help it any longer.

"What is your deal?" Sam asked as they rode.

"What?"

"I mean, with *him*," Sam said. He remembered that Cassidy needed simple talk. Direct. "How'd you get involved with a man like Casey Calhoun?"

"Would knowing help you do your job?" she snapped.

"Well, possibly. Even if it doesn't, I'd still like to be familiar with the dangerous outlaw at my side."

"You first."

Sam sighed. "Alright."

He thought on it for a while before answering. What was he comfortable telling this woman? Should he tell her about moving west with his family as a teenager, about how they disliked it and ultimately moved back east? Would she sympathize with him, knowing that he fell in love with Kootala, and that his family abandoned him for it? Would she be searching for truth, or might she believe a fabrication? He looked at her often, and knew the strength of perception in her eyes. He decided to tell the truth.

"Well, I'm a German-Irish queer who escaped into the freedom of the west. I fell in love with a Hoki man and foolishly stole my way into his heart. I tried robbing Casey in pursuit of a better life for Kootala. Casey nearly killed me, but decided to conscript me instead. I received his debt in exchange for my and Kootala's life." Sam sighed. "Now I go home and lie to the man I love, because I tried to make his life better."

Cassidy scrunched her mouth to one side, making the face of empathetic understanding. "Ain't that a bitch," she said.

"Your turn." Sam reminded her.

"Alright."

Cassidy had always been a brutally honest person, often to her detriment, Sam thought. She cared little about how others perceived her, and she spoke openly, with restraint only for herself.

"My parents were slaves down near Tucson, well after the war ended," she said. "There are still slaves out there today, if you'd believe it. They're technically free, but nobody told *them* that."

Sam figured as much.

"Anyway, my parents got their freedom, eventually. They went out on their own with nothin' but rags for clothes, a blue bead necklace from my mother's mother around her neck, and me in her womb. They worked hard, managed to buy some land near Phoenix, and started a small farm of their own. When I was fifteen, a group of corporate ranchers killed my parents and stole their land. They burned the house to the ground and left my parents hangin' from a tree." Cassidy took a deep breath, then said, "The goats ate my mother's feet."

"Oh." Sam was stunned, speechless at the wickedness of men. Looking at the woman before him, it was no wonder she had gone so wrong.

"Now..." Cassidy continued. "I'm getting back at the white motherfuckers who did that to us, my family, *and* all the other Black folk done wrong. These people up in this town are just the same; rich white folk who owned my people as property, and still do in some cases. I'm out here taking back what's mine. And as a bonus, I might someday find the ones took my mother's beads, and I'll string them up a tree just the same!"

Sam found his words then. "I guess that's as good a reason as any."

"That's the difference between *us* and *him*," Cassidy said. "Casey's in it for the money. And the sick satisfaction of ruining other people's lives, I think. But if he can help me in *my* endeavors, well, then why not return the favor?"

Was that supposed to make everything she'd done justified? Clearly she thought so, but Sam couldn't bridge that gap for himself. He said, "Well, I'm nearly free of my debt. After that, I'm done with this life. I'm not made for this."

"You sure about that?" Cassidy looked over her shoulder. She raised a questioning eyebrow.

Honestly, Sam wasn't so sure after all. The outlaw life had done him well so far. He figured he would just have to wait and see.

Cassidy turned forward again. "Tell yourself whatever you want, hun, but at the end of it all you're still a damn good thief."

Changing the subject, Sam said, "I still don't understand why we have to do this *at* the bank. I mean, why couldn't we ambush them a few miles outside of town instead?"

"Think a minute as if you was them. Wouldn't you expect *that*? Would you think anyone could be brave or stupid enough to steal from them at the bank itself? Nah, they'll let their guard down for sure."

That was quite a leap in logic, Sam thought.

"And besides, this is what Casey said to do, and his word is final."

"Alright, alright." Sam conceded. "So how is this gonna go down?"

"There will be an armed caravan coming through around noon. The bank will empty their vault, including the bonds and stocks and whatever else is in there, and transfer it through the back door to a safe within the caravan. The safe will probably be in a covered cart like the one we're pulling.

"Your job is to wait until they go inside, then climb into their cart and hide behind the safe. Once they leave, you shove the safe out the back and I'll come along and pick it up. We then ride back here, I'll take the score, and you can return home with no incident."

Sam stared slack-jawed at the stupidity of the plan. It was ridiculous, and it was irresponsible. "You don't think they are going to notice a heavy safe fall out the back of their cart?" he asked.

"No," Cassidy said with a smile. "Because I'm going to cause a little distraction. You'll push the safe out when you hear my signal."

"Okay..." Sam hesitated. "And what is the signal?"

"You'll know it when you hear it. Trust me."

"Oh, well, you *are* a very trustworthy person after all." Sam groaned. "I don't like this one bit. Not a single detail. Couldn't Casey come do this, just wave his hand around and do some shit with the dirt, and be out before anyone even knew what happened?"

"Quit your bitchin' and just do it, okay?"

"Fine. I expect a big cut for this." *Enough to pay off my debt for good,* he thought.

"You can count on that," Cassidy said. "Are you ready?"

"I guess so." Sam ran his thumb across his lip scar, then pulled the bandanna up over his nose.

***

Sam dismounted Cassidy's horse. His boot heels sunk into the soft, moist ground of a back street. No one had seen them come through. Cassidy tipped her hat and continued on, while Sam made his way to the alley behind the bank.

He searched the alley for a spot to hide, and found someone's porch steps with a good view of the bank's back door. Sam crawled under the porch and found himself up to his wrists in mud. The space smelled musty with ancient wood, mold, and the bones of long-dead rodents. There, he waited. *Like a damn rodent, myself,* he thought.

After some time, Sam felt as if he might doze off. He slapped himself awake.

A flicker of light caught his eye. He looked down the alley and saw the Deetmans' barn in the distance. Up in the hayloft, a reflection of sunlight pulsed with a consistent rhythm. Cassidy was up there, letting Sam know that she was in position. She could see him, and she was ready. Perhaps, also, she meant to warn him that he was too visible. He sunk further into the shadows.

Sam couldn't begin to imagine what the woman was doing up in a hay loft. Whatever her plans, he didn't think Vanessa Deetman was going to be too happy at the end of the day.

Not long after, the bank caravan rounded the corner into the alley. There was a stagecoach in the lead, followed by a covered wagon pulled by two horses, and another stagecoach at the rear.

Sheriff Brooks and Kootala followed close behind.

"Shit." Sam cursed through clenched teeth. Of course they were with the wagon! Why hadn't he thought they'd be there too? Wishful thinking or dumb blind ignorance?

Sam scanned back to Cassidy's position, hoping she might come running from the barn, or flash her light again, or *something*, anything at all.

Why would she?

There were no signs from her location.

Alright, Sam told himself, *we are doing this, then*.

The caravan stopped outside the back door of the bank. Sam's blood pounded hard, echoing through his head, likely to give him a headache later that evening. The caravan men dismounted their rides along with Sheriff Brooks, then went into the bank. Kootala remained outside, on his horse, watching the alley.

If he sees me...

Kootala turned, rode a few paces up the alley, and remained there, still as stone. He was watching Main Street, and likely wouldn't turn again for some time.

"Oh, I love you. I really love you!" Sam said aloud, though quietly under his breath.

Slowly, Sam crawled out from under the porch and removed his vest, which he used to wipe the mud from his arms and legs, then threw it back under the porch.

How much easier would it be, he wondered, if *he* had the power of Grit. Like Casey Calhoun, he could bring forth a sandstorm to conceal himself.

I wonder...

Sam focused on the dirt floor of the alley, which was still moist and rutted from the passing caravan. He tensed his muscles, his mind, and tried to force the dirt and dust to his will.

Nothing happened.

Sam groaned, then continued on. No mystical power to be had today.

He crossed the alley without a sound, and found purchase next to the covered wagon. In a single swift motion, he pulled back the canvas, climbed inside and wedged himself behind the safe, then threw the canvas back.

Then Sam waited.

It felt like ages, but he was sure that only minutes had passed. Yet in those few minutes, Sam had come to a terrible realization; there was a stagecoach *behind* the safe wagon. If he were to push the safe out while they were moving, they would notice immediately. It was likely that the coach's horses would trip on the safe, and Sam would find lead in his head, regardless of the distraction Cassidy had planned.

What a foolish idea! Sam was stupid to have gone along with this! He should have said no, could have figured something else out. There was no way this was going to work. He needed to get out of there right away!

Sam gathered his courage and reached up to remove the canvas once again.

The bank's door opened.

"—and I told him, 'you want some damn fine tobacco, take a trip down to Tijuana,'" someone said.

Another laughed.

"Alright, let's get this in here and be on our way." A third voice.

Sheriff Brooks spoke. "Kootala, go along Main and make sure these fellas got a clear path."

"Sir," Kootala said, then Sam heard the squishing of horse hooves walking away through the mud.

The canvas fluttered, and someone began working on the safe. *Scuff scuff, click. Scuff, click. Scuff scuff.*

What have I gotten myself into? Sam wondered.

The safe creaked open, something heavy was placed inside, and the door closed again. The canvas fluttered a final time, then was still.

"That's that," someone said.

"Kootala and I will follow y'all until you're out of town." The sheriff. "Then, you're on your own."

"Load up, fellas."

Sam heard everyone mount their rides again, and felt his cart jolt into motion.

What was Sam to do? Stick with the plan and get caught? Improvise and... get caught? Perhaps he could stay hidden until they stopped at Lonely, then sneak away? Would they even stop in Lonely? Is Cassidy still—

KA-BOOM!

The world shook. Sam's ears rang and his skull vibrated in tune with the air around him. The wagon lurched, sped up, swerved, tipped, swerved again. Sam's teeth crashed together and pinched the inside of his cheeks with a sharp *crunch*.

I guess I'm improvising!

Sam threw back the canvas and looked up. In the distance, the Deetmans' barn was raining down from the sky as shrapnel over a rising column of black smoke.

"Holy shit, Cassidy!" Sam cried out.

The wagon lurched again and the driver emerged from underneath its wheels. He rolled limply through the mud. Behind him, the drivers of the stagecoach struggled to calm their horses. The sheriff's mule bucked wildly, sending him into the mud as well.

I guess I'm taking the whole damn cart!

Sam crawled to the front and took purchase upon the bucket seat. He took hold of the reins and got the horses under control, then sailed out onto Main Street, turning the corner sharply. The wagon tipped up on two wheels, then crashed back down again. Sam continued, heading out of town along Main.

But where is Kootala?

Cassidy rounded the corner, joining Sam, yelling, "Hey, cowboy!"

"What the hell was *that*?" Sam shouted, nodding back toward the blown-up barn.

"That was supposed to be my *little* distraction. Seems God had other plans today." Cassidy howled with laughter.

Sam looked back and saw nobody following. "As stupid as this was, I think it worked after all!"

They rode on, seemingly without further incident. They were going to get away with it.

As they passed the last house on Main, Kootala and his horse jumped out into the road ahead of them. Kootala held out his gun, aiming toward Sam and Cassidy.

"Stop!" Kootala shouted.

Sam's eyes darted between his husband and his associate.

Cassidy drew her own gun.

"No!" Sam yelled, and steered his horse into hers, pushing Cassidy to the side and breaking her aim. He pulled hard on the reins, stopping the horses in their tracks. The wagon Sam was pulling slid sideways through the mud, wrapping around his side, and came to a stop in front of Cassidy. She reared her horse and came to a stop herself.

"Please, Cassidy. Don't," Sam said, his voice quivering.

Cassidy looked back up at Kootala, called out to him. "Are you willing to kill us for a little sum of cash?"

"There is more in there than money," Kootala shouted back. "And I am willing to do what I can to uphold the law."

Sam leaned toward Cassidy and said, only loud enough for her to hear, "He won't shoot us. We can just walk around him."

Cassidy lowered her weapon. "How about you just let us by, and we won't cause any more trouble, eh, kid?"

Sheriff Brooks shouted from the distance. "Shoot her, Kootala!" He was riding fast up their rear. "That's Cassidy Reeve! Don't let her get away!"

In a lighting swift motion, Cassidy turned, raised her gun again, and shot.

KA-BLAM!

The report echoed across the desert.

Brooks flew backward off his mule and landed face-first in the mud with a wet, limp *thump*.

"*NO!*" Kootala and Sam yelled in unison.

"Let's go," Cassidy said calmly, and took off again. She rode slowly around Kootala, who only stood there in disbelief. Though he still raised his weapon, he did not shoot.

He would never shoot.

Sam slapped the reins and followed after Cassidy. He turned his face away as he passed Kootala, and did not look back as he left.

They continued out of town.

9

When Sam and Cassidy reached the outcropping of rocks, Sam looked back toward town, following the tracks of wheel channels and hoof prints.

They had not been followed.

Finally, Sam spoke. He tried to remain calm, though he couldn't keep the pure hatred from his voice. "What the hell, Cassidy? You... you killed the sheriff."

"I've killed many men." Cassidy replied, softly. "You know that. Would you have preferred I killed your lover instead?"

Sam's anger boiled over and he shouted. "No! I would have preferred you kill nobody! What were you thinking?"

"I was thinking I didn't want to hang like my parents! Now shut the hell up and help me with this safe!"

Sam's voice caught in his throat. Then, said simply, "Fine."

They lifted the safe and moved it to Cassidy's cart with great effort. It was heavy, both with its own thickness and with the contents inside. They secured the safe with a rope and threw a tarp over the top. Cassidy unhooked the horses from the bank's wagon, then slapped them on the rear. They kicked at the air and bolted out into the desert.

Cassidy turned to Sam. "You'll get your cut in a few days. Keep an eye on the mail."

"I don't want a penny of this... this... *blood money*! Tell Casey he can keep my cut, and consider my debt paid. It should more than cover it. I'm out. I'm done."

"You know that ain't how this works, Sam. You get a cut, whether you want it or not, and he keeps you in service. That's your deal."

"Don't you tell me about my deal! He can keep my cut whether *he* wants it or not." Sam ripped off his disguise and threw it into the dirt. He put his own clothes back on, then mounted his own horse. "Excuse me, now. I have to go pretend like I don't know what the hell happened back there."

Luke spit into the dirt at Cassidy's feet, then rode back through Bluff's Reach, passing the Newports' property on the way through.

Cassidy shouted as he left. "Don't be stupid, kid!"

As if he hadn't been stupid all along, he thought.

***

Kootala fell to his knees before his sheriff. He ran a hand over the man's chest, then flinched when he felt the wound; a hole, directly through the heart. Cassidy's aim had been true.

"No. No!" Kootala moaned.

He took a handful of sand—skimmed from the ground what dry material he could find—and held it to the bubbling bullet hole. With great effort, Kootala focused all his energy on the injury. He drew deep upon the well of power within his own heart, then pushed outward. His hand quivered. The smell of apples erupted from the wound, but it was sour. Rotten. Black sludge gargled up between Kootala's fingers: blood and mud.

Abner Brooks remained still. Dust could do many things. Could seal cuts, could sooth pain, but it could not mend a fatal wound. It could not revive the dead. Nor could Grit, for that matter.

A weary sound came from Kootala's chest, not quite a cry, not quite a groan. It was the sound of defeat, plain and simple. Of giving up. "I'm... so sorry," Kootala said, then covered the sheriff's wound with his own hand.

A crowd had gathered around the fallen sheriff and his clerk. They murmured among themselves. *What a sight to see*, Kootala thought. There would be much talk, that night. The next. For quite some time. Rumors. Fears.

Someone was shouting, pushing their way through the crowd. "—happened? Kootala! What happened?" The onlookers parted, and Luke shoved his way to Kootala. "I heard an explosion, and a gunshot. I... Oh." Luke stopped, looked down. "Kootala," he said softly. "What can we do?"

"Get these people to clear out." Kootala commanded. The force of his voice surprised even himself. Never had he spoken so directly and with such authority!

"Alright, everyone," Luke called out. "Go on and get home. Give this man some respect and quit your gawking."

The crowd murmured, but didn't seem all that interested in leaving.

Kootala stood, then shouted. "*GO!*"

They flinched and reluctantly started to disperse. Kootala could hear the fear and uncertainty in their voices as they left.

Someone handed Kootala a quilted blanket.

"Thank you," Kootala said. He reached down and removed Abner's hat and badge, said a quiet Hoki prayer, then covered the man with the quilt.

Kootala stood. He looked down the street, out to the open desert beyond, where Cassidy Reeve and Sam Clangour had escaped.

Is there such a truth as justice, he wondered as he affixed the sheriff's badge upon his vest.

10

Casey Calhoun rode slowly across the desert just north of Graben. A posse of three others rode at his side. The boy, Buck, rode closest. He was a young man of around twenty, stupidly ambitious, and trying hard to impress. His green eyes watched Casey intently, searching for the smallest hint of approval—Casey could feel the look piercing his side. Buck irritated Casey immensely. He was weak, utterly dependent on the strength of another man. Still, Casey knew the boy's value and was happy to use him thus.

The group rode north until they came upon a shallow dip in the land. A channel, a few feet deep and some fifteen feet across, stretched east to west as far as they could see. It would appear to many as an old, dried-up river bed.

Casey knew otherwise.

He had recently come into the possession of an old map, one which was hidden for years in the back of a safe deposit box belonging to a man in Bluff's Reach—along with a load of other treasures. Judging by the state of the map, Casey figured it had been long forgotten by its previous owner: just a dusty scroll in a pile of shimmering gold. Casey, however, had been hunting this for quite some time. Most people in his search had been uncooperative, evidenced by the little *quarrel* with Thomas Abernathy. Yet Casey was a man who got what he wanted, whether with help or without, and so it was *their* fault that he sometimes had to be *persuasive*.

Now, here it was at last.

Casey dismounted his Arabian and threw the reins to Buck. The boy fumbled, but managed to get hold of the ropes. Casey shook his head, knowing it would distress the boy, and walked down into the ditch.

The bottom of the channel was filled with a soft layer of fine sand that had settled from years of passing desert winds. He let the powder sift through his fingers and float back to the ground. The formation was even, with no large rocks or blemishes in its structure. In fact, Casey noted no natural features at all. This was man-made.

Casey walked to the center and knelt. He removed the buck knife from its sheath at his waist, then ran it through the sand, perpendicular to the direction of the channel. The knife struck something solid. Casey brushed away a bit of sand to reveal a steel beam.

He smiled, stood, then held his hand out over the metal, palm down. Casey focused. The fine sand at his feet began to shiver, as if quaking before an approaching train. Then Casey pushed, and threw his hand to the side. The sand flew open like a huge, tumbling wave, and revealed two sets of parallel rail tracks, hidden under the desert for decades.

Casey Calhoun had *parted* the desert, just as Moses did the Red Sea. *Wasn't that something*, he thought. A man, under the favor of God.

He smiled, then turned and walked up out of the track's ditch. Casey brushed his knife across his pant leg, cleaning the sand that clung to it with dry static.

"Good job, sir," Buck said, returning Casey his horse's reins.

The boy would eat out of my hand if I willed it, Casey thought. *He would eat out of my ass!*

"Sir, would you like—"

"Enough." Casey interrupted. "Leave us, Buck. Go to Graben at once, and find someone who can cut us a lot of lumber for cheap." He shoved a small paper ledger at the boy. "Cutting specs."

"But what—"

"Go!" Casey said, not quite a shout, but strong and demanding.

"Sir," Buck said, nodded, and left.

Casey could feel his plans coming to fruition. Looking east, following the path of the tracks, he imagined a locomotive racing toward the mighty Colorado River. He nearly felt his hair blowing back as the train passed, kicking out a wake of hot air and sand. Then, the train turned, and headed directly for the bluff, upon which Bluff's Reach was perched high above. Casey watched the train fly across the desert. It raced toward the wall of rock. It was going to crash.

Casey shook the image from his head, and shuddered. "Come along," he said to the remaining two men in his posse.

They followed without a word, northwest toward Lonely.

11

Darkness had long since fallen through their bedroom window, yet Luke Morgan laid awake, visions of the dead sheriff haunting his eyes every time he blinked. Kootala lay at Luke's side, facing away. The Hoki man was still, breathing steadily. Luke wondered if *he* was sleeping, or staring at the wall too. Luke did not ask.

He was restless for what seemed like hours. Eventually, he could take it no longer and decided to get out of bed. From the icebox he retrieved himself a glass of cold milk, which he then drank slowly while seated at the table. His mind was turning over and over with endless thoughts, and he felt in that moment that he might go mad.

Milk foam dripped from Luke's lip. He licked it off, and was once again reminded of his scar. And of how he got it.

It had been a cool winter day, and the train's smoke hung in a low haze that smelled sweet like tobacco...

Several Years Ago

Luke Morgan stepped up to the train platform. He wandered for a moment, then found a lonely seat on a bench near the ticket counter. The station was busy that day, crawling with businessmen and families out on travel. Luke watched them all carefully, analyzing their behavior, trying to determine who might be easy pickings.

He had only stolen once as a young boy with his friends back east. It was simple enough, back then. Luke's friend Maxwell distracted the candy man, and Luke filled his pockets with licorice and lemon drops. It couldn't have been more than a dollar's worth, in all. Yet when Max's parents found out, they told Luke's. Both boys had their bare asses beat with a wooden spoon with holes drilled into it. The holes, Luke learned quickly, made it sting and helped the lesson sink in quicker. But now was different. That first time, he was just a stupid kid, doing things kid boys do. Now he was a man, still young, sure, but an adult nonetheless. And if he got caught, he would get more than a spoon to the rear.

Luke noticed a man take a seat on a bench opposite the station platform. He wore a nice suit, had his hair slicked neatly back, and flashed an exquisite gold watch on his wrist. The man read the train ticket in his hand, then folded it and tucked it into his jacket pocket. Strangely enough, he carried no luggage: same as Luke.

After some time, the strange man pulled out a newspaper, held it up, and pretended to read. He never flipped the page. Instead, he stole peeks out from behind the paper, watching the crowd with great interest. He was certainly an interesting sight, and Luke wondered if he was up to no good. Perhaps he was there for the very same reason that Luke was. Perhaps he would make a good target. He certainly wouldn't expect that!

Luke occasionally had to remind himself why here was there. This was not a spurred whim, not a crime of opportunity. No, this was necessity. This was for Kootala.

Luke had chosen to stay with Kootala against his parents' requests. They had fled back east and left Luke in Arizona, with nothing but shame in his heart and dust in his pockets. He and Kootala lived poor, and though they both moved from job to job, it never seemed enough.

That was when Luke turned to pickpocketing. As it turns out, he was a natural. One man's wallet usually held more than Luke or Kootala could earn in a month, and so Luke continued down that path of crime. And it was all for Kootala, so that someday he wouldn't have to come home with knuckles bloodied from factory work. This was all for love.

Luke noticed the strange man stir. He ruffled his newspaper, then held it higher, concealing his face. Another man walked by, carrying a bulky briefcase at his side, which he placed at the first man's feet, then walked away. The first man—the one with the slick black hair and gold watch—casually slid the briefcase under the bench with his feet. Not once did he look up from his paper.

Luke smiled at the scene. Whatever was in that briefcase had to be worth a fortune. For Luke at least. Those men would likely be fine without it. Luke had to have it.

They waited for some time, until the next train pulled into the station. It squealed to a stop, and locomotive smoke filled the air.

Luke's target got up, with his briefcase, and boarded the train. Luke waited until nearly all the other passengers had boarded, then stepped up into the car as well.

The cab was filled with more smoke—real tobacco smoke, more harsh than what came from the engine. On the left were rows of bucket seats, three per row, all facing forward. On the right, bench seats faced small tables on both sides, like semi-private booths. The man with the briefcase was sat alone at one of these booths. Luke approached and gestured to the open bench across the table. "May I?" he asked pleasantly. "All the other seats have been taken."

The man looked annoyed, said nothing, but nodded his acceptance.

Luke took the seat, and noticed the briefcase tucked between the man and the window. He would be able to grab it easily enough. He only had to wait until the train started moving, then he could snatch it and run off. Luke stared at the case, wondering what treasures it might contain. Cash? Gold?

The man coughed. Luke looked up at him, and he was staring right back. His face held no readable expression.

A steward approached their booth. "Gentlemen," he said with a nod, then started when he recognized the man across from Luke. "Casey! So nice to have you again.

Casey spoke with a voice smooth and pleasant like fine Swiss chocolate. "Bring me a bottle of brandy and two glasses. Fill one with ice and leave the other without."

"Absolutely. And you sir?" The steward tipped toward Luke.

"Nothing for me, thank you," Luke said. He wasn't planning on sticking around for a drink.

"Very well." The steward walked off.

The train vibrated and hissed as the engine was worked up to full power. The passengers settled into their seats for departure. All the while, Luke stared intently at the briefcase. His palms grew sweaty, and he wiped the moisture off on his pants.

Quickly, the steward returned and placed a bottle of brandy and two crystal glasses—one filled with ice—onto the table. Casey gave the man a dollar and a thanks.

The train lurched and began creeping forward.

Casey filled the ice glass with brandy, swirled it, then put his fingers over the top and strained the cold liquid into the other glass.

"Where you headed?" Casey asked suddenly.

Luke stammered, startled. He had been so focused on the briefcase that he never thought the man might start conversation. "Oh. Uh. Well, I'm going down to Marble Springs to visit family," Luke said, unconvincingly.

Casey dumped the brandy into his mouth and swallowed it all in a single gulp. "Hmm. I was just curious, beings you have no luggage."

He's on to me, Luke thought. *Now is the time.*

Their train car approached the end of the station. Outside, a railing divided the loading platform from a three-foot drop to the ground. Luke had to time it just right. If he could step off the train right before that railing, he could walk away with his score, and this *Casey* fella couldn't follow.

Luke jumped from the seat and lunged for the briefcase.

Casey stood at the same time and drove the stock of his pistol into Luke's upper lip.

Luke fell back into his seat with a grunt.

"If you let air under your ass, you'll be getting off this train in a burlap sack," Casey said, aiming his gun at Luke's chest.

Luke tasted the sting of iron on his teeth. He put his hand under his chin to catch the sieve of blood that ran from his split lip. Casey bent, removed one of his boots and a sock, then handed the sock over to Luke. Repulsed, but as his only option, Luke held the sweaty cotton to his lip.

An older couple across the aisle gasped at the sight, then whispered to each other. Their eyes darted back and forth between Luke and Casey. The man began to stand, but the woman caught his arm and pulled him back down. Her eyes pleaded. *This is none of our business.* She was smart, and she was correct.

"You must think me stupid," Casey said. "You've been staring at me since I sat down at the station almost an hour ago. Your eyes haven't left my briefcase this entire time. You were drooling over it, boy. I could see your plans in your eyes."

"I'm sorry, sir," Luke said, muffled through Casey's sock. He was somewhat thankful for the blood in his mouth, for it masked the disgusting taste of foot sweat. "Are you going to turn me in?" he asked.

"Now, that *would* make me stupid! I want the law to know about this briefcase about as much as you want to spend the night in a moldy cell. So no, we can resolve this dispute on our own."

Casey grabbed the two glasses and split the ice between them. He filled both with brandy, stirred them with his finger, then sucked his finger dry. He pushed one of the glasses to Luke. "That wound is going to leave a handsome scar, kid. The ladies will like that."

"Right." Luke muffled. "What do you want from me, then?"

"First, put down that drink I so generously made for you. It is impolite to refuse a drink from someone while negotiating a deal."

Luke hesitated for a moment, then dropped the sock. It was soaked halfway with fresh blood, and made a mess on their table. He tipped back the drink and guzzled through the sharp pain of ice and alcohol on open flesh. When finished, he set the glass down and saw its ice had turned a vibrant pink. He put the dry side of Casey's sock back to his lip.

Casey drank his brandy slowly, then sighed with satisfaction and leaned back into his seat. "You're lucky my briefcase is still at my side, if I'm being honest with you. I *would* have killed you, had you managed to leave this train with it. I might kill you yet, just for the hell of it."

"Please, sir. Casey. I'll do whatever I can to make this right. I don't have money, but I can work hard! Please, whatever you need." Luke's *whatever* came out wet and unintelligible. He could feel the glob of spit and blood pooling around his teeth.

"I like your proposition," Casey said. He bent again and removed his other boot and sock, and handed the fresh cotton to Luke. "You made a mistake trying to steal from me, but I can see that you aren't *too* foolish. You had this all planned out. And, it likely would have worked on anyone else. But, you see, I'm a professional. I figured you out the minute I saw you at the station. I also figure you have potential, and that is something I find very valuable. So, here is *my* proposition.

"I will pay you a significant sum of money today, enough to go stitch up that lip and pay off any bills you may have. It's enough to live on for a time. In return, you will owe me a debt of ten times the amount, and you will work for me to pay it back. You will complete any task that I give you, and along with reducing your debt, you will receive payment for each job, whether you want it or not. My other offer, if you so choose, is your life."

Luke groaned. "I'll take the debt," he said.

"Good choice." Casey laid the briefcase on the table and unlatched it. He opened it, revealing an uncountable sum of money from which he grabbed a single bound stack and handed it to Luke. Casey then latched the case and returned it to his side. "That is five thousand dollars. You take that home with you, or to the family you say you are visiting. Honestly, I don't give a damn what you do with it."

Luke pulled his hand away from his face, his mouth open, frozen in awe. A clot of blood plopped down into his lap.

"You will be in my debt for fifty thousand dollars," Casey said. "Depending on your cut from each job, of which I decide, you can expect to earn, say, another ten thousand by the time your debt is clear."

Luke drooled blood. He had hardly ever conceived of so much money. He was unsure if he should be ecstatic or terrified.

"Like I said earlier, you're lucky you did not leave here with my briefcase. In fact, you have stumbled into a rather lucrative business opportunity, kid. You're welcome." Casey smiled. His teeth were clean white and perfectly straight.

The train had long since pulled out of the station, and was now chasing hard through the desert. Casey and Luke hashed out the details of their agreement, although there was little negotiation. Casey continued to fill Luke's glass with liquor, and Luke continued to drink despite the pain it caused to his lip. Casey's socks became heavily saturated, and Luke eventually switched to his own. All the while, heavy coal smoke left a slug trail behind the train as it made its way to Marble Springs.

***

Luke had just finished his glass of milk when Kootala emerged from their room and joined him at the table. The Hoki man's eyes were red and puffy. He had not slept, either.

Neither man said a word, but Kootala took Luke's hand into his own and squeezed tightly. No words *needed* to be said, as that touch was clear enough. *Come back to bed.*

Luke followed Kootala back to their room, where they held each other under a warm quilt. Neither could find rest that night, but they found comfort enough, for a while.

12

*C*assidy Reeve was in a garden with her hand wrapped lightly around a deep reed tomato. She plucked it and added it to her basket.

The garden's canopy cast a wide shadow over her, protecting her from the wicked sun above. She grabbed another tomato. It glistened with cool sweat, taunting her to take a bite of its sweetness. She looked around, saw nobody, and sunk her teeth into its flesh. Sweet red juice dribbled down her chin.

A pair of boots stepped into her vision.

"Cass," her father said. "Your Mam would turn your rear purple if she saw you eating that."

Cassidy looked up at the silhouette of her father. The sun radiated from behind his head like a majestic halo: black against gold.

She smiled with tomato seeds in her teeth. "Don't tell, Daddy."

The towering man knelt down to her, took the half-eaten tomato from her little hands, and bit into it himself. "I won't tell if you won't," said he.

The girl giggled.

Her father wiped the tomato juice from his face, then lifted her up onto his hip.

The ground raced away, and she clung to his waist as tightly as possible. Though she was scared, she knew she was safe in his arms.

***

Cassidy Reeve was in the kitchen, washing a bucket of potatoes. She could feel the gritty sand from the spuds under her fingernails. The water was steaming hot, and she could only submerge her hands for a few seconds at a time.

She handed a clean potato to her mother, who peeled and diced it, then tossed it into a bowl. The woman wiped her wet hands on her apron, where a starch stain had bloomed, then began snapping the stems off a handful of string beans.

Cassidy plunged her hands back into the grainy water.

Cassidy's mother placed a loving grip on the girl's shoulder. She squeezed, and the touch told a love story stronger than any words ever could.

***

Cassidy Reeve wept at the foot of her bed. She prayed, asking God what she had done wrong. Her folded hands were red from the blood that she had just found in her pants.

Her mother found her like that, and consoled her. "No need praying," Mam said. "You did nothing wrong, babygirl."

Cassidy's mother made up a bucket of soapy water, and helped the girl clean the blood from her hands.

Cassidy changed into fresh clothes, and her mother taught her about growing up.

"You are a young woman, now, Cass," Mam said as she removed her necklace. She held it out to Cassidy. Its blue beads glistened with

generations of history. "*My Mam gave me these beads when I became a woman. Now, I'm giving them to you.*"

"*Not yet,*" *Cassidy said, pushing her mother's hands back.* "*You keep them for now. I like how they look on you, anyways.*"

***

Cassidy Reeve crouched inside a thicket of brambles, thorns pulling at her hair and scratching her cheeks, turning her constellation of freckles into shooting stars with streaks of blood, and she held her breath low and steady while her eyes reflected the orange of flames that engulfed her house, hot on her face. The girl grasped at her neck, feeling for her mother's beads, but they were not there. Men ran by, hollering and shouting with vile hate and exultation while they kicked up dirt into Cassidy's face and tangled hair.

They did not notice her hiding in the bush.

Cassidy Reeve peered out from the darkness and saw the silhouette of her parents swinging limply from a Joshua tree.

***

Cassidy Reeve woke up, gasping for air. Her lungs felt as if they had been filled with smoke, and her dreadlocks were damp with night sweats. She had been having that same nightmare again, the one that always seemed to haunt her after putting someone down. *Keep trying,* her subconscious seemed to be saying. *Find them, and get back what is yours. The sheriff was not the one.*

Her room at the Lonely Outpost hotel was dark, and the old building creaked and moaned as its wood contracted with the night's cool air. Neither could *it* seem to find rest that night.

Cassidy rolled over, curled her knees to her chest, and tried to sleep once more.

13

The Bluff's Reach Cemetery was far northwest of town, alone, a blemish on the face of the large plateau. The cemetery itself was small, housing only a handful of graves and a lonely sycamore tree, under which mourners would gather in the shade. Small tufts of pampas grass grew above each grave, having taken root on the upturned soil. All else was bare rock and dirt.

Kootala had arrived early, long before the procession carried Abner Brooks' casket to the grounds. The young man lingered among the granite, quiet, deep in thought.

Like everything in Arizona, the graveyard would grow, too. New generations would set their roots up on the plateau, and time would pass. Grandchildren of grandchildren would eventually know only of the town that always was: its settlement and growth no more than a footnote in a history book. *Yet it all started small, one member at a time*, Kootala thought. And that day, the Bluff's Reach Cemetery gained another member. The Brooks name would forever be a foundation of Bluff's Reach, literately etched in stone.

The procession arrived around noon, and the ceremony started soon after.

Kootala found Etta Brooks, draped in black silks and tulle. He took her arm, and held her in silence.

Many others had also gathered to observe the ceremony. Some family, many friends, and many more strangers. They cried, mostly with sadness at Abner's death, the loss of a loved one, the end of a friendship. But Kootala felt another somber note in the air. These people also wept with fear. Fear of uncertainty. Horror with a sense of impending doom, a terrible realization that this funeral implied; the violence in Bluff's Reach was just getting started.

Reverend Mattson spoke quietly and clearly throughout the ceremony, giving no indication of grief. He had performed countless funerals, and this was just another. The dispassionate tone in his voice proved that. He prayed over a man and comforted a family that he hardly knew.

When the reverend finished his speech, he invited Etta up to the pit for final words. Kootala led her forward by the arm. She bowed at the lip of the pit and muttered a quiet prayer, then took a handful of soil from the upturned pile and sprinkled it over the casket. Pebbles clinked off the wooden lid with a saddening, hollow sound. Etta stared down into the pit for a moment longer, perhaps thinking a final prayer, then retreated.

Missy came forward, said a prayer, and threw in a handful of dirt, same as her mother.

Kootala followed, going third. He left a prayer for Waasam, that Abner might see a mask of jewels at his gate, then threw in some dirt. Kootala looked at his hand, at the filth left on his palm, and thought to soothe the crowd with his Dust. He decided against it—this was not the time—instead holding a handful of powder to his nose alone. He took in a deep breath of sweet plum and ease.

Others went up in turn, each throwing a small amount of soil over the casket. Soon, only a corner of the box remained uncovered. A few of the men finished the job with shovels, then raked the ground flat.

The funeral was over, and the congregation dissipated slowly. The sun moved forward in the sky, and the shadow of the sycamore grew long and thin. After a time, only Etta, Missy, Kootala, and Luke remained. They exchanged kind words, hugs, and shared looks of longing and grief.

Kootala held Abner's hat in his trembling hands. Its brim had long since worn to fraying and was stained blotchy from years of sweat. Kootala traced the hat band with his finger, lingering on the bullet tucked within. He looked down, remembering the sheriff's badge that was pinned to his vest. Then Kootala removed Abner's bullet from his hat, wondering, and tucked the shell into his own. He handed Abner's hat to Etta.

"You know, Kootala," Etta said, taking him by the hand. "I only wish this had happened differently. I would like to have been with him."

"Come, Mother," Missy said.

The two women took off, leaving Kootala and Luke alone in the cemetery.

Luke reached for Kootala's badge, but did not touch the thing. It was as if he thought it were sharp. Or poisonous. Dangerous, either way. And perhaps it was, Kootala thought.

"So," Luke said.

"So." Kootala turned and began walking toward town. "Let's go home."

***

The next day, Etta Brooks felt the calm warmth of morning sun on her face. She held her eyes closed, yet her vision was orange with the bright light that filtered through her eyelids. The old woman daydreamed of younger days, back when her bones did not ache and the world had been kinder. She opened her eyes and looked out into the town park.

A pair of boys were running laps, slapping a hoop with a stick and chasing it through the dirt.

Etta ran her hand along the arm of the bench, tracing the cracks of age in the wood. Her other hand was empty; something she thought she might never get accustomed to.

Missy found a seat next to Etta on the bench. The young woman pulled her dress up and folded one leg over the other. She placed a soft hand on her mother's shoulder.

"It is curious," Etta said.

"What's that?" Missy replied.

"How quickly everything can change." Etta rolled her wedding ring around her finger. "For decades, we lived a static life. Every day was essentially the same. We had coffee in the morning, his always as strong as I could make it. He worked an easy day, I did my chores and hobbies. He would come home. We'd have supper. Then we'd go to bed, happy in each other's arms. And that was it, every day, again and again. We got comfortable and I wouldn't have traded that for anything. And then, within a minute, maybe less, it all changed."

Missy said nothing. Both women watched the kids playing with their hoop.

Etta's chest turned over and over on itself. It felt like her lungs were filled with rats, chewing at her throat, scratching against her ribs. "What am I supposed to do now?" she asked. "I don't know anything else."

Etta begged for her daughter's wisdom. Yes, it was *Missy* that offered the best words in times of need. She had an uncanny talent of guiding people through their emotions, and Etta always wondered where she had gotten that ability. It wasn't from *her*, and certainly not from Abner. Yet Missy was smart, much smarter than she led people to believe, and she often connected to others on a profound level. It was what made her so successful in her... *business*. She knew people deeply, and she often found the right words to say. In this instance, none came.

Etta continued instead. "*You* will move on, Missy. And so will everyone else. You all have your own lives, goals, futures. Those kids over there, they have their whole lives yet to come."

Missy finally spoke. "Those kids don't have a purpose, nor goals, other than to *be kids*. They play with that hoop because it's fun, not because it's meaningful in some profound way. Perhaps that is what's different about them and us. They don't worry about what comes next."

"And what about you, Missy? What is next for you? What are *your* goals?" For a moment, Etta was more sad for her daughter than for herself. Missy had lost a father, and a great one at that.

Again, Missy seemed to be at a loss for words. Perhaps she had no answer to Etta's question. Perhaps it wasn't Etta's business to know.

"Never mind," Etta said.

They sat in silence for a while, watching the kids play. Eventually, the boys ran off to some other adventure.

Etta spoke again. "You know, it's funny that we feel so strongly about how our lives turn out, as if ours are unique from anyone else's. How many women find themselves in my exact situation every day? And here I am, wondering how I can possibly live on, while all the others do just that."

Missy was staring up at the still, blue sky, where a single cotton cloud drifted lazily along some unknowable course. "They've had time," she said. "Maybe the answers come with time. Maybe they never come at all. I really don't know. But you can't just sit here on this bench until you die, too. You don't have to move on, Mother, but you've got to move forward. Give it time, and maybe, just maybe, you'll manage."

Etta looked up at the young woman. Her skin was smooth and vibrant, with orange freckles as fresh as morning dew. Her red hair was still full and luscious. But Etta could see age behind Missy's eyes, and she was captivated by the extraordinary wisdom within. In that moment, she wondered how it was possible that Missy had ever come to be. It was a miracle, by God.

Etta asked her, "Can you move on so quickly?"

"No. I grieve in my own way, and in my own privacy."

"Yet you are so willing to help others."

"They could write a hundred philosophy books about me." Missy laughed. "But they would all be wrong, wouldn't they? No man can claim to know the mind of a woman."

Etta laughed back. "You are right about that."

"Would it be so bad to be more like those kids?"

"Not worried about their future?" Etta did not understand.

"No. I mean, not worried about *worrying* about things." Missy laughed again. "That doesn't make sense, does it?"

"Actually," Etta said with a smile. "It makes more sense than anything else I've heard."

"And you've heard a *lot*, haven't you?"

"Are you saying I'm old?"

"I would never say that to you."

They laughed again, fully from their chests. Etta grabbed her daughter and hugged her deeply. She smelled nice, like cinnamon and plums and... tobacco.

"Have you been smoking?" Etta exclaimed.

"No, no! It's my... perfume. I promise!"

Etta took Missy's hand and smelled her palm. *Sweet, fresh dew and apples. Plum. Cinnamon. Tobacco.* Etta instantly felt better. Missy *was* telling the truth. In fact, Etta noticed fine sand stuck to Missy's palm, tacked to the oils of her perfume.

Missy pulled her hand back and wiped it against her dress. "So, you will be alright?" she asked.

"I believe so. Thank you."

"Good. Come visit me more often," Missy said. "We've got each other, Mom. Let's not lose that."

Etta nodded. She *hadn't* been spending much time with her daughter recently. That needed to change.

Missy stood, twirled her dress lightly, and walked gracefully away.

Etta sat on the bench for a while longer, watching the park, watching kids come and go as they pleased.

She *did* wonder what the future held for her, but only a little.

14

Buck pulled his hat down, shading his eyes as he walked through the south streets of Graben. It was a dirty, industrious area with a sharp, pungent stink. The streets ran red with runoff from copper smelting, and almost everything was stained black with the soot from men's filthy hands. The people there were rough, gruesome creatures. Buck loved everything about it. He was drawn to the filth, and to the strength of the men who lived in it. He made his way to a sawmill along the river, his green eyes peering out from the shadow of his hat like a hungry gator.

Buck entered through the gates of the sawmill and the foreman waved him over. He was a bulky man with muscles that threatened to escape his cotton work shirt. They shook hands, and Buck thought his arm might come free of its socket. The man's hand was tough and callused from hard work, but had a sense of softness that could easily be overlooked.

"You sure look out of place," the foreman said, looking Buck up and down. "You come from northtown?"

"I come from out of town, actually. I was told your mill can supply custom cuts?" Buck looked at his hand, which had turned brown with dirt from their handshake.

"Aye, we can. But it'll cost you."

"That's fine. We aren't too worried about that, as long as you can get the job done quickly."

"Quick costs more. Quality too." The foreman wiped sweat from his hairline. "Follow me to my office so I can write this down."

They walked through the mill yard while they spoke. Some other men waved at them as they passed, but most kept focus on their work. "Keep the wood cheap, if you can. No building quality, we're gonna destroy it anyway," Buck said.

The foreman looked confused and humored. "What are you making anyway?"

Buck thought of saying a smart reply like, *You do the cutting and leave my business to me*, or, *You'll make a casket if you keep asking questions*. Instead, he deflected kindly. "I don't know any more than what I've already said. I'm just the messenger boy." He smiled at the foreman, and that was genuine.

"Alright, alright," the foreman said, patting Buck on the back.

They entered the mill office, which was small and lit with only two small windows on either side of the door. A metal desk was pushed up along the wall on its short edge, and a row of cabinets lined the wall behind. Opposite the desk was a long couch with dark stains spotting its fabric. The foreman wiped his hands clean and began to write in his ledger. He was leaning over his desk, and Buck could see down his shirt collar at the rug of thick hair that covered his chest. Buck felt strange – perhaps envious of the man's masculinity, he thought.

"Dimensions?" the foreman asked without looking up from his ledger.

"Whatever it takes to build a crate six feet wide and long, and four feet high. Two-inch plank thickness all around."

"And how many crates would you need?"

"Two hundred and sixteen."

The foreman paused and looked up at Buck inquisitively. "Not two hundred, not two-fifty, but two-sixteen exactly?"

"Well, give us extra in case some break."

"Alright, say, two-fifty then?"

"Yeah, that's fine."

The foreman shook his pencil at Buck. "That sure is a strange request, mister. And a large amount, coming from a man without a single scratch on his hands. You plan on putting all that together yourself?"

Buck was frustrated at first, as he always was when pestered. But when the foreman laughed, he couldn't help but laugh along with him. Something about the man made Buck nicer, or want to be nicer, anyway.

"I'm just fuckin' with you, guy. I honestly don't give a damn what you plan on doing, as long as me and my men get paid." He smiled at Buck with warm, dry-cracked lips. Buck licked his own lips, which were smooth and soft.

"I'll make sure of it," Buck said. "Can we pay you when we pick up? I'm good for it, I can guarantee that."

"Certainly, when do you want it by?"

"Can you have it done in five days?"

The foreman stood silent for a moment, waiting for Buck to laugh at his own joke. When the laugh never came, he spoke again. "You serious? Five days to cut thirty-five hundred feet of lumber?"

"You said quick work costs more, and we can pay."

"Damn, alright. My men will piss and moan, but we'll have it done by then."

"Thank you, eh, what was your name?" Buck asked, not that it mattered much for the purposes of a business transaction.

"Charlie Rose, please to meet you. And your name?"

"Buck. Just Buck."

They shook hands again. Their grip lingered.

A desire stole over Buck's body, sudden and intense. He wanted to grab Charlie by the collar and pull him close. He wanted to smell the sweat that was steaming up from the hair on his chest. He wanted to taste the salty sawdust on his lips.

Charlie's brown eyes stared back intensely, almost begging Buck to give in to his desires. He stepped closer, and Buck could feel his breath on his own lips.

In that moment, Buck wanted nothing more than to feel the powerful hand of another man. He craved it, had been searching for it for so long, and he hadn't ever known until now.

No, that was wrong. This was the lie of the devil. Satan was here, tempting them with his wicked ways, testing the men to see if they were strong enough to resist his power. It was sin.

Charlie grabbed one of the buttons on Buck's vest and pulled him close. Buck felt the weight in Charlie's jeans against his own.

Buck leaned into it, lingered, then fought against the desire and pushed away. He straightened his collar.

Charlie looked away, his cheeks turning pink. He straightened some papers on his desk as if nothing had happened.

"Do you know where I can find someone who can weld?" Buck asked casually.

Charlie cleared his throat, then spoke with a deep voice. "There are a few men down at the shipyard that can weld."

"Thank you, Charlie."

"My pleasure," Charlie replied, his eyes sad and shameful and sorry.

With that, Buck left the lumber yard. He walked quickly past the gates and back into the muddy streets of Graben, leaving the evil temptations behind. But the devil would follow and tempt him again and again. Buck would win in the end. He would fight back against that evil, and he knew when and where it would happen.

He smiled triumphantly.

15

Luke and Kootala hadn't spoken since Abner's funeral, two days prior. Neither knew what to say. Instead, they pouted silently.

The last time Luke had felt so low was when his parents abandoned him. *That* was tough.

They had moved to Arizona for a better life, for opportunity, but the west wasn't what they expected. The Morgans were built for eastern living, where you could always get a hot bath and a cool drink. Work was harder out west. In Arizona, you were always dirty; you were always sore. Pennsylvania was civilized, clean, easy. They *had* to go back. But Luke had found his reason to stay. The Hoki man. Luke's mother had cried. His father called him *an abomination*, *a pervert*, and *no son of mine*.

Now, Luke could feel that sinking shame and self-hatred once again. He could see Kootala was feeling similar, likely blaming himself for Abner's death. That made Luke feel even worse, and the two continued to spiral into depression.

Eventually, Luke could stand it no further. He had to say something, anything, to Kootala. He had to break the tension between them.

They were standing in the kitchen together, wandering, aimless. Luke said, "Our buyer backed out. We lost a huge opportunity. I... won't be traveling to Graben for a while."

Kootala said nothing.

"Are you going to be alright?" Luke asked, finally. It was a question they had both been avoiding, but it had to be asked, eventually.

Kootala collapsed into a dining chair and laid his face down on the kitchen table. He sobbed.

Luke sat next to him, rubbed his back, said, "I'm sorry." That was all. What more could be said?

"I was there when he got shot," Kootala said, muffled. "That woman shot him and I just let it happen. All because *I* couldn't pull the trigger."

"Cassidy Reeve is a murderer. You didn't kill anyone, Kootala. She did."

"Is there much of a difference if I let it happen?" Kootala asked. He sat up. His eyes were swollen and red.

Luke did not know the answer to Kootala's question. Thinking back, Luke remembered Cassidy raising her gun at Kootala. If she had... Well, Luke would have stopped her. He would have stopped her for Kootala, yet he hadn't for Abner. Did that make Luke... *No.* He shook the thought away.

Kootala groaned. "Now, *I'm* the sheriff. How am I supposed to protect this town? I can't do this job, Luke!"

"Then give it up." The solution was simple enough.

"I... can't do that either. It's my duty now, and I can't abandon that."

Then why ask? Luke nearly said. Instead, "I don't have an answer for you, then."

"I took the clerk position because I thought it would be easy and safe. It *was* safe. I never expected this, but I *did* make an oath to protect this town. I'll keep my word. I just don't know how."

Luke sighed. He didn't have a solution for Kootala. To Luke, the problem was simple, binary: protect the town with the gun, or quit. But he knew Kootala well, and for the Hoki man, the problem was unsolvable. Kootala was a man of peace over all else, but he was also a man of promise, of honor. He would not easily relinquish his duty, whatever he imagined that to be.

"Use your Dust." Luke offered. "Calm your nerves."

"I have. It doesn't help." Kootala shook his head. "Some things are so ingrained in our nature that they cannot be altered, no matter how hard I try."

Then there was nothing left to do.

Luke took Kootala by the hand. "Do you want to go to the saloon and forget about all this, just for tonight?"

"I'd like that," Kootala said with a reluctant smile.

***

Katie Lybuck watched Luke and Kootala enter the saloon. They walked with heavy feet, dragging their boots across the hardwood floor, leaving scuff marks of shoe oil. Kootala's shirt was soaked down to the second button and his eyes were glossy and red. Luke pulled a stool from the bar and sat Kootala down.

He is such a gentleman, Katie thought.

The men ordered a round of drinks and Bill filled two tumbler glasses with a clear liquor. Katie remembered her own drink, tipped it back, and gulped down a sickening amount. She belched the sourness out of her stomach, and it lingered as acid in the back of her throat.

Katie stared at Luke's backside, drooling over his tight jeans and full buttocks. She fantasized about having a life with him. *He could love her*, she thought. She could show him what it was like to love a woman, show him what he was missing, something Kootala could never give. She would take Luke into her, and be with his child. Yes, she would. They would be forced to marry! Oh, he would be hers forever. Only Kootala stood between her and lifelong happiness. Kootala, the lily-livered Indian who let the sheriff die.

Katie saw her opportunity. She would confront them, prove to everyone else in the bar that Kootala was not worthy of this town. The people would chase him out, yes they would! And Luke would let him go, and he would search for someone better to love. She would be there, ready to be swept up into his arms.

She belched again. Her stomach swam sickly.

***

Luke ordered himself and Kootala another round of moonshine. As Bill Williams poured, Luke thought he could see the liquor vapor wafting out over the lip of the glasses. His head was beginning to swim, and his sorrows would soon sink away, too.

"Hey, Lucas!" Someone called.

He and Kootala turned to see Katie standing with her hands on her hips and a pout on her lips. "There is a pretty young lass sitting alone at the bar, and you walk right past her without an offer to dance." She attempted a graceful twirl, but wobbled drunkenly instead. Her right heel slipped, and she stumbled, barely catching herself on a bar stool.

"We aren't in the mood for your jokes tonight, Katie," Kootala said. "If you want, I'll buy you a drink."

"I sure wouldn't take a drink from *you*!" She hiccuped. "From Luke, sure. He's a *real* man."

The smell on Katie's breath told Luke that she had had enough to drink already. "Go sit back down," he told her.

Katie broke into tears. "I could treat you so much better than he does." She pointed at Kootala. "What can he do besides let people die? He's a pity, Lucas!"

"The only pity here is you," Kootala said. "You should go sit down, have some water. We are all broken up about Abner's death, but it's no reason to act a fool."

"I'm no fool," Katie said. "These people here are fools for letting you be sheriff. You're not right for this town, and everyone will see that sooner or later. Let's—" She hiccuped again. "Let's hope it's sooner, before you let more of us die."

Luke looked at Kootala, wondering what the man might do. Whether Katie thought it was right, Kootala *was* the sheriff. He could bring her to a cell to sober up. Plenty of men would do just that. What would *he* do? And would it be the right move?

Powerful heels clicked across the hardwood as Missy came up from behind. She placed a hand on Katie's shoulder: firm, but not yet combative.

Kootala stood from the bar, posture high and important. "I think you'd better go home, Lybuck," he said.

Katie shook free of Missy's grip. She looked around at everyone with seething anger and, Luke thought, a deep sadness. "Fine!" She shouted. She turned to Luke, her eyes rolling as they tried to focus. "I thought you to be a smarter man. If you come to your senses, you know where to find me. Although I can't say you'd be welcome anymore." She turned and stormed off into the night.

"What a pleasant evening," Missy said, taking a seat next to Kootala. She nodded at Bill, and he brought her a drink. "Cheers, boys," she said, rolled up her dress sleeves, and dumped the liquor down her throat.

"Are you worried about her?" Luke asked. "Going off that drunk?"

"She'll be fine," Kootala said. "She just needs to sleep it off."

Missy thumped Kootala on the arm. "Hey, don't let what she said put a knot in your drawers. She's a drunken wretch tonight. She was going to act up with *someone*, and you simply caught her eye first."

Kootala sighed. "She's right, though. This town needs a braver man than me. I'm not the one for these people."

Missy grabbed Kootala and turned his face to hers. Luke saw her eyes burning with a passion. She loved her friend, and wanted the best for him. There was also sadness in there, though Luke didn't think it was grief he saw. No, it was empathy. She felt Kootala's hurt, yet she smiled, and spoke with utter sincerity.

"What makes a man? What makes a hero?" she asked. "Is he a man because he can piss on a bramble bush with a cigarette in one hand and a whiskey in the other? Is he a hero because he has the balls of a bull and the courage to match? Out here, none of that matters. Out here, women drink moonshine and hold tobacco between their missing teeth. The bravest gunslingers are young boys with more notches on their pistol than hairs on their chin. These are renegade lands, and there are no rules on how you aught to be."

They were quiet for a moment. Missy sipped her whiskey, watching wheels grind against rusty tracks inside Kootala's mind, working against his refusal to believe in himself.

"I'm supposed to be the sheriff. How can I do that and—"

"Kootala, your beliefs tell you to be a steward of the earth, to foster peace. Right?" Missy shook her head. "Does a sheriff go around creating mischief and violence? Hell no! They protect their town *from* violence. You have more good in your heart than anyone else in this town. If anyone deserves to protect this place, it is you. You can't be bought or swayed from your beliefs, and *that* makes you a hero. I know you will find your own way to succeed. I trust that, and so does everyone else, no matter what they might say."

Kootala was silent for a full minute before saying, "Thank you, Missy. You always know what to say." There was still a small doubt lingering behind his eyes, but Luke saw that it was shadowed by beaming pride.

"Well, you're the only one who gets that for free," Missy said, winking at him. "Now enough with the philosophizing, let's have some fun. You in, Luke?"

"For sure!" Luke called Bill over and ordered another round of drinks.

The trio of friends took their glasses in hand and crashed them together above their heads.

"For Kootala!" Luke shouted.

"For Abner Brooks!" Kootala joined in.

Missy finished. "For Bluff's Reach!"

They chugged until their glasses were empty.

Bill Williams called out from behind the bar. "Hey, why don't we get some music going? LeAnn!"

LeAnn Cheek, who had been eating dinner alone, stood and made her way to the piano. She cracked her knuckles and began to play an upbeat tune.

Missy grabbed the boys and led them to the middle of the room. She twirled and dipped and jumped, and her frilly dress waved like an ocean in a violent tempest. LeAnn played the cancan, and they kicked along in a line. Luke went to refresh their glasses, and LeAnn played 'She Wore A Yellow Ribbon'. Everyone danced and sang along.

Around her knee
She wore a purple garter.
She wore it in the springtime
And in the month of May.
Hey hey!
And if
You ask
Her why they heck she wore it;
She wore it for her lover
Who was far, far away!
Far away. Far away.
Oh, she wore it for her lover
Who was far, far away!

Steve and Sue Barlow joined the dance, both getting lost in Missy's dress. Luke pointed this out to Kootala, and they laughed together. When the song was finished, Missy wished the boys a good evening, then left with the Barlows. As they walked out, Missy slipped one hand down the back of Steve's pants and the other hand down the neck of Sue's dress.

LeAnn slowed it down and played a Strauss waltz. Luke and Kootala waltzed together, hand in hand and shoulders together. Kootala spun Luke out, then pulled him back. Luke dipped Kootala. Their boots flitted gracefully across the floor. Their dancing was light, as if they had been suspended from the sky. Or perhaps it was just the moonshine. Kootala pushed away, then raced back and dove into Luke's arms. Luke hoisted Kootala up over his head and...

They crashed into the floor. The moonshine had won out in the end. The men dusted themselves off and laughed along with the rest of the saloon.

Jim McCready called them over to a nearby table, where a friendly game of poker had started. A light brown velvet had been draped over the table and tied tight around the corners. On it, neat stacks of coins and cards waited to be played. Luke and Kootala took seats across from Mark and Vanessa Deetman. They all threw a handful of nickels onto the table.

They played several hands with low stakes, more for fun than for money. Conversation was light, and they avoided talk of the bank robbery or the murder. The Deetmans never brought up their barn. They had money enough to replace it, and so it really was not that big of a deal after all. For that, at least, Luke was grateful. Jim McCready hit a flush on the river and won a two-dollar pot. He bought the table a round of drinks.

A stranger walked to the table and threw fifty dollars into the middle. The man removed his hat and hung it from the back of a chair. "Deal me in," he said with a sweetly smooth voice, then took the seat next to Luke. "Mr. Morgan, I thought I might find you here. Looks like a lovely little game y'all've got going. Mind if I raise the stakes?"

Luke looked up from his cards and held back a gasp. "Casey! It's... good to see you." Luke was cautious. Casey had never come to Bluff's Reach before, and Luke knew instantly that this was not a cordial affair.

Luke turned to Kootala. "Uh, Kootala, this is one of my business partners."

"Casey Calhoun," Casey said, offering Kootala his hand.

Kootala smiled and shook the man's hand. "Well, it is nice to finally meet you, sir. I've been waiting so long to meet some of Luke's friends."

Luke had always feared these two meeting. Kootala, smart in so many ways, was naïve in others. He was no businessman, and had never found himself in discussion about people like Casey Calhoun.

"And I've been waiting a long time to meet *you*, Kootala," Casey said. "Are you in?" He gestured to the table. "Or are you boys going to make me play by myself?"

Jim, Mark, and Vanessa pulled their money close to their chests and gestured that they would skip the hand. They had plenty of money to play, but they knew better. *This is between Luke Morgan and Casey Calhoun*, they were surely thinking. Luke figured they knew of Casey—if not personally, then by reputation. Casey was not officially an *outlaw*. He had no definitive connections to Cassidy Reeve or Sam Clangour, but there were rumors. They would certainly be skeptical of Luke's association with the man. Yet they dared not speak of it. What this meant for Luke's future in this town, he did not know.

"I'm sorry, Casey," Luke said. "But we don't have that kind of money right now. I can't bet that much."

"That's alright," Casey said. He dug into his vest pocket, then threw an additional fifty dollars onto the table. "I owe you, anyway."

Luke smiled uncomfortably. His palms began to sweat and his stomach turned in on itself. He thought he might puke.

Jim dealt the hand.

Luke picked up his cards and fanned them slightly to show Kootala: pocket queens. He laid them back down on the velvet, then folded his arms so that his trembling hands were hidden in his armpits.

Casey peeled the corner of his own cards up from the table with his thumb. He peeked quickly, then let them down again. Remaining as still as the desert air, he gave no indication of what he held.

"Kootala, Luke has told me so much about you," Casey said. "Do you enjoy working with the sheriff here in town?" An evil shimmered in his eyes that only Luke noticed.

"Actually, there was some trouble the other day, and Sheriff Brooks passed away. I am acting sheriff now." Kootala's eyes fell to the floor.

"Oh, such a shame." Casey pouted. "Well, I hope you are up for the job. It's getting dangerous out there. Plenty of monstrous people about these days. You might not even know if they were sat before you." Casey faked a shudder.

"Well said." Kootala nodded in agreement.

Though Casey was speaking to Kootala, Luke knew the actual message was directed to himself. It was not very subtle, after all. He was sure the others in the saloon could see it. Only Kootala seemed to be oblivious to the situation. Oh, innocent Kootala.

Jim dealt the flop; a deuce, an ace, and a seven. He laid the cards out in the middle of the table and aligned them in a perfect row.

"I'll check that," Casey said.

"Yep, same." Luke followed, not that he had the money to raise, anyway.

"Mr. Calhoun," Kootala said. "Luke told me your deal fell through."

"Please, just Casey. And yes, that is correct." He looked at Luke with utter contempt. "But I've got a task that Luke is going to help me with down in Graben in a couple of days. If all goes well, I think you boys will be sitting quite comfortably. Luke may even be able to retire."

"Wow, that is great news!" Kootala exclaimed. "Luke, you didn't mention any of this to me."

Jim dealt the turn; a five. Neither man reacted to the card in any noticeable way. In fact, the cards themselves hardly mattered, Luke thought.

"Well," Luke said. "I told Casey here that I was going to have to take some time away from the business. Our last deal went wrong and I—"

"He got cold feet is all, Kootala." Casey interrupted. "Every man goes through it. Not knowing if they are good enough to perform their job successfully, that is. Check."

Kootala was silent.

"Check," Luke said in turn.

"But of course, if Luke wants to back out of his business deal, that's his prerogative. Personally, I think it would be exceedingly foolish. Especially since this particular client has significant influence around here."

Jim dealt the river; another seven.

"Oh, man!" Casey cried out, startling everyone. "What do you have, Luke? Three of a kind? Two pair? I might just want to raise the pot!" His eyes were on fire. Behind his handsome and pleasant mask hid a face that was monstrous and hungry with malice. "What are you willing to risk, Lucas? Are you in, or are you out?" He demanded with a deceivingly calm voice.

"I... I..." Luke stammered. "Give me a minute."

Kootala leaned and whispered into Luke's ear. "There is dust in the air. If you want, I could—"

"No!" Luke choked. "I mean... hold on. I need to think."

There was a horrible threat concealed beneath Casey's smile. What would he do if Luke made the wrong choice? What *was* the wrong choice? Fold? Call? He saw Casey's arm bent in a crook, his hand at his hip. The minute flexing of his right bicep told Lucas that Casey was rubbing his pistol with his thumb. He was obvious about it, at least to Luke. There was no question here. Casey was *not* bluffing.

"All in," Luke said, then held his breath.

"We don't have any more cash." Kootala pointed out.

Luke and Casey stared at each other for a long time, judging the other's intentions and sizing him up.

Casey threw his cards to the center of the table, face down. "I fold," he said.

Kootala cheered. "A hundred dollars! Wee, doggy!"

"Congratulations, Lucas," Casey said. "You play a mean hand of poker." He turned to Kootala. "This deal Luke and I are working on is worth a hell of a lot more than a hundred dollars." To Luke again: "I expect to see you in Graben soon. Don't disappoint me. You both stay safe in the meantime."

With that, Casey Calhoun stood and grabbed his hat off the back of the chair. He folded his black hair across his head and slid his hat on top. Then he walked out of the saloon without another word. He had already told Luke all he needed.

"You *are* going to take that job, aren't you?" Kootala asked, almost pleading.

"Of course." Luke's throat filled with acid. "He makes a rather persuasive offer. It's hard to say no to him."

"What did he have?" Mark Deetman asked.

Jim flipped Casey's cards: pocket aces.

"I don't understand," Kootala said. "He had a full house. Aces over sevens. Luke, you really must have intimidated him. He would have won that hand."

He did win, Luke thought.

"Well, let's celebrate." Kootala took Luke's hand and led him back to the bar top.

They drank again, danced again, and Kootala continued to have a great night. He played the piano when LeAnn was done, but the song was a jumbled mess. All the while, a deep dread grew in Luke's chest. Throughout the evening, he stole glances at the other patrons. Jim and Mark, Vanessa, LeAnn, even Bill Williams snuck curious glances back. They whispered behind Luke's back. They would be talking about him, about his connection to Casey Calhoun. *What were they thinking?* Luke wondered. Nothing good, that was for sure.

Eventually, Luke and Kootala went home. They were good and liquored up, far drunker than either man had been in quite a while. Luke's stomach was terribly twisted, but he managed to hold it down.

When they went to bed, Luke loved Kootala like he never had before, afraid that he might never get to again.

16

Katie Lybuck wandered the dark streets of Bluff's Reach, moonlight reflecting off her tears as they fell from her cheeks. She was hysterical, babbling the broken and incomplete thoughts of a drunkard. Her heart was shattered. The man she loved did not love her back, and his friends had humiliated her in public. She flip-flopped between hate for them, for ruining her life, and for herself, for being so dense.

She could not go home and face her father. He would belittle her for the state she was in. Though she thought she might deserve a good lecture, she wanted anything but. Her bed called out to her, but she would not go home. Not tonight. She was too wicked, too wretched for such a nice respite. No, she would sleep in the dirt like a snake. It was what she deserved. Yet even the streets of Bluff's Reach were too nice for her.

Outside of town—shallowly into the surrounding desert—Katie Lybuck searched for a good place to wallow through the night. The desert sand was still warm from the day, and a low fog oozed from deep within the earth. Katie's feet kicked up swirls of fog as she walked. She soon found an outcropping of rocks, next to which was parked an abandoned wagon.

Had Katie Lybuck been sober, or at least been searching in the light of day, she would have noticed the wagon was new. It had been moved there recently, not more than a few days ago. And if she had searched the wagon, she might have found the clean and dry canvas inside. Indeed, she could have covered herself and slept comfortably until a mild headache woke her with the rising sun. Instead, Katie Lybuck sat back against the outcropping of rocks and closed her eyes. The ground pulsed underneath her in a dizzying pattern. She bowed to the side and heaved stomach bile and liquor into the sand.

She felt a cold breeze on her back and heard the light whisper of swirling air. Interested, she turned and pulled away some loose rocks, revealing the entrance to a small cave. The smell of ancient petrichor and guano filled her nose, but it was subtle and strangely inviting. It settled the gurgling of her stomach. She removed more rocks and crawled into the tunnel. It was cool inside the cave and more comfortable than the dry heat of the desert. *She could cry in here*, she thought, *wail like a siren, and nobody would hear her*. It was perfect, so she crawled deeper. The earth was soft and loose beneath her fingers. A chitter of bats echoed from somewhere deep within.

Had Katie Lybuck been sober, she would have noticed a small sign, writ on an old board above her head, that read *Danger—Condemned*. But Katie Lybuck had swallowed enough liquor to kill a cactus, and she, of course, did not notice. In fact, she likely would not have cared either way. Instead, she crawled right under the warning and deeper into the cave.

Katie's hand struck something solid. She felt what she thought to be hardwood, like a timber, that stretched upward along the wall of the cave. She stood, using the timber as a guide, until she felt something metallic hanging from the wall. From the faint glow of moonlight, she recognized an oil lamp. She shook the contraption and heard a liquid sloshing within. *Surely this can't work*, she thought. She spun the flint wheel and was disappointed, but correct. She spun the wheel again, and though it sparked, it caught no flame. She replaced the lamp on its hook and continued to walk deeper into the cave. She felt the walls as she went, holding herself upright against the spins.

The soil under Katie's feet slipped away. She stumbled, slid down a slope of loose gravel, then was in freefall with no ground beneath her at all. A timber beam slammed into her side, which she tumbled over. A rock found her elbow. Then she hit ground again. A whipcrack echoed through unseen tunnels as her leg folded sideways, broken at the shin. She cried out in agony. The darkness cried a twisted, haunting echo in response. Bats fluttered.

Katie grasped at her leg. She felt bone pushing up under the skin.

She fainted at the bottom of the shaft, her body mangled in full dark, where not even the faint glow of moonlight could reach.

17

Howard rocked back and forth on his chair swing. A dry breeze blew through his open porch and ruffled the curls of his mustache. He looked to the north and watched as a cavalcade of criminals rode toward his outpost, kicking up a trail of dust as they approached.

It was a sight that Howard was always conflicted to see. He welcomed the company, sure, and he would never complain about the money—in fact, he dared not complain about anything involving Casey. Howard's job was easy enough, and Casey's gang protected him. He was happy for that, at least. Yet, Howard was not a bad man, not really—or so he liked to believe. The extent of *his* violence was a single bar fight as a young man, and nothing since. He never participated in Casey's crimes, only provided the food and lodging for his men. Still, Howard felt ashamed every time he saw Casey and his crew riding toward Lonely.

He got up and went to the kitchen to prepare a quick meal for the men: salted ham and dinner rolls. It was still early in the day, and they wouldn't stay in Lonely any longer than necessary. They would eat lunch, drink furiously, exchange payment, and continue on their way toward Devil's Gulch. On Sunday, Howard would ride down to Graben with an envelope of cash and mail it back east. East, where he had left his previous mistakes behind.

Howard had built a decent life, years ago. He had it all; the beautiful wife, smart kids, a wholesome job, a nice home. But he was young then, stupid and impulsive. And when his wife caught him with another woman, she kicked him out and sent him west, keeping the kids for herself. Yet he still loved them, and sent them money when he could, though he would be surprised if the kids saw a nickel on the dollar. Brenna had been a good mother back then, but people change. God knows Howard did.

Casey and the others arrived in Lonely. They tied up their horses at Howard's stable, but left the saddles and gear on their backs. The men weren't on the run, but they were always ready to go if necessary. Casey led them into the hotel. He stomped the dirt off his boots and greeted Howard with a smile.

"Howard, are we too early for lunch?"

"No, not at all. I saw youse coming some while ago. Hopefully all went well?"

"Better than expected," Casey said, removing an envelope from his vest pocket. "There's an extra fifty in here. I'd like you to make us up a real nice feast next time we ride through. My men could use a hearty meal."

"I think I can accommodate that, sir," Howard said, taking the envelope. "Lu— Sam is joining you again?"

Casey narrowed his eyes at Howard, and Howard flinched. Casey did not often like to talk *details*. "That situation is handled. And, I had other business in Bluff's Reach while I was there. You are soon for the post office in Graben?"

"Yes, sir."

"Good. Could I trouble you to take this?" Casey produced a small package and handed it to Howard. "It's pre-addressed. Just needs postage, which you should be able to cover."

"Oh. Sure." Howard turned the package over in his hands. "What is it, if I might ask?"

"That is really none of your business," Casey said.

Howard cringed.

Casey sighed. "Although, you *are* doing me a favor... Would you believe me if I told you it was someone's scalp? From an old friend to another?"

Howard held the package at arm's length. "Eh, yeah, I'd believe you. Is that what's in here, really?"

Casey shrugged. "I guess they will find out when they get it in the mail."

"Right." Howard set the mysterious package aside. "If it *is that*, I'd say you don't fuck around."

"Nope. Never have. My daddy taught me to be a *real* man. Slapped me straight when I was a boy, he did." Casey gazed longingly, as if reliving a fond memory. "He was a good man, Howard. I thank him every day. Lucky for me, nobody else seems to have learned the same lesson. Well... makes my job easier, doesn't it?"

Howard, cautious of his words, said, "Not everyone is so fortunate to have such a wise and strong upbringing." It was always in Howard's favor to kiss Casey's ass, and that day, he seemed particularly generous.

"Pah!" Casey cried out, causing Howard to flinch again. "My father taught me much, but even he was weak. He got along too well with other men, let them walk all over him on occasion. But not me, no sir. I do what I want. I take what I want. And people fear and respect me for it. Only God can tell me what to do, and even *He's* been awfully quiet for some time."

Howard said nothing. What could he possibly say to that? Casey was a crazed man—unhinged for sure.

"What would you know about any of that?" Casey asked. He picked at his teeth, dislodging the dirt that had collected during their ride. Then he froze still, staring at Howard intently.

Howard stared back uneasily. Something in Casey's brain seemed to have switched, and Howard did not know how to respond. Casey was unpredictable, and Howard feared the man more than anything in his life.

"*BWAH!*" Casey shouted and jumped at Howard, snarling with a twisted and wicked face. Then he tipped his head back and laughed.

"Ha! Very funny, sir." Howard's hands trembled. "You got me good."

"You crack me up, Howie." Casey caught his breath and wiped a tear from his eye. "I think I'll take my lunch outside today."

"Sir." Howard said, then fled to his kitchen.

18

Sam Clangour rode toward Bluff's Reach, Cassidy Reeve at his side. They had met up in Lonely the night prior, Luke having *left for Graben on important business.* They had ridden quickly all morning, and came upon Bluff's Reach early in the day. Their horses kicked up dirt as they galloped, and the smell of cool dirt rushed through Sam's nose. He was breathing heavily, pushing his ride fast, excited to complete his final score. After this, Sam's debt would be paid off, on *official* terms, and he would finally be free of Casey's influence. Compared to their last job, this one promised to be as easy as the east.

Their target was Jerome Carlotta, owner of a large copper mine to the northwest. Casey was interested in Jerome's mine, and had requested a map of its layout. What Casey would want with a map of a copper mine was unclear to Sam, but it wasn't his business to know. He didn't care to know, either. The only thing that mattered to Sam that day was completing his task and keeping Kootala safe. And, he figured, the only real threat to Kootala was the woman riding at his side.

Sam glanced over at Cassidy. He wondered if she really thought Jerome was worthy of her retribution; that he had somehow wronged her. Based on how Cassidy treated everyone else, Sam didn't think it mattered. She was a machine, built for killing. It was her nature, and she would justify any action in her own twisted way. *Though*, he thought, *the same might be said about me.*

"Hey," Sam called to Cassidy, shouting over the roar of hoof beats and wind. "How long do you plan on working for him? How far are you willing to go?"

She replied without turning. "As long and as far as my search takes me."

"Your search?"

"My mother's bead necklace. Her killers will have it."

"It is really that simple?" Sam slowed his horse to a basic trot. He did not wish to shout. To his surprise, Cassidy slowed as well. He continued. "Don't you want to do something else with your life? Make something good of yourself?"

"I *had* a good life ahead of me. *They* took that away," Cassidy said, never one to hide her thoughts.

She sure was blunt, Sam thought. That was something nobody could take away from her. He spoke again. "Cass, your life is not your past. They may have taken something from you back then, maybe everything. I don't know. But you are in control of what you have *now*. Until you let go of the past, you will forever be a slave to it."

Cassidy pulled hard and stopped her horse. "Don't you ever tell me about slavery! How god-damned dare you? You, of all people, have got fucking nerve to lecture me."

"I'm sorry. I didn't mean—"

"Stop." She demanded. She kicked her heels and rode on. "Keep my past out of your mouth and out of your mind, or I'm likely to put a bullet in it."

"Okay. Sorry," Sam said, shamefully. He kicked his horse and followed.

"How about this? You mind your business and I'll mind mine. When we're done today, you go your way and I'll do the same. That's all."

Sam nodded. "Agreed. I can't say it's been a pleasure working with you, but I will wish you the best, anyway."

"Well put. I'll say the same to you." Cassidy was damn angry, yet Sam noticed a faint smile twitch at the corner of her lip.

They continued riding swiftly toward town, eager to complete their final job in Bluff's Reach.

The sun beat down on them as it peeked around a lonely cotton cloud in an otherwise empty sky.

***

Jerome Carlotta was home, waiting for his wife to return from the butcher with a venison roast for dinner. He was in his study; bookshelves wrapped all around him like a bank vault filled with paper instead of gold. He sat comfortably in a leather reclining chair, reading Mary Shelley's *Frankenstein* and smoking a thick cigar. He puffed out a cloud of smoke that curled its fingers around the edges of his open book. Through the haze of light blue smoke, he read:

But success shall crown my endeavors. Wherefore not? Thus far I have gone, tracing a secure way over the pathless seas, the very stars themselves being witnesses and testimonies of my triumph. Why not still proceed over the untamed yet obedient element? What can stop the determined heart and resolved will of man?

He puffed another breath of smoke that bounced off the pages before joining the haze of the room.

There was a knock at the door.

Jerome folded the book, marking the passage at the corner of the page. "One moment!" he called out, then placed the book on a side table. He grabbed his cane, which leaned against his chair. With great effort he stood and hobbled to his front door. He opened it, revealing a young white man and a Black woman waiting on the other side. They were both wearing bandannas over their noses.

Jerome slammed the door, but the woman's boot struck it open before it could latch, knocking him to the floor. His cane clattered and slid across the marble tiles.

He held his side, groaning at the flare of pain in his ribs. "Just what in the hell do you think you are doing?"

The woman pointed the barrel of a shotgun at his head. Jerome got a good look at her, and though she wore a bandanna, he knew her well enough from the posters in town. Dread filled his chest as he realized; Cassidy Reeve had come knocking. And the man, what was his name again? Sean something? Dan?

The young man crouched and bound Jerome's hands in his lap, then pulled him to his feet. The rope, he noticed, was hard and frayed with age. He could feel his blood throbbing in his constricted wrists, and his hands began to tingle. He might have been able to break free, but not now. Not with a gun to his head. And, while most people might protest, try kicking and screaming, Jerome was a smart enough man to know it would do him no good. For now, he kept silent.

They led him to a chair in his dining room, unbound his hands, and sat him down. They then tied his ankles and wrists to the chair. The rope was not as tight on his wrists this time, but still tight enough to hurt. Though now, without the extra leverage that free elbows afforded, he did not think he could so easily break free. No, *now* he was stuck.

"Alright." The woman, Cassidy, spoke. "This is going to go quick and easy. We don't want to be here, just as much as you do, so just cooperate and we will be out momentarily." She crouched to Jerome's level. "We want a map of your copper mine, or blueprints, doesn't matter. You tell us where it is, we retrieve it, and we leave. That is all. Now speak."

"What do you want with a map?" Jerome asked.

The masked man spoke with a rough, though clearly fake voice. "We ain't having a discussion. Tell us where it is."

Jerome thought about it for a brief moment. It was a strange situation he found himself in, but he figured himself smart enough to work through this dilemma.

These people had come to his home—likely from quite a distance—knowing that he had many valuables and lots of cash. Yet, they were only here for a map of his mine. They could tear up the floorboards and pull out a lifetime's worth of money, but they were not here for that. Whatever business they had with his mine, it was worth much more than whatever money he had. And though he couldn't know their motives, he knew they were dastardly beyond speculation. He would not give them what they sought. And he would not negotiate either.

Jerome smiled. "You can find what you're looking for, jammed clear up my ass." He laughed. "Oh, but you're really gonna have to dig for it."

Cassidy sighed. She would know he wasn't going to cooperate. Now, she would have to work for it. "Do you really want to fuck around with the bitch that killed your sheriff? I'm not going to spend all day here, so you can tell us now... or in five minutes. Trust me, I'm a brutally honest woman. I can get a lot done in five minutes."

"Cassidy." Her accomplice growled. "No."

"Do you want to be here all day, Sam?" she asked. "You want to wait around for his wife to come home and run off screaming, to go get the sheriff? The *new* sheriff? You want to deal with that, or do you want to get this done *now*?"

Sam was silent for a moment, clearly boiling in anger. Then, he said, "Fine. But I won't participate. I'm gonna start searching on my own." He left the room and began ransacking Jerome's house.

"Tell me." Cassidy demanded as she pulled a hoof nipper from her bag.

So, she meant to torture him. To cut off his finger. Go figure. Well, Jerome had known pain like that before, yessir. He had been in the war. They amputated his leg with a wood saw after a bullet wound went gangrenous. He knew pain, that was for sure. But was he willing to suffer that kind of pain again, all for a stupid map? What would they even use it for?

They wouldn't steal the copper. Not enough to be worth the trouble, anyway. And any equipment would be too heavy to move without getting caught. The only thing they could steal other than the earth itself was...

The dynamite.

Jerome's mine kept a supply of dynamite—several train cars' worth—to blow open the gaping pits. In fact, he thought there might be enough to blow a pit the size of Graben into the ground. But the dynamite was well protected, fortified, and hidden. His pit mine was a maze of trails and chasms, and you'd need a map to find your way around, if you were not already familiar.

To think what these people could do with all that explosive power... No. No. Jerome would not let them have *that*.

The amused defiance fell away from Jerome's face. He spoke slowly and clearly so that the Black bitch could hear him well. "I am not going to give you a damn thing. Whatever you are planning, I see a lot of people in danger. I'll die at your hand before I let that happen."

"If that's how it has to be." Cassidy sighed, then held up the hoof nipper. "All I know is I have a map to retrieve, and that's what I'm going to do. How I get it is up to you."

Jerome spit into her face—a thick gob of snot that stuck right above her eyebrow. She wiped the spit off with the back of her hand.

"Fine, then," she said.

Cassidy opened the nippers and placed Jerome's left pinky between the blades. The stoic determination on her face disappeared. She looked away and squeezed.

Unlike the tough keratin of a horse's hoof, Jerome's finger gave little resistance. The blades lopped through his knuckle like a twig and the top half of his pinky fell to the floor with a soft, wet thump. Jerome cried out and thrashed violently in his restraints.

"*You bitch!*" he cried.

Cassidy grabbed the bleeding stump and pinched it as hard as she could. "Where is the god-dammed map?" she demanded.

Jerome screamed and thrashed again. "It's hidden in a book in my study! *Moby Dick*. Huge book, you can't miss it." he sobbed.

"You could have just said that from the start." Cassidy placed the nippers on the table in front of Jerome—a warning—and left for the study.

But she would not find the book. Jerome had lied. He didn't own a copy of *Moby Dick*. And she believed him so easily! Yet, he knew she would realize his deception after a short search. She would return, bursting with fury, and she would probably take the rest of his fingers. But Jerome had felt pain before, and he could manage the fingers. What he could *not* do is manage a step up from that. She might go for his penis, just for the trouble he caused her.

Still, Jerome would not give in to her terror. He wasn't going to wait around for her to come back for his manhood, either. No, he had to end it all right there. He needed to show her that the torture would be in vain. He needed to show that *he* was in control, even if he was tied up like an animal.

Jerome scooted his chair closer to the table. He stretched out with his right hand and just managed to grab hold of the nipper. It was hot and damp with Cassidy's sweat. Clearly, she wasn't used to this after all.

With his arms tied to the chair, there was little room for movement. Still, there was room enough. He held the nippers in his right hand and placed the tip of his left thumb between the blades. He closed his eyes and clenched his jaw—what he wouldn't give to have something to bite down on. Jerome thought of green pastures and sprawling libraries and venison roast, then squeezed.

The tip of his thumb gave more resistance than the pinky knuckle had. He felt the bone splinter as the blades crushed it from either side. A primal scream rose up in his throat, but he held it back with the strength only a man at war could know. He squeezed again. The blades met in the middle, and the tip of his thumb joined his pinky on the floor. Searing pain shot up his arm and into his chest, causing hot vomit to spew into his lap. His vision spun and went blurry for a moment, then returned. His ears rang out with the echoes of artillery fire.

Jerome placed his first finger into the nippers and chopped it off.

Then the middle.

Then the ring.

His blood poured out onto the floor and began coating his naked toes.

The man was no longer Jerome Carlotta of Bluff's Reach. No, he was now Jerome Carlotta of Herbert's Battalion, Arizona Confederate Cavalry. He was a man at war! The future of his nation and the lives of a thousand men were at stake. He'd be damned if the Yanks got one word out of his mouth!

The Yankee captain was shouting from the other room. "It's not here! He lied! He lied!"

She was coming for him, and she would bear down on him with all the force of the north.

This ended here.

Jerome bent over in his chair and grasped his front tooth with the nippers. The metal was cold and sour.

The woman burst into the room, shouting obscenities.

Jerome squeezed.

His head exploded with cannon fire as his tooth erupted into shrapnel. Shockwaves of searing heat filled his brain and he howled with the screams of all the souls in hell.

His vision swam to black.

***

Cassidy returned to the dining room, filled with fury, ready to beat Jerome senseless. He had lied to her, had wasted her time. She was done with his fucking around. Now, she would get answers, even if it killed him.

She stopped quick when she saw Jerome doubled over in his chair with the hoof nippers in his mouth. His left hand laid limply at his side and all the fingers had been clipped at the tip. His open knuckles dripped blood, adding to the growing shadow of red on the floor.

Jerome squeezed the nippers and let out a howl that echoed in his open mouth. Cassidy heard the crack of his tooth like gravel under a wagon wheel. The sound made her own teeth ache and sent shrieks down her spine. The man sat bolt upright and screamed into the air. He shook violently. Blood and spit flew from his mouth and peppered the room around him. Then he laid back limp and passed out.

"Hey!" Cassidy yelled and ran to Jerome. She removed his bindings, pulled his limp body from the chair, and shook him vigorously. He remained unresponsive, and Cassidy stared in awe at the man, wondering what strength had possessed him to do such a thing to himself.

Sam crashed into the room. "Cassidy, what the hell are you doing to—" He stopped short when he saw the gruesome scene. The blood drained from Sam's face, and he looked like he might wretch.

"He—he—" Cassidy stammered. "He did this to himself."

Sam gagged. "Well, fuck! Now what are we supposed to do?"

"Tear this house apart!" Cassidy said, her eyes darting from wall to wall. "Someone could have heard him scream. Be quick!"

The two criminals scoured the Carlotta residence with ultimate fury. Sam threw open cabinets and slammed them closed again. Cassidy thumbed through books, then threw them to the floor, landing with bent and open spines. They ransacked the manor nearly to its studs and found all manner of gold, cash, jewelry, but no map. Cassidy could feel success slipping away with the clock.

She saw two futures take shape in her mind; abandon the job and suffer Casey's retribution, or stay and possibly get caught. She didn't know which was worse. Panic set in like a shadow over her heart.

"I doubt the damn thing is even here," Sam said with his head deep in a wooden chest. He stood and pulled at his wig in frustration. "Why would someone keep a map of a mine that's a hundred miles away?

It isn't the Holy Grail! They probably don't even *make* maps of pit mines."

Cassidy slapped the wall and shouted in anger. "He *has* to have *something*! A mine that size, well, you could get lost there. There *must* be some form of direction. Thousands of acres of pits and roads and rails, you'd need a fucking atlas!"

Jerome gargled, blowing bubbles of pink spit from his shattered mouth.

"Wait," Sam said. "We're thinking like criminals, Cass. Think like *him*."

"Crazy?"

"No! Like a businessman. You don't *hide* a map of your own property, that's ridiculous. Casey would, but that's because he'd have things to hide. Jerome would just leave it out on a table or something. In a stack of other random crap."

"We've searched everything." Cassidy was getting fed up with this whole fiasco. If only she had started on Jerome's balls...

Sam growled. "No, we've been digging like rats. We need—"

"Shit." Cassidy rolled her eyes, then ran to the study. She had been so focused on looking for secrets, that she had overlooked everything obvious.

Sam followed after her.

Cassidy went to Jerome's desk, where a stack of papers sat, barely disturbed. She had rifled through them before, but only briefly. The stack contained transaction receipts, ledger notes, and telegrams. All mundane things. She hadn't considered them at first. Now, she shuffled through the papers in a frenzy.

"Is it there?" Sam asked, leaning over Cassidy's shoulder.

She paged through the documents. Harvest report. Junk. Rock slide notice. Junk. New pit order. Junk, junk, junk. Then, among the litter of other useless business records, she saw something that caught her eye.

Blasting Order

Pit six requires ten crates of explosives
moved at Noon on the 3rd, Tuesday

—

Road A-5 out of service due to ditch water erosion.
Utilize alternative route
See attached map

A woman screamed from the other room.

"Shit!" Sam cried. "The wife!"

"Go!" Cassidy said, grabbing the entire stack of papers. They could sort through it later.

They ran back to Jerome, still slumped in the chair. Cassidy could see through the front door, hanging wide open, Jerome's wife running down the street. She was screaming and flailing her arms above her head like she was swatting bees.

"Did you get it?" Sam asked.

"I grabbed the stack. Let's get the hell out of here!"

They headed for the door.

CRACK!

Something crashed behind Cassidy. She turned to see Sam and Jerome on the floor, thrashing, wrestling. Jerome was on top, scratching furiously at Sam's face with his finger stumps. Blood flew, smearing Sam's face and clothes. Jerome drooled blood, and his eyes were wild like a rabid hound.

Cassidy watched, slow in time, as if they were underwater. Her hand drew the pistol from her hip, and she leveled it at the rolling bodies.

Sam was going to be furious with her.

She fired.

KA-BLAM!

Jerome's throat burst open and he was thrown off to the side. He flailed over the marble floor, grasping at his neck. All was crimson, and Cassidy couldn't tell the man's hand from his throat.

Sam rolled, kneeling, as he wiped the mask of blood off his face and eyes.

"Come now, or I'll leave you here!" Cassidy shouted.

Sam took her hand and she pulled him up and out of the front door. They mounted their horses and took off.

19

Kootala was sat atop his brown, watching over the southern edge of the bluff. In the distance, a band of dust marched its way up the valley toward Lonely.

The Hoki man had made a habit of watching over the valley. Other men might have done so with arrogance, believing themselves to be better than those below. They would feel larger than life, standing watch high above. Kootala was not that kind of man. He looked over the valley, at first in admiration of its beauty, and recently with curiosity. He had noticed that every few days, a group of riders would go back and forth between Graben and Lonely. *It was curious*, he thought, *that they never came up the bluff*. What was their business in Lonely, a worthless outpost with no business to be had, if not as a rest stop on their way to Bluff's Reach?

Kootala removed his hat and wiped the sweat from his forehead. He brushed his long black hair back over his ears before putting the hat back on, then surveyed the rest of the valley. It had been green and lush two days before, the plants still holding their moisture from recent rain. But when their leaves had finally given up their water, it went all at once. They had burped it up yesterday, and the air had been humid for a few hours. In several days' time, the humidity would condense again and rain down over Amarillo, Texas. The water would quickly evaporate, there, too, and the cycle would continue, bouncing its way east across the country. Eventually, the water, including the sweat from Kootala's brow, would rain over a peach tree in Georgia. The peaches would be canned and sent west, where a prospector in Temecula would eat them with a full copper mug of moonshine. He would vomit the peach and liquor slurry into the dirt, and the water would evaporate again. And so on.

A gunshot echoed through the air, taking Kootala out of his daydream.

He had not anticipated any excitement that day, but he was ready anyway. There had been too much going on in this town recently, and it was time the criminals were stopped. However the day might turn out, Kootala fully intended to end this business once and for all. He didn't know *how* he would accomplish that, but he was ready to find out.

He took off, this time heading directly for the road out of town. Kootala knew that running toward the gunshot would put him behind the fleeing targets, where he would surely fail the upcoming chase.

The horse galloped hard, and they soon passed the shadow on Main Street where Abner Brooks had stained the earth with his blood.

The outlaws ran around a corner out in front of Kootala, riding quickly out of town. Kootala pursued. He *would* catch Cassidy Reeve and Sam Clangour.

They rode hard. The horses frothed saliva from their mouths and nostrils. Kootala was close behind the outlaws. He felt their freshly kicked-up dirt raining on his face.

It was now, or not at all.

Kootala drew his gun, took a deep breath, and fired up into the sky.

His memory flashed back to his last encounter with these criminals. Kootala remembered seeing Brooks draw his gun, Cassidy firing her own, and the stain in the street. Would he be able to shoot that woman this time? If not, would he leave his own stain upon the desert sand?

Kootala let up slightly, waiting for Cassidy's bullet to tear through his heart.

It never came. Instead, Sam had drawn his own iron and had it aimed at Cassidy. Though the man's face was concealed under a bandanna and sunglasses, the lines on his temples spoke with unmistakable clarity. He would kill Cassidy if she drew on Kootala.

The chase continued, and Kootala began to fall behind as he grew less sure of himself. What could he possibly do if he *did* catch up to them? They were smart by now, and they would know that he would not fire upon them. They would keep riding, hoping that he would eventually back off and end the pursuit. And they were right, weren't they? That is exactly what Kootala would do. He would ride back to town in defeat, declare someone else sheriff, and never go outside again. All would know him as the failure of a man, who had let their town fall into the darkness of the wild west.

Kootala slowed, watching as Cassidy and Sam gained distance on him. Could he use his Dust in some way? Take control of their emotions, make a mirage of some sort? No. There wasn't time for that. As a last resort, thinking of nothing else he could do, Kootala aimed at the ground in front of Sam's horse and fired.

The horse faltered. One of its hooves slid across a rock and it fell as its leg folded underneath its own weight. They went down hard, and Sam slid across the sand. Kootala cringed. He had only meant to startle the ride... not injure it. Yet it was *their fault*, not his. If they hadn't run...

Cassidy continued riding hard, not looking back.

Sam's horse writhed and flopped on the ground, kicking up a cloud of dust. Sam drew and fired three times. His horse fell still, the dust settled, and the gunshots ricocheted across the otherwise silent desert.

Kootala drew his gun and dismounted his horse. He whispered a quick prayer for the poor beast before approaching Sam on foot. "Discard your weapon," he said, making his voice as deep and as threatening as possible.

Sam threw his gun into the sand.

"Are you injured?" Kootala asked.

"No," Sam said with a muffled voice.

Kootala took a few cautious steps closer. "Remove your bandanna."

Sam did not move. Instead, a tear crawled out from under his sunglasses and fell down his cheek.

"Remove your mask, or I will do it for you." Kootala demanded.

With trembling hands, Sam pulled down his bandanna, revealing a slash scar on his upper lip. He removed his sunglasses and white wig.

Luke Morgan stared up at Kootala. His wet eyes swelled with shame and regret.

Kootala was speechless. He stood frozen with his gun pointed at Luke. His grip tightened as he filled with anger, then anger gave way to sadness and he dropped his gun to his side.

"Lucas," Kootala said, nearly whispering. "This whole time…"

"I'm so sorry," Luke said.

Kootala was silent for a moment, his brain spinning in every direction, mainly toward disbelief. Finally, he found his words. "You lied to me. All this time, I thought you were on my side, but you've been a nasty, wicked liar. And you've been… you…" Kootala's anger returned. "You killed people!" he yelled.

"No! I never killed anyone! It was always Cassidy!" Luke pleaded.

"It's just the same. You helped her. You are a very bad person, Luke. I... I can hardly believe this."

"I had no choice!" Luke cried. "They threatened to hurt you. I had to do this to protect you."

Luke went to stand. Kootala motioned for him to remain sitting in the dirt. "How long?" he asked. "How long have you been doing this?"

"Years." Luke conceded. "Since before we moved to Bluff's Reach. This is how I afforded the move, actually."

"Our entire relationship, our entire lives, was built on deception? You know how I feel about violence. You knew that, and you hurt people anyway."

Luke—quiet until then—yelled. "I was keeping *you* safe!"

"No!" Kootala yelled back. "You are the reason I was in danger in the first place. And for what, a bit of money?"

"I never did this for myself. The money, the house—that was all for you. Everything I have done had been for you, Kootala. I wanted to give you the world. It was love."

"You showed your love by lying and stealing and hurting others? People are *dead*, Lucas! And you're saying that this is for me?" Kootala had started crying. "No, you did this for yourself. Maybe you used to think it was for me, maybe you still believe that. But I think you came to enjoy it."

Did Kootala really believe that? He had known Luke well, possibly more than anyone in the world. Luke was a compassionate person. He loved. Still, he did this, knowing how Kootala would feel. He should have known! Kootala would rather live on the streets again, eating garbage, than *this*!

Luke sank away, defeated. "Kootala, I don't know what to say to you. I don't think I *could* say anything to fix what I've done. If there is anything I can do, please tell me."

Kootala shook his head. "Your actions are beyond redemption, Luke. You've hurt others, and you've hurt me more than you could ever know."

"What do I do now?" Luke asked, almost pleading.

Kootala tossed a canteen of water into Luke's lap. "Take my horse, go to Graben, or even beyond. Do not return to Bluff's Reach."

"Kootala, please."

"No! Leave here and never come back. If I see you in my town again, you will be the only man I kill. Don't make me do that."

"And then what?" Luke cried. "You are all I have. You are my life. There is nothing for me out there!"

"That is not my problem anymore," Kootala said. He took a few belongings from his saddlebags and began walking back to Bluff's Reach.

Luke called out from behind. "I love you, Kootala! I'll never stop loving you!"

Kootala did not look back, for Luke would have seen the tears coursing down his face. He loved Luke too, and knew that he always would.

END OF PART ONE

Intermission

C asey sat comfortably in the boardroom, waiting for the other members to trickle in. He had been working toward this meeting for quite some time by then, had put in great effort to secure his position, and was ready to make a big move. In one hand, he held a fat cigar that trailed blue smoke, and though he did not suck on the tobacco, he liked how it looked in his grasp. His other hand rested on a small box that was set on the table before him. This day, Casey wore more gold than ever before, though it was not meant as a display of wealth. He had something else in mind that day.

The final board members took their seat.

"Welcome," Ennin Grey said, taking his place at the head of the long table. "I hope you all had good travels to be here today. Philadelphia is happy to have you."

Grey was the executive director and majority owner of the East-West Excavation and Rail Company. He was the man in charge, and might have been the only man on Earth that Casey admired. *He* was tough! He was power incarnate. To have such control over the railroads... what an awesome position. Casey would have such power, too, some day. Hopefully, someday soon, if all went well.

Ennin continued. "It is with great thanks that I see you all here again, and for such an important decision, no less! These are fortunate times for the company, as for the United States. This country grows, and we do with it. That said, I want to say how saddened I am by the loss of board member Spike, but I have faith that his replacement will serve us just as well. Casey Calhoun, it is good to have you."

"Thank you," Casey said. "I just hope I can be as tenacious as Spike was; that I can fill his boots, so to say."

"You will do fine," Ennin said. "Now, I'm sure you all have other business, so let's not waste too much time. I—"

Someone interrupted. "The judge has ruled in the commissioner's favor. I received the telegram three days ago. The Department of the Interior will not allow excavation through the bluff. We must find another route."

Ennin sighed. "I figured as much. What of the alternative proposal?"

Another member spoke. "Union Pacific has agreed upon the preliminary joint proposal to reroute south through Tucson. Excavation on that route has already been approved by the DOI."

Someone slammed their fist down onto the table. "Bureaucrats! What percentage has Union Pacific promised the commissioner? And to subsidize his own pocket. That is corruption at its finest!"

"It is only business," Ennin said.

Casey quite liked that answer.

"However," Ennin said, consulting a ledger. "While the alternative route will increase our total revenue, the split costs with Union Pacific, as well as increased manpower, will severely cut into our profits. The extra three hundred miles required to route south would cut our profits by some forty percent."

Most of the room groaned at the figure. It was nearly a half million dollar pay cut per board member.

"Could we borrow men from Central Pacific?" someone asked. "They have many Chinese."

"Might we be able to cut a deal with some of the businesses in Tucson?" someone else offered.

Casey put out his cigar, which he had not sucked on the entire time. "There is another option," he said. "That we might yet be able to cut north along the original proposed route to Denver."

"But the DOI has already ruled—"

"Hush," Ennin said. "Casey and I have discussed a solution to that issue in private, and I'd have you all hear him now. But know this conversation does not leave this room."

"Thank you," Casey said. "Now, I feel that the DOI's decision is fair, and that they are right to reject our proposal. A bridge around the bluff would be more expensive than the alternative route, and yes, to excavate under the bluff would be irresponsible. I agree with those presumptions. However, I also think that the original route is in the best interest of this company, and of the United States as a whole. This country is expanding, and damn all who stand in the way. The rewards we have before us are too great to let them slip away. Therefore, I propose a *different* solution."

Casey continued to tell the board his plan, mostly to the horror of the men before him. He could see weakness in them, in the way they gaped, in the fear their eyes held. Were they truly good men, astonished at Casey's proposal, or were they scared that they could be held responsible if Casey's plans went astray? Regardless of how they felt, their greed stayed their mouths until Casey had finished.

"... and for my trouble, I expect to be compensated fairly," Casey said. "Say, ten percent of cost savings, on top of my shareholder dividends."

The room was quiet for a moment, until one of the members finally spoke up. He was a small man, who Casey thought looked much like a little desert lizard. "This is madness. It will never work. You, Casey

Calhoun, would be the downfall of this company. It is lunacy to even consider!"

"Such a small mind," Casey said. "Do you think this great country was founded on worry? Or did the brave men of the commonwealth revolt against tyranny? We have an opportunity here, and we should not squander it."

"But..." The man stammered. "How many people are we willing to hurt?"

Casey caressed the box in front of him. He had waited so long for this moment, and now it was finally upon him. His face twisted with malice. "In losing the war against the North, we lost a great resource. And all because men like you wanted to relinquish ownership of those... *beasts*." Casey snarled, spit flying from his lips. "All because you didn't want to *hurt* those *people* anymore. Bawh! You, sir, are a poison to the principles of this country. You would bring death to the machine of the free market."

"Alright, now, Casey," Ennin said. "That's quite—"

Casey slammed his hand on the lid of his box. "No! I will show you men what it means to *earn*!"

He threw open the box, revealing nothing inside but a small pile of sand.

The lizard man scoffed. "You have truly lost your mind," he said, shaking his head.

Casey took a deep breath, then scooped the sand into his hand. "My will be done," he said plainly.

Power surged through Casey's arm, drawing strength from the gold around his neck, on his wrists, his fingers, in his pockets. He focused his will upon the sand, and it began to lift from his palm. He imagined his future, his plan in action, and the sand coalesced into the shape of a locomotive, as large as a toy model, blowing a geyser of fine dust from its smokestack.

The board room erupted in gasps.

"What in God's name!" the lizard man cried.

Casey pushed, and he felt an awful arousal growing in his chest. The train chugged forward and crashed into the lizard man's face. Casey sucked in air. The train tunneled into the other man's mouth, up his nostrils. He began choking, scratching at his face and throat. His eyes bulged.

"Casey!" Ennin shouted.

He paid Ennin no mind. Nothing would stop Casey Calhoun's will this day.

The lizard man fell back out of his chair, rolling on the floor, trying desperately to cough free the sand that had filled his lungs. But Casey held his breath, and the man continued thrashing on the floor.

Casey's head grew light, and he thought he might faint. His vision grew blurry, but he did not let out his breath.

The man on the floor threw a final spasm, then was still.

Casey let out a huff, and breathed normally again. He stood, peering over the table at the man he had killed. The man had thick mud dripping from his mouth; a mix of sand and blood. His eyes were rolled back to the whites, but they were bleeding, too, and covered with crust like a bad case of conjunctivitis.

It would have been easier, Casey thought, to kill the man with a bullet. In fact, that was usually his preferred method. But the men in this room needed to see his *true* power. They needed to know who was really in charge. Killing this man with a gun would have just turned the others off even more. But now, they could not oppose Casey. They wouldn't dare.

"You…" Ennin gagged. "To give you a place on this board, what a mistake!"

Casey smiled, wiping a small bead of blood off his own lip. *That* was new, he thought. He was exhausted. This performance had taken a lot out of him. However, he made no indication that the others could see as weakness. He sat tall and straight. "Would you all accept my proposal, now? Or must I be more persuasive?"

None dared speak against him.

"Very well," Casey said. "You may distribute this man's shares among yourselves as you see fit. I, however, do not want his leavings."

Ennin stood, though in a subdued manner. He would not impose upon Casey. "We will not take the fall for you if your plan goes south. Know that."

Casey shrugged. "That's fine, but I'm not worried. My will has not led me astray yet. If it should now, then I am the desert's cruel joke." He scrubbed the remaining sand from his fingertips. "Yet, I think the desert will do me just fine in the end."

The board meeting was done. Nothing more needed to be said. Casey straightened himself, running his hand through his hair, fixing his watch that had slipped around his wrist, tucking his necklace back into place. "Clean up, if you will," he said as he left the board room. Though he was ecstatic inside, he showed no emotion on his face. His wealth had just grown immensely, and with it, his gold, and his power over the world. That day, Casey Calhoun had become unstoppable. All among the desert, and the desert itself, would kneel before him. That, or they would fall. To him, it made no difference.

PART TWO

VENGEANCE

20

Luke turned over the coals of his campfire, exposing the reds to the evening air. They flickered and brightened as they sucked in the fresh oxygen of the open desert.

He was camped on the western boundary of the plateau; he'd gone as far from Bluff's Reach as he could without making that final descent to Lonely. Cassidy would surely be there for the night, and Luke wished to see her no more than he wished to have a scorpion in his pants.

As Luke's stomach grumbled, he cut open a can of beans and set it up over the heat of the renewed coals. The can turned dark on the bottom and the sludge inside began to bubble.

Kootala's horse snorted in the darkness.

Luke hushed the creature, then shoveled a spoonful of steaming beans into his mouth. The mush was unpleasant: Luke had never really liked beans all that much. He wished instead for a deep bowl of Kootala's stew, with fresh carrots and potatoes, instead.

But Kootala had sent Luke away, out into the desert. Where would he go now? What would he do? He thought for a moment about remaining in Casey's employ, but shook the thought away just as quickly as it had come. Damn that man, damn Casey Calhoun for everything. *He* was responsible for Luke's situation. *He* had forced Luke to do all those things! Couldn't Kootala see that?

Luke took another bite of beans.

The horse snorted again, louder this time, almost impatient.

"Look, I'm just as unhappy about our situation as you. You aren't the animal that got put down today, so be happy about that at least."

Luke set aside the beans and walked to Kootala's horse. He stroked its neck and shoulders, and felt her muscles tight and trembling under the coarse, dusty hair. *Was it fear or anger in those muscles?* Luke wondered. It was hard to tell, as they were often one and the same. Luke patted the horse and hushed it with a calm voice, then retrieved a hand saw from a saddlebag. He walked into the darkness and found a dead-dry chaparral shrub. The saw made quick work of its brittle branches, and Luke soon had an armload of tinder. He added the wood to the fire and returned the saw to its saddlebag, which made the horse flinch. Its eyes had grown wide and it pinned its ears back.

"You scared of the dark?" Luke asked.

The horse stomped a hoof in reply.

"Well, listen. If you're gonna get all worked up, I'm gonna throw my bedroll over your head. I'd rather sleep in the sand than have you run off on me tonight." Luke tied the horse's reins around the trunk of a dead shrub.

A scream echoed in the distant dark; a primal sound that sent ice coursing through Luke's heart. He was instantly on alert. That ancestral nature that had been lost to civilization—the deep and ancient instinct—came rushing back, pure and true.

Fear.

Again the scream echoed through the dark, as if a woman were having her guts spilled upon the sand. The horror of it hung in the air like a fog.

Luke had heard the cry of a mountain lion once before. Then, he had been helping family hunt the hills for a lost calf. They had found the poor thing, split open, guts spilled out like a can of beans. Its killer had cried from the hills, but it had not scared Luke back then. He had been in a large group, and a cat wouldn't attack that many men. This time, however, his fear was tangible, thick in his blood.

Kootala's horse stamped its hooves and shook its head wildly. Luke calmed it with one hand and drew his pistol with the other.

He stood there, frozen and silent, for what seemed like hours. In reality, it was probably only a few minutes. When a man feels that level of fear, it fills him, pushing out any true sense of time.

Another scream never came. Instead, Luke felt something worse than a scream. He sensed eyes watching him from the dark. The beast was out there, waiting for Luke to falter (or relax) so it could have an easy kill.

It was ready for him, and Luke had to do something to send it away. He aimed his gun into the air and fired. The shot cracked the air and echoed throughout the land.

But the creature remained, still lurking in the dark.

Or was it?

Luke was suddenly sure that it had been his imagination. There was no mountain lion out there. There never was one to begin with. All his stress, all the turmoil, had finally broken his mind. He had snapped, and now he was imagining creatures in the dark; creatures that reflected the haunted state of his soul.

A shadow passed through the brush to his right. Luke heard the crunch of gravel under its... Paw? Foot? Claws?

Maybe there was something out there after all, something much worse than a mountain lion. Instead of fluffy cat ears, Luke imagined a set of wicked, curly horns. A demon, hungry and evil, had come to drag Lucas to hell. This was his reckoning, his reward for all the trouble he had caused.

Tears began coursing down Luke's face, carving clean channels across his dusty cheeks. He tipped his head back and screamed into the darkness. Kootala's horse reared up, bucking wildly with terror. It tried to pull free, but the rope, the knot, and the shrub held strong.

The demon came for Luke then, pouncing from out of the darkness. A set of ivory fangs shimmered with firelight.

Luke jumped to the side. Instead of fangs landing in his throat, a set of sharp claws sliced through his right arm, leaving three parallel rifts in his flesh. He fell to the ground, filling those carvings with dirt.

The mountain lion tumbled across the ground, then skittered to its feet and pounced again. This time, Luke couldn't jump to the side. The beast's trajectory would fall true.

KA-BLAM!

Luke sent a bullet through the creature as it came down on top of him. It writhed and scratched furiously, slicing Luke's leg this time. The mountain lion howled an injured screech then pounced back into the night. Luke heard the scuttling of claws in dirt as it ran away. Soon only the crackle of the fire remained.

That feeling of being watched was gone, too.

The horse remained alert.

Luke waited, his gun gripped tightly in his hand, until a scream came again. It was more distant that before, hungry and defeated and painful.

Relaxing, Luke holstered his weapon.

The cuts on his arm and leg didn't hurt—his adrenaline was high—but they would soon enough. He poured canteen water over the wounds to clear off the dirt. They were shallow, and would not give up much blood. Luke had been lucky.

He cut more tinder and built up the fire until it was a blazing pyramid that lit up the desert. Hopefully, that would deter any other creatures that might be lurking about.

The can of beans had grown cold, and Luke choked them down reluctantly. When he was done, he wiped the can clean with some sand and a rag, then stored it back into his bags. Even in his awful state, he wouldn't leave trash out in the desert.

Warm firelight at his back, Luke searched for a blood trail around the perimeter of his camp. He found a few drops leading away, but nothing more than that. The mountain lion had been injured, probably not enough to kill it, but certainly enough to send it away for good. Likely, Luke had only grazed the cat, as it had done to him.

Something else caught Luke's eye, buried almost completely in the sand. He went to it and brushed away the loose soil, revealing a jagged clump of green glass. He pulled it free from the ground. It was strange, rock-like, just smaller than his palm, slightly oblong in shape. Its edges sparkled with dull firelight.

Luke had heard myths of lightning glass, but he had never seen any in person. It was said to be a thousand times rarer than gold, and most people were skeptical that *any* of the material even existed. But now, holding the strange thing in his hand, he knew the myths to be true, and was in awe at its beauty. There was only one thing in the world that Luke found more beautiful...

He returned to his camp and carefully packed the lightning glass into his saddlebag. He wondered at the thing's value. It was fragile, could not be turned into jewelry or coin like gold could. Still, there was value in its beauty and rarity. Luke saw that well enough, and he wondered if Kootala would too. Luke decided to keep the glass, never sell it, and if he never saw Kootala again, at least he would have something *almost* as wonderful.

Luke laid out his bedroll as close to the fire as he could manage and crawled inside. After some time, he heard the horse snoring.

Staring up at the stars, Luke wondered if Kootala was looking at them too.

He closed his eyes and slept restlessly. That primal being deep down waited for the predator to return, and would snap Luke awake at the first hint of danger. Yet Luke's heart was calm, beating a different rhythm, yearning for the beating of another in his arms.

21

Cassidy Reeve awoke in one of Lonely's rooms, buried under a thick layer of quilts. Morning sunlight filtered through the dusty air, warming her face. Like most nights, the nightmares kept her from a decent sleep; though Cassidy was tired, she was happy to get on with another day.

It was the morning after abandoning Sam outside Bluff's Reach. She rightly assumed he had been caught. Although she was not one to struggle with guilt or empathy for white men, she had come to enjoy working with Sam—even though they fought—and had some lingering shreds of remorse for how things ended.

Howard soon brought a breakfast of oats and sugar, which Cassidy ate furiously, like flies on shit. She washed each bite down with a sip of hot black coffee. After breakfast, she sorted through the stack of papers that she had taken from Jerome Carlotta. The records were mostly useless, the ledgers unimportant. Those she threw into the room's fireplace. They crackled and hissed as they burned. Jerome would not miss them. What remained, then, was a few transport orders, written directions, and a couple of crude maps indicating washed-out and newly carved roads. She folded those few papers and tucked them into her pocket.

Cassidy freshened up with a bowl of warm water, scrubbing stray sand from the scalp between her braids. Howard retrieved her horse from the stable and helped her saddle the creature. Cassidy thanked him for his hospitality, handed him five dollars, mounted her white, and headed west along the secret route to Devil's Gulch.

The stallion was quick and had decent stamina, but Cassidy rode him slow. She was fast when a job was due—faster than most, she liked to believe. But, she preferred to take her time when given the opportunity. She longed to be alone in the silence of nature. The empty desert calmed her, and so she often took it easy when returning to the gulch.

Casey would be grouchy, of course. He hated waiting for Cassidy, for anyone, really. He was the most impatient man she had ever known, except when patience served him directly. Yes, Casey would be upset that she took the extra time to bring him his score, but that would be dust compared to his fury when he found out about Sam.

She should have shot them both. Instead, she left Sam behind. She didn't think him capable of attacking Kootala to defend his identity. And Kootala wouldn't have killed him, no matter how angry he would have been. It was a risk to leave them. Who knows what Sam revealed? Would he have revealed the location of Devil's Gulch or the inner workings of Casey's gang? She hoped not, for Casey would have her head on a pole. But now, removed from the event, Cassidy's mind was clearer. It would be silly to think that Sam—Luke—wouldn't squeal to save his own hide.

Dammit. Cassidy growled under her breath. She had killed so many people before, with no reservations. But she pitied those two, and truth be told, that is why she ran away.

But it was all behind her now. Sam Clangour was, in all ways that mattered, dead. Luke Morgan had paid off his debt. And, as far as Cassidy knew, Casey had no further plans with Bluff's Reach. She had already stolen everything of note in that town. Her work there was done.

And she had gotten no closer to finding her parents' killers.

She would continue on, with hope of more luck in the next town.

A mile west of Lonely, Cassidy came upon the great wall of the western plateau. On her right, the wall stretched north along the path toward Bluff's Reach. To the left, the wall ran south until it hit the tracks leading to California. A mile south of that, and you'd be in the Colorado River. Cassidy took neither direction. Instead, she continued west through a small slot canyon, where a stream had carved its way through the plateau long ago. The stream had since dried, but a winding channel in the earth remained, no more than three stagecoaches wide. Cassidy took this path and walked for a time. The air was cool and the path was shadowed from the cliffs on either side. Only at noon, when the sun was at its peak, would light reach the floor of the canyon. But that was hours away, and Cassidy would be on the other side by then.

She stopped, watered her horse, urinated, and carried on.

As Cassidy approached the end of the passage, a breeze began to blow through the walls. Her dreadlocks swung in the wind like the branches of a willow tree. Her heart sank in her stomach, and fear began to crawl up her back.

Cassidy wasn't afraid of much: not of death, not of pain, but she *was* afraid of ghosts. And she was afraid of this section along the route to Devil's Gulch. Ahead of her, the canyon opened into a sprawling valley filled with mesas, buttes, and rocky spires. Casey's gang called this place the Howling Valley, for if the wind blew just right, it made a haunting, howling sound as it echoed around the strange geology. To Cassidy, it sounded like a thousand spirits crying out as they wandered aimlessly through a god-forsaken wasteland.

She shuddered, took a deep breath, told herself that it was just the wind, and entered the valley.

The valley cried.

Cassidy continued westward, picking up her pace slightly.

A gust blew. Swirls of dust danced off the ground like phantoms. The wind shrieked a siren song. Cassidy imagined the spirit of her mother out there, lost in the wind, calling out to her for guidance. She wondered if other people heard their loved ones out there. Mothers passing through would search for lost children. Widows would scour the sands for departed husbands. They would get lost themselves, and become another member of the chorus of the damned.

There *was* a power in this valley. Cassidy could feel it as sure as she could hear the wind. And she wondered—strangely enough, for the first time—if this place held any connection to the talents of people like Casey Calhoun and Kootala Morgan. Did they draw upon some supernatural power, gifted somehow by the spirits of this place? And if so, could *Cassidy* find that power as well?

It was certainly possible, but she did not wish to stay long enough to find out.

Cassidy rode to the rock formation the gang had named Big Butte. It was a juvenile name, not even pronounced properly, but it kept the travelers in a good mood and left their sanity intact. Cassidy stopped under Big Butte's shadow, chuckled, ate a cold can of beans for lunch, drank some water, and waited.

The shadows shrunk as mid-day approached, and after a time became no more than a sliver on the ground. Just after noon, the shadow returned and the butte became a compass. Cassidy walked around to the oppose side and headed south.

After some time, she came to the wall of a plateau once again and found the continuation of the ancient river canyon. Into this she went, leaving the valley behind as it howled the hungry tune of a creature who's lunch had just escaped. Through this passage she rode yet another hour and finally approached Devil's Gulch. There, the walls had closed in on Cassidy, the passage shrinking down to a skinny ravine. Above, the lip of the ancient crevasse loomed, with ledges jutting randomly here and there.

A voice called from above. "Cassidy, are you riding alone?"

Cassidy looked up and saw a man leaning out over one of the ledges. He wore a dusty brown blanket over his head, which he used to blend in with the rocky surroundings. Cassidy called back up to him. "Just me. The other was left behind. Is Casey here?"

"Yes," the man said. "He came through not long since, from the river north. He is in his quarters, has been waiting for you. I think he is itching to leave soon again."

"Fine. I'll be going then," Cassidy said. A bit further up, she hitched her horse and continued on foot.

At the terminus of the ravine, a slot-like gulch twisted open into a maze of channels and pillars. It was quite obvious that an ancient current had once swirled there, carving the strange and intricate formations. Among this scaffolding, Casey and his band of outlaws had built their hideout, Devil's Gulch.

Their base was by no means a city, but it was not Lonely, either. Small wooden buildings populated the cliffs on either side, and hanging bridges connected the structures overhead. Several members went about their own business, and Cassidy noted one of the newer members carrying a large box over one of the boardwalks.

Years ago, Cassidy had claimed a room up along one of those ridges, but she had since given it up for the freedom and solitude of the desert. Permanent residence had never set well with Cassidy. Not since the loss of her parents, anyway.

At the very end of the gulch, a cliff edge gave way to coursing water below—an unnamed river that flowed into the Colorado, downstream. A zigzagging staircase followed the cliff down to the water, where a small dock and some boats waited for a quick escape. Casey would occasionally enter the gulch from upstream, when it was too much trouble to take the route around and through Lonely. *How much easier would it be*, Cassidy thought, *if they could go straight north to Promontory instead of south first, around the plateaus?*

Along the cliff face, another set of stairs led upwards to the top lip of the gulch, where the quarters of Casey Calhoun nested. Cassidy climbed and came, at last, to deliver Casey his prize. She pulled herself up to a small balcony looking out over the river. A heavy canvas acted as a door to Casey's room, with a cowbell hung nearby. Cassidy rang the bell with the barrel of her gun, and Casey's voice beckoned her in.

***

Casey's quarters were not as fancy as most people would expect. Sure, he had a couple pieces of fine furniture, mainly his desk and bed, but everything else was purely utilitarian. In fact, most of Devil's Gulch was the same; simple, practical, with rare bits of comfort. Yet the one thing about Casey's quarters that followed his character was the *neatness* of it all. He was an organized man, and his room reflected that. Shelves were stacked with precision, and most of his belongings were put away in simple cabinets or chests. Next to Casey's bed, a locked chest contained his most valuable treasures. He was locking this particular piece when Cassidy entered the chamber.

Casey's eyes glistened as Cassidy handed him the stack of Jerome's papers. "You sure these are accurate?" he asked, taking his prize delicately.

"I'm sure," Cassidy said. "Their roads are constantly changing, but these maps should provide assistance enough to navigate the pits."

"Very good. You've done well, my love." Casey took Cassidy's hand into his own. "You are trembling, girl."

"About Sam," Cassidy said, trying to remain stoic.

"His debt is paid, then. He's done?"

"About that. Well, Sam got caught. The sheriff, Kootala, found out Sam's true identity."

"And?" Casey's smile tightened into a purse, and his grip constricted around Cassidy's hand.

"Last I saw, Luke Morgan was kneeling in the dust before the sheriff. I... left them behind."

Casey's mouth twisted into a snarl. "You let them go? You stupid bitch! What if Luke squeals to that pissant sheriff? What if they take their info to the state marshal?"

Casey dropped Cassidy's hand and slapped her hard across the face. She stumbled back.

"You should have killed them!" Casey shouted.

Cassidy felt tears leap into her eyes, but she held them in. She would not let Casey see them fall. And her cheek, fuck it stung. Yet she didn't rub it. Instead, she just stared back at Casey without a word.

He growled. "You'd better fix this, Cassidy. I want both those boys dead. You have a week."

Cassidy resolved herself. "Tell me what you are planning with that mine, and I will have Luke and Kootala's heads here in three days."

"Fine. I suppose you have a right to know, anyway." Casey sighed, then opened a drawer in his desk and retrieved a long, thick cigar. He bit the tip off and spat it into his hand, then tucked the nub into his pocket; he would not dirty his own quarters. Casey lit the cigar with a match and began to reveal his plan with blue smoke pouring from his mouth.

"Out here, everything starts and ends with the railroad. The rail connects *everything*, and is currently the most powerful force in the nation. The west is growing, and it is growing fast.

"Three years ago, they finished building the Overland Route. The *Transcontinental Railroad*, they call it. Poetic, isn't it? Well, this route they built is the *only* direct rail between the east and the west, joining the two in Promontory, Utah. The businessmen in Promontory have grown very wealthy in the few years since the rail's construction." Casey took a big drag of the cigar. "Understand?"

"Sure," Cassidy said. "Capitalize on the growing rail industry. But what with the copper mine?"

"I'm getting to that soon," Casey said. "The Department of the Interior and the railroad companies have been planning *another* route to connect southern California to the Overland Route in Denver. The optimal, cheapest path would be to follow the Colorado River through Graben and northeast from there. However, what happens when you follow the river north of Graben?"

Cassidy thought, following the geography in her mind. "You run into the Powell Bluff."

"Exactly!" Casey smiled. "It is too expensive to build a bridge over Lake Powell. They can't go around the bluff, so they would instead have to tunnel *through* it. However, that brings up another problem. Do you know the origins of Graben?"

"No. I don't."

Casey's face lit up. "Gold, Cassidy. Gold!" He giggled. "When the prospectors first came west, they found it inside the land underneath

Bluff's Reach. They mined vast networks under the bluff, and built the town of Graben along the river. Since then, Graben has grown into a fully fledged city, and the mine has long since been abandoned, and mostly forgotten."

"The railroad?" Cassidy encouraged.

"Cannot tunnel underneath Bluff's Reach without collapsing the mine and destroying the town in the process. The cost to relocate the population is unthinkable."

"Of course. And—"

"Instead," Casey interrupted, "they will be forced to build another route, detouring south through Tucson and avoiding Graben entirely. The city will be cut off, and would waste away with time. I have much invested here, and I do not want that future, you see."

"The copper mine, Casey. What about that? What about these maps?" Cassidy was getting impatient.

"Building a detour through Tucson will be expensive. Not so much as a bridge or relocation of Bluff's Reach, but still a sizable sum. And I have made an... agreement of sorts, to provide the opportunity to build the original route through Graben, in exchange for a percentage of the railroad's cost savings."

"The copper mine!" Cassidy nearly shouted.

"Fine." Casey ashed his cigar. "They have dynamite, and lots of it. And that old gold mine underneath Bluff's Reach, well it is quite fragile, I suspect. So, I am going to—"

"You are going to blow up the bluff?" Cassidy's ears grew hot with blood, her heart cold with ice.

"More or less. With the bluff collapsed, the route can proceed north. It's dirty work, sure, but progress demands compromise."

"Surely the government won't let that happen! There will be investigations."

"Money talks," Casey said. "Or rather, it keeps people *from* talking."

"How much?" Cassidy asked.

"By my math, and my investment in the railroad, close to a million dollars."

A million! That was not a figure Cassidy had ever imagined, not in a hundred lifetimes. It was asinine.

"And," Casey said. "I am in a position to obtain many assets from the people of Bluff's Reach. Imagine, Cassidy, owning *all* of Graben as it grows to one of the biggest cities in the country!"

Cassidy felt sick to her stomach. "You'd kill all those people?"

Casey frowned. "Have you never studied the history of this country? You think one town makes a difference? Think of all the Chinese that die every day, laying down track. The natives, the slaves, all those people that died so that we can live as we do today. This world is not kind, not made for the weak. God has shown us again and again that it is our duty to make progress, regardless of who is in our way. *That*, love, is the way of the world."

Cassidy said nothing to that.

"Anyway, my *employees* will get a big cut of my profits. Enough, I would think, to quiet your silly conscience."

"I should hope so," Cassidy said. "How long is this all going to take?"

Casey laughed. "Why, it is already in motion, my girl! If I take a crew out today, I can have the dynamite here in three days. We can float it down the river from the north and retrieve it here. Then, we ride the explosives to the mine under the bluff. Altogether, Bluff's Reach will be a pile of rubble in five days' time."

He was certainly efficient. Cassidy could commend him for that. But to collapse the bluff... that was evil. Cassidy was no saint, and she had no qualms about killing, when someone *needed* killing. But a whole town? Yet... a town of rich white folk...

Casey's face turned sour again. "I will be leaving now. I will be back in three days. I expect to see you here. And if there aren't two dead sissies up on that bluff—"

"Stop," Cassidy said, remembering the sting of her cheek. "I understand. It will be done."

"Good." Casey smiled pleasantly. "If I don't see you, I'll assume the worst." He looked Cassidy up and down. "And please, clean yourself up for when I return. You are filthy."

"Of course."

Casey put an arm around Cassidy's waist and pulled her close. He slipped his tongue into her mouth. She returned the favor, though she was utterly repulsed. The feeling was nothing new, so she maintained the ruse.

They separated, and Casey left his quarters to gather his crew.

Cassidy was left standing alone in Casey's quarters. After a few minutes, certain that Casey would not return, Cassidy began to sob. She wavered, almost collapsing, then took a seat on Casey's desk. Her cheek ached, and had likely started to turn purple in the shape of Casey's hand. She rubbed the sore spot and cried more, though not in pain, but with shame and embarrassment and hot anger. Casey had never struck her before. It was humiliating.

She also cried in fear, but not for herself. No, Cassidy feared for Bluff's Reach, and for Luke and Kootala. As her emotions came bursting forth, she realized she had become friends with Sam Clangour, and, in turn, with Luke Morgan. She realized, too, that the two men were not so different from herself. They had all been wronged, all had a desperate urge to find a way to make things right, and the only difference was *how* they went about it. Suddenly, and with exceptional clarity, Cassidy Reeve decided that she wanted to help all those people.

And Cassidy cried for the most visceral reason of all. She had become the very thing that her parents escaped from all those years ago. She was a slave to Casey, not in the traditional sense, but through her own actions and desires. She was bound to the man by her unbreakable drive to avenge her parents. She had been his pawn, had fallen right into his charismatic grip. He had *used* her, as a man uses a tool. Like she was his... property.

Cassidy's blood boiled.

She had another thought, then, that stung equally as harsh as a slap to the face. Casey had desired Cassidy's services, and Cassidy desired her mother's necklace. Casey knew that she would do his bidding until she found what she was looking for. Should Cassidy find the necklace and avenge her parents, Casey would lose her. What better way to keep her in his service, then, but to keep her from her one and only goal? And how would he do *that*, without keeping the necklace for himself?

He couldn't, Cassidy thought. *And yet...*

She burst into an intense rage and began tearing through Casey's quarters. Cassidy smashed the man's belongings, throwing books, ripping doors off cabinets, tearing his clothes to shreds. She destroyed Casey's possessions with all the anger of her ancestors.

What was she doing? She had clearly lost her mind! She was not thinking clearly. There is no way that—

The locked chest!

Cassidy flew to the chest beside Casey's bed and began waling on the lock. It was tough, but it would break.

Casey would kill her if he returned. What she was doing was crazy. It was nonsense!

As she brought her boot down on the lock, she remembered the night her parents were killed. Cassidy saw her parents in that tree, saw her home engulfed in flames. But a fog had been lifted, and she remembered with clarity what she had never noticed before. There was a man there: young, handsome, with slick black hair. She had seen Casey that day. She was sure of it. He had pulled the rope upon which her parents hung while she watched from the bushes. And that same man, Casey Calhoun, had found her soon after, had taken her in, taught her his ways, of vengeance, of violence.

With a final blow, Cassidy's boot busted through the lock on the chest. With trembling hands, she lifted the lid.

More boxes. A gold watch in one. Snakeskin boots in another. Deeds. Stocks. Silver. Regular, unassuming valuables. Cash. A—

A pouch, sown into the very bottom of the chest. Cassidy reached into the pouch, then pulled out a crude necklace, strung with blue beads.

Her mother's necklace.

Casey had it all along.

The explosive rage settled, nestling softly into Cassidy's heart. She had, at long last, found one of her parents' killers, and he would know the others. She had found the necklace, and she found her resolve once again. The woman had only one purpose in life, and now she knew how to accomplish that goal.

Smiling, Cassidy Reeve strung the beads around her neck.

***

Cassidy Reeve followed Casey Calhoun and his gang until they got to Lonely. She kept her distance, knowing she could not take them all by herself. The men slept the night in Lonely, and she slept out in the desert with no fire to keep her warm. Her nightmares and the echoes of the Howling Valley kept her from a decent night's sleep.

In the morning, Casey took his men south. They would eventually turn west along the road to California, would travel for a day, then turn north once again toward the Carlotta copper mine.

Cassidy rode into Lonely not long after Casey had left.

Howard greeted her as she rode up. "Good noon, Cass. Casey just left; you should be able to catch up if you're quick."

"I'm on a different job today," Cassidy said. She hopped off her horse and tied it to the hitching post in front of Howard's home. "What did Casey tell you?"

"Nothing involving you." Howard replied.

Cassidy scanned his voice, and found it to be honest. "Have you seen Sam... eh, Luke?" she asked.

"Sure. He rode through recently, heading down to Graben. He was in a rough way. Had a different horse, too."

"Thanks."

"Did something happen?" Howard asked.

"Do you have anything to eat?" Cassidy asked. "I'm starving."

"I've got some roast chicken left over from last night. Casey and the guys are like hogs, but I made sure to set some aside."

Cassidy's stomach growled. "That would be wonderful. Did they drink, too?"

"Of course. Though there isn't much left in that regard."

"Fine. Get me a bunch of bottles. I'll be out back."

Howard regarded Cassidy with understanding, then went inside.

Cassidy retrieved two boxes of ammo from her saddlebags, then walked around the back of Howard's house. He came out the back door with a wooden box full of empty bottles. They worked together, setting up two dozen bottles in the sand. Cassidy then loaded fresh, clean rounds into one of her shotguns. Howard stuck his fingers into his ears.

Cassidy fired at the closest bottles, turning them into a spray of brown and green glass. She quickly reloaded and then let off another set. Then once more. All shots hit with deadly accuracy, and no bottles escaped her fire.

"I think that last one jumped in front of your spray," Howard said.

Cassidy slung her hot iron across her back, then drew the other. She loaded two shells. "Let's see if I can hit them when they're jumping away."

Howard grabbed two bottles by their necks and held them with one hand. He pulled back, then swung and threw them high into the air.

Cassidy waited. The bottles peaked in the sky, then began to fall again. She pulled the trigger once, and both bottles turned to clouds of glitter in the air. She cocked the shotgun open and the unfired shell popped out, which she caught in her hand. She tossed it to Howard, said, "Guess I don't need this one."

"Lord, remind me to stay out of your way," Howard said.

"I'll clean up the glass," Cassidy said. "Then I'll be in for that chicken."

22

Kootala slid a citation under the tailor's door. It read:

By the order of, and enforceable by, the Bluff's Reach Sheriff's Office.

Fine in the amount of:

Five dollars. For,

Failure to adhere to town cleanliness standards for public establishments. i.e. dusty windows, mud on front steps.

Ten dollars. For,

Unsafe dwelling or structure. i.e. loose railing around porch.

Fines to be paid or resolved at town Sheriff's Office.

Kootala tucked his notebook and pen into his shirt pocket, then started back down the porch stairs.

The door swung open with a crash, and the tailor stood on the other side with the fine paper in hand. "What the hell is this?" he shouted at Kootala.

Kootala stopped and turned halfway down the steps. "It is a citation. You let your place go to hell. We've got standards around here, you know."

"You're just being an asshole, all because you—"

"Watch your mouth." Kootala cautioned, then turned again and continued down to Main Street. "Have a nice day," he said over his shoulder.

The tailor grumbled and retreated, slamming the door behind him.

Kootala continued toward his next victim: the general store. *Surely*, he thought, *they would be breaking several regulations.*

When Bluff's Reach was being built, its founders had written absurd regulations into the local law. They were designed to keep property values high, but were found to be unreasonable and had never really been enforced. That is, until Kootala decided that these people needed to learn some responsibility. They would be upset, of course. Would they think Kootala was searching for some sense of control, especially after having lost Luke? Or would they think it just juvenile anger? Possibly neither were too far from the truth.

Kootala kicked the mud off his boots and went inside the general store.

The Deetmans were at the counter, talking with Todd Lybuck. Kootala rummaged through the shelves, pretending to shop while listening to their conversation.

"—and three cases of number two nails," Mark Deetman was saying.

Todd wrote something on a slip of paper. "Do you need any new tack?"

"No," Vanessa said. "That all survived the explosion, though the leather still smells like smoke."

"Alright. I will send out your order with the next round of mail. I'd expect the lumber to be shipped within the week. The sheet metal might be another after that. It'll save you fifty dollars or so, if you wait and have them bring it all at once."

"That's fine."

"Alright. If you need anything else, just let me know before the mail goes out."

"Thanks, Todd."

"Oh, by the way," Todd said. "You two haven't seen Katie around, have you?"

Mark and Vanessa exchanged a questioning look, then together, said, "No. Why?"

"She didn't come home a few nights ago, and I haven't seen her since. If she's been staying with someone, that's fine. I've been waiting for her to get with a nice man anyway. But I would have expected her to be around by now."

Kootala was bent down, looking over a crate of various hardware. Hearing talk about Katie, he snapped up. He interrupted the ongoing conversation. "Todd, when did you last see Katie?"

"Oh, Kootala. I, uh... Last I saw Katie was at Abner's funeral. I came back here to work the desk, and she must have stayed out. Haven't seen her after that, and it ain't like her to go off without telling me."

Kootala remembered that day clearly. He remembered Katie having a drunken fit in the saloon. "I saw her that night," Kootala said. "She was at the saloon, quite drunk if I'm being honest. She was upset, we all were, with the funeral and such. We got into a little spat and she stormed out of the saloon."

"You think she hurt herself? Or someone might have taken advantage of her! Oh God!" Todd started to panic.

"I wouldn't worry too much, yet," Kootala said. "But we'd better ask around town, see if anyone has seen her. Could be she's hiding out for whatever reason."

Mark Deetman chimed in. "Hey, Sheriff, we can go spread the word, try and get some information or a search going."

"Yes, that's good." Kootala agreed. "See if you can get a party to search south of Main Street. Todd and I can get a search going north. Todd, you'd better lock up for now."

They closed the general store and went out onto the street. Kootala spoke again. "Alright, try to get as much information as possible. If you find her or learn that she is safe, come find us. We will do the same. If we don't find anything, meet back at my office before dark."

They separated.

Kootala felt a sinking feeling in his heart: failure. He had been so worried about his own problems that he had neglected those of his people. He had not protected this town, and now people were dead and missing. Kootala had not protected Abner. He had not protected Jerome. And he hadn't protected Katie. Who would be next?

Kootala *had* protected himself and his own feelings. Luke had broken his heart, and that was all he had cared about. He had beat himself up over it, had recounted all the little hints he overlooked, or even ignored, over and over again. But no longer. Kootala *was* the sheriff of this town, and his people's safety was more important than a broken heart. He would still hurt, but it would be on his own time.

Kootala and Todd went door to door, asking for information and spreading word of Katie's disappearance.

Nobody knew anything. Nobody had seen her.

Within an hour, nearly the entire town was searching for Katie Lybuck. They dug under bushes, under porches, in their barns. Someone found a muddy jacket under a porch in the alley behind the bank, but nothing else.

The evening grew closer, and nobody had been successful in finding the girl. It was as if she had vanished like a shadow in the night.

Everyone gathered outside the sheriff's office as the sun began to set. Kootala told them to keep their eyes and ears open for any information. He told them not to worry too much, that without signs of an attack, she most likely just up and left for Graben in the night. They decided to wait a few days for news, and if they heard nothing, would go from there.

Kootala was less optimistic than he let show. Things had changed around Bluff's Reach, and wickedness seemed to have grabbed hold of their town. He couldn't be sure what happened to Katie, but something told him it wasn't good.

That *something* was a feeling he had felt once before; the day his mother died. Kootala had woken up in a dirty Graben alley, and his mother was not at his side. Sickness filled him, either by some divine gift or just subconscious knowledge, he did not know. But he knew something bad had happened. And he had been correct. Kootala had found his mother later that day. The details escaped him now: probably repressed long ago. Still, the feeling was the same.

Was he somehow using his Dust in another way? Was there more to that power than he knew?

Kootala disbanded the search party, then went home himself. He drew a steaming bath to soak his muscles, but they refused to loosen.

How Kootala would proceed, he had no idea.

23

Katie Lybuck awoke inside the cave.

She had gone in and out of consciousness several times as the agony of her broken leg ebbed and flowed like the tides. Her hangover had passed silently behind the pain. She thought mainly of her stupidity, and the streak of bad luck that brought her down into the depths of the earth. It was beyond dark, and she couldn't be sure if her eyes were open or closed. Without the light of day, her only judgment of time was the hunger growing in her stomach and the dryness on her lips. She knew that people would be looking for her soon enough—maybe they already were—but the chances of finding her were slim. Someone might stumble upon this cave decades from now and find only her bones. If she wanted any chance of escape, she would have to drag herself out. And she needed water and food.

"I don't know if I can do this," she said, possibly out loud, possibly only in her head. In the dark, she couldn't really tell the difference.

"Yes you can," she bargained with herself. "You are the strongest woman you know. Remember back on the farm, when that momma cow chased you up a tree? You stayed up there for hours, and the cow waited you out. What did you finally do?" she asked herself.

"I jumped down and twisted my ankle. I ran away anyway, and jumped the fence. My foot was swollen for weeks."

"And you continued to work anyway, didn't you? You threw hay and chopped firewood. You even managed to break a young mare, all the while with a bum foot."

"What ever happened to that momma cow?"

"You chopped her up and ate her, every last piece."

"I'm the toughest woman I know, aren't I?"

"Damn right. Now buck up and drag yourself out of this stinking pit!"

With great effort, Katie got on her hands and one knee, and began to crawl further into the cave. For hours she crawled, dragging her busted leg behind. Somehow, she sensed a gradual slope downwards.

"We wouldn't want to go down, right? Don't you go up to get out of a cave?"

"Do you think you can go up?"

"No, I guess not."

Katie continued downwards, and soon found remnants of old human activity as she went. At first, there were only timbers and the occasional dried-up oil lamp. But as she crawled deeper into the earth, she found empty crates, a lonely shoe, a pickaxe. The tunnels got wider. She learned to see with the sound of her pained grunting echoing off the cave walls. At one point, she thought she was in a massive cavern, her echo distant and quiet and lonely.

"Who's in here?" she asked.

"Who's in here, here?" the darkness responded.

She crawled, dragging her busted limb behind her. Every little protrusion or crevasse she crossed was agony on her leg.

At one point, Katie crawled headfirst into a wall of metal and it rang out like a steel drum. She felt it, pulling herself up and standing on her good leg, and was able to identify an old minecart. It must have been on the very end of its track, its wheels welded in place with rust. She felt inside but it was empty. Condensation clung to the metal where it was still smooth. She had found water. With great effort, Katie worked her way around the cart and licked the water off its surface. The water had a sharp, metallic taste, but was refreshing nonetheless.

"That tastes like getting punched in the teeth," she told the dark.

Katie filled her stomach with the rustwater. She searched more, and found the metal rails that the cart had moved along many years ago. Again she crawled, following the track, and eventually came upon a small encampment. There was what felt like benches made of half logs, a couple old denim jackets, a single boot. Men would have gathered here to have their lunch and sharpen their tools. Katie searched for an old lunch sack, hoping for even a scrap of mummified jerky. She had no such luck. She crawled again, groping at the darkness as she went.

A small crate found her grasp. She picked it up, shook it, and heard something clattering inside. Its lid was secured with nails, but she managed to get her fingernails inside the gap. She pulled hard and the lid pried open, one of her fingernails ripping back in the process. Her fingers gave her no troubles though, as a bent-up fingernail was no comparison to a broken leg. She reached into the box and her hand curled around an insect. It writhed and struggled, then stabbed her in the back of the hand with its tail. She winced, more so in fear than pain. She had been stabbed by a scorpion. If it was venomous, she hoped it would kill her quickly. If not, she still had hope of escape.

Her hunger took her, hard and fast. She hesitated slightly, and held the squirming thing in front of her mouth.

"Mmm, this will be so tasty!" she lied. "If only I had some relish."

She threw the scorpion into her mouth and chomped furiously, as if someone might come and take it from her. It gushed, sour and cold, but tasted fine enough and went down her throat rather easily. She wiped the goo that dripped down her chin, and continued crawling.

Hours, probably, and Katie had not felt any effects from the scorpion's sting nor a stomachache from its consumption. She felt incredibly lucky, given the circumstances. Her luck was confirmed when, at one point, she was able to see again. Though minimal, she could make out the very basic details of the tunnel. She could see the shapes of beams and crates. She continued and soon was able to make out more details. She saw individual tools now and could follow the cart tracks visually. The track and tunnel curved, and she could see the light of day in the distance. Katie crawled quickly, the pain of her broken leg falling into the back of her perception as euphoria took over.

Finally, she exited the mine. It had almost been her tomb, and now she was free again.

She rolled her back onto the sand and splayed out, collecting sunlight like a blooming flower.

Death hadn't taken her in the darkness, but she knew well enough that the desert could take her just as easily.

Yet it felt nice, so she let the hot sun warm her skin.

24

A small grove of Joshua trees grew just north of Bluff's Reach, not all that far from the cemetery. Under the sparse shade of the trees, Kootala built a small fire with dead dried logs and sticks. He sat by the flames, watching them lap at the dusty air.

Kootala had been grieving for the past few days. Luke Morgan, the man Kootala *had* known, was gone. Dead, in a way. Kootala mourned the loss appropriately, grieving over the man Luke had been. The good Luke. Kootala would not think on the man that Luke *truly* was. It would only make things worse.

"Oh, Tama." Kootala groaned, kneeling by the fire. "What should I do? Kongwuti, guide the way."

Typically, Kootala would confide in Luke. But now...

This was something Kootala had never done, though his mother had on many occasions. She would often look to Kongwuti for guidance, finding the Grandmother in the flames, in the clouds, the wind, the stars and moon. Though Kootala had never *seen* what his mother did, he believed she saw *something*. Now it was his turn, though he was not confident he would see anything in the fire. There was always that doubt in Kootala's mind, that perhaps it was all just *myth*. Tradition, rather than truth.

"Show me," he again whispered, watching the embers shimmer.

Nothing emerged but smoke, and even then, no figures could be found in its swirls.

What was Kootala doing here? This was pointless.

A small breeze came through, kicking up a light wave of desert dust.

Could it be so simple?

Kootala took a handful of sand from the ground, held it in an open palm, and studied it carefully. He took in each grain, imagining how they had formed, the history of each rock, slowly tumbled to fine powder over the eons. In that short instant, he came to know the earth in his hand, became intimate with it, and understood its place in nature.

Then, Kootala threw the sand into the fire.

Kootala startled, nearly falling forward into the flames. A man was kneeling across the fire. He was naked except for a cloth around his waist and a fine bejeweled mask on his face.

"I—" Kootala began to stand.

"No," the masked man said. "Sit."

Kootala hesitated, but eventually did as told, crossing his legs under his rear. "You are Waasam?"

"Am I?"

Riddles, then.

"What is this?" Kootala asked. "A trick? Is this like the cloud I made. Some... illusion?"

"The Dust, Kootala. How do you do it?"

"I— What?"

"Never mind. Why are you out here?"

The jewels on the man's mask—the *eyes*—peered intently. They seemed to be looking *through* Kootala. Or perhaps, not looking at anything at all. How could they? The man wasn't *real*, after all.

"I came for guidance," Kootala said. "I'm... lost. I thought, at least, I could have some time to think."

The masked man—it *was* Waasam, wasn't it?—gestured to the fire. "Look."

In the flames, Kootala could see figures moving. Horses, galloping through town. Abner Brooks, falling into the dirt. Kootala, standing over the sheriff. Cassidy Reeve, riding through the desert. A wind picked up, crashing against the flames, sending burning ashes out of the pit and into the air. The flames grew. In there, Kootala saw Katie Lybuck wandering a flat, empty expanse.

Kootala did not want to see it, but he could not draw away his gaze. He fell deeper into the vision. The surroundings faded to darkness, except for the fire and the glistening mask on the other side.

"How can I save her?" Kootala asked. "I... don't know what to do. I don't know how."

"Is that your worry? The girl?" Waasam asked.

"Of course! It is my duty to protect my people. But... I have failed. I need help."

"No," Waasam said, suddenly appearing at Kootala's side. "Look deeper."

The flames blew away, leaving only red embers. Kootala fell into them, and saw himself sitting alone in the saloon. The other patrons sneered at him.

Worthless.

He can't do it.

He let the sheriff die.

Sissy.

We *will be next.*

"What do you see, Kootala?" Waasam asked. "It is not about the girl, is it?"

"No." Kootala shuddered.

The images changed, and Kootala was standing in the desert with his gun raised at Cassidy Reeve.

Then, Sam Clangour.

And Luke Morgan.

Kootala aimed at them all, and he could not pull the trigger. Around him, the world burned.

"Violence." Kootala muttered. "Is that the way?"

"That is not who you are," Waasam said. "You are good."

"Then what can I do?"

The smoke and ash swirled around Kootala, changing, and became a whirlwind of dust.

Dust.

"This is your strength, Kootala," Waasam said.

"Sure, my Dust can heal. Can soothe. But I can't protect with it. At least, I don't think I can. Not against true strength. Not against Grit."

"Do you really not understand?" Waasam asked. It seemed, perhaps, that his mask had grown sad.

"Dust is fragile. It's feminine. Is that my problem?"

A mighty sandstorm howled around them and Waasam's mask turned angry. Its jewels fell off into darkness and left only sour horror in its expression.

"Please!" Kootala cried.

Waasam reached up and removed the mask. Beneath, the face of an ancient woman emerged.

"Kongwuti." Kootala awed, bowing his head. "Grandmother."

The old woman raised a knobbly hand and held it, palm up, before her mouth. Her mouth moved, as if she were speaking, but no voice came forth.

"What?" Kootala asked, leaning close.

Dust poured from Kongwuti's mouth, falling into her hand. She extended this to Kootala, and poured the dust into *his* hand. He looked into his palm and saw that the dust had organized into a small script. Ancient Hoki glyphs, and somehow Kootala could read it.

From where do you draw your powers? What gives you your Dust?

"I... from my connection with nature. Harmony," Kootala said. "I see what *can* be, and let nature take that form on its own. It comes from my values. Peace and connectedness with nature."

Kongwuti gestured to Kootala's palm.

The script changed.

Wrong. From where does a man get his Grit?

"Strength," Kootala said, though he was not so sure now as he once was. "Power, greed, control."

Wrong again, his palm said. *Your strength, be it Grit or Dust, comes from your belief in yourself. Your power to alter the world is not a factor of values, nor of skill.*

"Then what from, if strength does not come from what I am?"

What are you?

"I... don't know. Is that my problem?"

Something like that.

"Must I be more of a man?"

Man, woman, Dust, Grit. It is all the same when broken down to the most basic grains. You are what you are, so be sure of yourself, and don't let the notions of others change that. For what change can you make in the world, if you let the world change you first?

"I am no hero," Kootala said. "I can't stop evil. I can't even stop a robbery. Not with Dust. Perhaps, if I had Grit."

Forcing change does not make a hero. Nor does Grit come from your strength or ability to force change.

"Then where? Please, tell me."

I already have.

The script on Kootala's hand blew away.

"Wait!"

The sandstorm raged, grinding at Kongwuti's ancient skin, sanding it smooth. The figure lost all features, and soon became only a glowing, radiant form. The sandstorm settled, and only the darkness, the bright figure, and Kootala remained.

"Tama?" Kootala asked, though he thought he already knew the answer. "Is this real? Did I create some hallucinogen from the Dust?"

The figure did not answer.

"I'm confused. More so than before."

Again, the figure only loomed.

Kootala wondered what the purpose of this was? Whether it was his own mind playing tricks, or actually Tama providing guidance, what was he supposed to have learned?

Without warning, the figure disappeared.

And Kootala was again kneeling by the fire, alone.

He *had* learned something, hadn't he? What was it? What did Tama want Kootala to know? Something about his Dust, how he used it, how his place in the world changed things. Yet, he couldn't quite place that knowledge. He would have to think on it further. Let it settle.

The visions Kootala had seen: those were surely hallucinations. But that figure... it had seemed so real. Had *felt* real. He truly thought that he could have reached out and touched them. They *were* physical. But Kootala had created them with Dust, right? Only Grit could make physical objects.

He stomped out the fire, kicking sand over the ashes, and walked slowly back to town. What he would do to save Katie, and how to move forward with his life, was still unknown. But, Kootala thought, there may be something he could do. He just had to figure it out. Still, it was all too much to understand at the moment, so Kootala let it go, for the time.

If only Luke were still around, Kootala thought.

Perhaps Missy could help.

25

Warm lamplight cast a hollow shadow on the saloon floor behind Luke Morgan. He was sat on a hard stool at the bar, slumped over with his fists holding up either side of his chin. The saloon stunk with the sweetness of booze and the industrial air of Graben. It mixed into the air, filling the dank establishment with sadness. Luke wallowed in it well.

He waved down the bartender—a slim and sullen man—then gulped down his glass of whiskey and ordered another.

A group of drunk men sat at a nearby table, laughing and hollering with idiot glee. They had worked a long day at some factory and had come to the saloon to have fun and relieve stress. Their boisterous laughter made Luke's head pound like a drum. Their shrill voices pinpricked his brain, but it was their happiness that irritated him most.

"Hey, could you fellas keep it down, just a little?" Luke said over his shoulder.

The men ignored him. They hooted and hollered, almost louder than before. Someone knocked their glass off the table. It shattered and threw shards of glass across the wood floor. Another man laughed so hard that he fell backward onto the floor himself.

Luke spun around on his stool with anger. He drew his pistol and fired, shooting a stein of beer out of one of the men's hand. "Shut the hell up!" Luke yelled, his face growing a deep red.

The saloon went silent and everyone stared at Luke. The silence broke with the click of another gun's hammer being pulled.

"That is not something we do around here, sir," the bartender said, pointing a shotgun at Luke's back. He spoke again, mimicking a southern drawl. "This ain't no backwoods ee-stablishment, stranger. We don't do no shootin' of no kind here, lest you end up swingin'." He spoke in his normal voice again. "So, put that iron away and relax."

Luke holstered his pistol, then asked for another drink.

"You have had enough, sir. You can stay here for as long as you want, but you drink water from here on."

Luke grunted and wobbled on his stool. He begrudgingly drank a glass of water, then slammed it down hard against the bar top.

"Goddamn, you look like shit," someone said, sitting down next to Luke.

He turned to see Cassidy Reeve glowering at him. "Fuck off, Cass," Luke said, and turned his back to her.

"No need to be rude, cowboy."

Luke turned to face her again, his face red with fury. "You ruined my life. I'm gonna be as rude as I wa-want." He hiccuped booze.

"No, I did not. You—"

Luke interrupted. "Oh, don't tell me. Say, '*You did this to yourself.*' Well fu-uck that."

"Yeah, that's basically it."

Luke rasped his empty glass against the bar top, then held it out at the bartender. "Whatever. Why'd ya come 'ere?" he asked.

"I need your help," she said.

"Oh no, I'm done helping you!" Luke shouted, nearly falling backward off his stool. "Forget it!"

"No, listen to me. I need your help to take down Casey."

Luke sat up, a degree less drunk. But not much. "Go o-*hyuk*-on."

"I'll give you the details later, but for now, let's just say that Casey screwed us both. Now he's about to do something big. And quite wicked, even for my tastes."

"Why should I care about what he does?"

The bartender refilled Luke's water.

"Because Kootala is in serious danger," Cassidy said.

Luke was silent. He stared at his reflection in his glass.

"I still love him," he said. "So—*hyuk*—damn much."

"Then let's go save him," Cassidy pleaded.

"He don't need me to save 'im. He's not some helpless damsel."

"Then he can join us. The entire town of Bluff's Reach is in danger."

"Since when do you care?" Luke scoffed. "You hate everyone up there anyway."

"No." She corrected. "I hate Casey Calhoun. I loathe him with every drop of blood in my heart, and I would do anything to see him fail. And..." Cassidy smiled. "I guess I've kinda grown a liking to you. Kootala, too."

Luke's eyes began to drift, drunk, though he tried his hardest to focus. "What kind of danger you talkin' about?"

"What else is there out here, other than life and death?"

"Alright, I'm in," Luke said without consideration. "But not for *you* or anyone else in B-*uh*-luff's Reach. I do this for Kootala, and that's all."

"Like you always have?"

"Yeah. Guess so."

"Alright," Cassidy said. She stood up and grabbed Luke by the arm. "Let's get you some sleep. We leave for Bluff's Reach at sunup. We only have a few days."

Cassidy dragged Luke out of the saloon by his arm. The rowdy men sneered at him as they passed. One of them spat in Luke's direction.

***

Luke and Cassidy rode out of Graben as the sun rose the next morning. Luke had a throbbing whiskey headache that intensified with each bounce of his saddle. His heart fluttered with fear and shame and anxiety about confronting Kootala again. His stomach bubbled with stale acid. Watching Cassidy from the corner of his eye, Luke could see that her heart baked with rage. Her trigger finger twitched with anticipation.

They rode west along the escarpments at the base of the plateau, then zig-zagged up the switchbacks toward Lonely.

Luke became slower with each step they scaled, until he had stopped completely. He leaned over the side of Kootala's horse and heaved yellow bile into the sand. They stopped at a mound of rocks and rested in its shadow.

Cassidy built a small fire and cooked a pan of flour biscuits. She forced Luke to eat a biscuit with some water. He held it down well enough.

After some time, Luke decided he could go on. Cassidy stomped out the fire, and they began to mount their horses again.

Someone called from the distance.

It was soft, and they almost missed it. Luke thought he was hearing the sound of his headache, but when Cassidy asked if he had said something, he knew it was not his imagination.

The voice called again, louder than before, almost desperate to be heard. Then a scream, deranged and bloodcurdling, like the mountain lion Luke had heard three nights before.

Cassidy climbed to the top of a pile of rocks and surveyed the land, then pointed out into the desert. In the distance, Luke saw a young woman crawling across the sand. He rubbed the headache out of his eyes, focused hard, and recognized Katie Lybuck.

They quickly mounted their horses and ran to her. Luke forgot all about his hangover.

"Katie, how are you here? What happened?" Luke called out as they approached. He noticed her leg dragging behind her, limp and crooked.

Katie tried to respond, but collapsed from exhaustion instead.

They picked her up and carefully loaded her onto Cassidy's lap, then rode back to their camp. Luke rolled out his bedroll in the shade of the rocks and laid Katie down, being extremely careful with her leg. Cassidy poured a splash of cold water from her canteen over Katie's dry lips. She sucked at the water in her unconscious sleep.

"We have to get her to a doctor," Luke said. "We have to ride back to Graben."

"We don't have the time," Cassidy reminded him. "I know that Howard has some medical supplies in Lonely. We can get her some morphine and splint her leg. I'm sure Howard would let us borrow a wagon to carry her in. Who knows how long she's been out here... but I think she'll be fine for another day until we get her to the doctor in Bluff's Reach."

"Fine, we'd better get going then," Luke said.

They mounted their horses and continued up the valley, taking turns riding with Katie on their lap. They took the switchbacks slow, so as not to hurt her any further.

***

Katie awoke that evening as the morphine began to wear off. Her leg was surely screaming in pain again. *Fortunately*, Luke thought, *she at least had a dry bed*. He took her hand, and she relaxed a little. Luke looked down at her with a smile. At seeing his face, Katie instantly became angry, then anger gave way to shame, then great, overflowing appreciation.

"Luke," Katie said wearily. "I'm sorry for before."

"Don't apologize." He told her. "I understand your anger."

Katie winced, her leg making itself well known.

"Do you need more morphine?"

"Not yet. Where am I?" she asked.

"We're in Lonely. You are going to be alright. Get some rest, and we will bring you to the doctor in the morning."

"I've rested enough for now. Did you come all the way from Bluff's Reach looking for me?"

Luke thought about telling her everything, but decided against it. She would learn the truth eventually. "No," he said, "I was traveling for other reasons. I had no idea you were missing. What happened to you?"

Katie tried to sit up on her elbows but couldn't manage. She laid back down with a sigh. "That night at the saloon. I was drunk and really angry. I was so stupid." She began to cry. "I wandered out of town to sleep in the desert. It was stupid, I know, but I was drunk and a little crazy. There was this cave, and I crawled inside to sleep. So dark... I fell down a shaft and broke my leg. Turns out I had stumbled into an old mine, I guess. I didn't even know there was a mine under town.

"I knew nobody would rescue me, so I had to get out on my own. I pulled myself through the tunnels. Licked water off the walls. Ate a scorpion. Oh, it was so dark. I followed a minecart track and eventually found my way out. When I crawled outside, I was at the bottom of the bluff. I didn't know where to go, and the river was on one side, so I crawled in the other direction until I saw you riding up the valley. I'm lucky you stopped for a while, otherwise you never would have heard me yelling."

Luke was slack-jawed. It was a stunning, arduous, and very impressive story, if it were true. Given her current state, Luke had no reason to believe it wasn't. "Katie, you went through hell," he said.

"No shit." She chuckled a little, then winced again. "I'll take that morphine now, please."

"Sure, sure," Luke said, and gave her more of the drug.

She soon fell asleep again and began to snore loudly and rattle-dry. Luke laid on the floor next to her, in case she needed anything throughout the night.

He wondered if this would have happened, had Katie's outburst in Bill Williams' saloon been different. Maybe, maybe not.

Luke fell asleep too.

***

Cassidy woke Luke in the early morning, before the sun had a chance to come up. Daylight would soon start the day, and their time would fade with the night.

"Come on, let's get going," Cassidy said. "Howard is letting us use his wagon, but we're going to be slow anyway. We need to get ahead of the heat of the day."

"I'll help you pack the wagon. We will need extra water," Luke said.

"It's all ready to go, and I paid Howard for the morphine."

They carefully loaded Katie into the wagon. She stirred in her sleep, but the drugs kept her from waking entirely. They thanked Howard, then rode north while it was still dark. The stars were beginning to fade, and a halo of what Luke called *less-dark* crept up in the east.

The going was slow, as Cassidy had predicted. They had to stop periodically to readjust Katie or give her more medicine to calm her screams. *This would be so much easier*, Luke thought, *if one of us had Grit. Or possibly even Dust.*

They rounded the final switchback at the top of the plateau and began riding east along its edge. On smooth ground, they were able to increase their pace.

By noon, Katie had developed a fever and had become unresponsive altogether. Her screaming ceased, which was a relief to their ears, but worrisome to their hearts.

The edge of the plateau never left their side.

It was a ride Luke had made many times before, almost always shadowed with guilt. Now, he rode it for the first time with a pure and good purpose in his heart. He looked out over the valley below and smiled.

They rode into Bluff's Reach as the sun began to set in the west. Cassidy hung back and made camp outside of town. They knew she would be welcomed with gun smoke if she tried to show her face, so she instead waited for Luke to return. Later, she could enter the town with the cover of night.

Luke pulled Katie to the town doctor, Ron Barker. He must have seen them from his window, because he was waiting at his door when they arrived.

"Luke Morgan, you found her? Bring her in, quick," Ron said.

Luke stopped and hoisted Katie from the cart. She had grown skinny from lack of food and water. He managed to carry her with ease, although he was careful not to injure her. He brought her inside and gently laid her down on one of the medical cots.

"She's had a lot of morphine," Luke said. "And little water. She's dehydrated for sure."

Ron dunked his hands in a bucket of lukewarm sudswater. A band of froth clung like a hoop skirt around the skunk tattoo on his forearm. Rumor was that he had gotten the tattoo during the war, where both Ron and the skunk had seen more bloodshed than Luke or Katie ever would.

Luke continued. "Her leg is broke bad, obviously. Also, she said she ate a scorpion."

"You know, scorpions are a delicacy in some places," Ron said with a light smile. He put a clean hand on Katie's forehead. "She's running hot. I don't see any signs of infection, so she should come out of her fever with some water and food. I'll put some iodine on her leg anyway."

"Can I do anything to help?" Luke asked.

"No. You've done well getting her here, and I can care for her now. She isn't too bad, and should recover well enough. She'll have a limp for life, but she gets to keep her leg, thanks to you."

"Thank you, Doctor."

"Todd would want to know that she's alright, Lucas."

"Right, I'd better go then," Luke said. "Bye, Katie."

Luke left the doctor's office and walked down Main Street toward the general store.

26

I t was another calm, bright night when Casey Calhoun and his
gang rode into the Carlotta mine pits. Above, the waxing moon
shone strong, letting the men see their path easily. Casey led the way,
and Buck followed annoyingly close. Another three dozen men trailed
further behind, steering a caravan of wagons large enough to collect
just over one hundred crates of dynamite. On their left, a tiered pit
carved its way fifty feet into the earth. On their right, the filtered dirt
was cast off into a man-made hillside.

They soon stopped at an intersection, where several access roads
diverged. Each road was marked with a small but legible sign, desig-
nating each road's number.

"Which way?" Casey asked.

Buck consulted the maps. "Three was under washout conditions as
of a couple weeks ago."

"I doubt they would have repaired it in that time," Casey said.
"What's the alternative?"

"Says..." Buck hummed as he read the ledgers. "Take Two until
pit G, and use the temporary crossroad back to Three up past the
washout."

"Fine."

They took the road marked *Two*.

So far, the gang had not come across anyone else. It was late, and most of the mine workers would be fast asleep in their lodges. Neither had they seen any patrols. What mine would ever need patrols, anyway?

Buck kept his nose to the papers, guiding the caravan around the pits and hills. They took the crossroad onto Three, and continued toward the deep pit which contained the store of explosives.

Not far past Pit J, the roads became flat and straight as the gang entered a major equipment yard. Rail tracks crisscrossed there, with small cars waiting to be filled with dirt. A row of buildings sat on the far side of the yard, where workers lived out their terms. Casey made sure his caravan did not get too close to the buildings, so as to not be seen. Though the moon helped light their way, it also made them easier to spot. Casey *could have* kicked up a sandstorm to conceal their passage, but he worried that would have gotten them incredibly lost. Especially with Buck guiding their way.

They looped wide around the equipment yard and pulled further away from the worker's quarters. By that time, they had ventured deep into the mine pit complex. It would be quite the trip back out the south entrance once they had their load. Fortunately, Casey had seen a north entrance in the maps. They could easily ride out that way and be gone long before sun up. From there, the river back to the gulch was not far.

"I'm amazed by the scale of this place," Casey told Buck at one point.

"Yes, sir. It's enormous," the boy said.

Though Casey was hard set on the task at hand, he couldn't help but let his mind wander. The Carlotta mines were impressive, and Casey was a hard man to impress. It was not the technology here, nor the science of extracting minerals from the ground, which impressed him. It was the scale that was most admirable. It was how well these men exerted their will over the earth. Jerome Carlotta had taken from nature with no qualms. He made this section of the world *his*. It was a bitter shame, then, that he had to die. Poor man. Cassidy would be punished for that.

Casey let his mind drift further, back to when he was a boy, just learning about his place in the world. He remembered his father, and how the man had taught Casey some of the most important lessons a boy could ever learn. He was only nine, maybe ten...

Thirty Years Ago

Casey flicked a shiny blue marble across the floor of his room. It clattered into a pile of other, smaller marbles, sending a little yellow one bouncing across the hardwood and out into the hallway. *Tack, tack, tack*, it sounded, bouncing down the stairs before coming to rest in front of his father's study.

He had seen the marble set in a toy catalog. There had been kites and nine-pins and toy soldiers, but he had been drawn to the shiny little spheres most of all. He didn't dare beg his father for money, so he had worked and saved on his own. A local farmer paid him to pick rocks from his field, at a nickel for every wheelbarrow full. After a month, he had saved five dollars, enough for the marble set and sending fee.

He knelt slowly and quietly, picked up the yellow marble, and tucked it into his pocket. He took a step toward his room again, and stopped when his father called out to him.

"Boy," his father said from his study. "Come in here."

Casey went in. His father stood, tidied his desk slightly, and gestured to come close. Casey stood opposite him near the desk, holding his hands stiff and awkward at his sides. He pulled his shoulders high, knowing poor posture was likely to get him slapped.

"What is that in your pocket?" his father asked. "Show it to me." His face was stern.

Casey showed his father the marble. "Father, sir, I was playing and it got away."

"Did you steal that, boy?"

"I bought it with my money from working at—"

His father interrupted with a mean-spirited laugh. "Stupidity. Waste of money. If you are old enough for work, you are too old for playthings. Give that to me."

Casey opened his palm, letting the cool ceramic ball roll out of his hand and into his father's. His father studied it, curious, like he had never seen such a thing in his life. Then he tipped his hand and dropped it into a metal wastebasket next to his desk. The marble clinked as it bounced inside the metal, then was still.

"How old are you, boy?" Casey's father asked.

"I'm ten this summer, sir."

"Then you are a man by fall," his father said. He walked to his bookshelf and ran his thumb across the spines. Casey recognized a few of the words on the books, like *the* and *land*, but most were too big for him to sound out. "Do you know what makes a man?" his father asked.

"Well, Tommy told me girls don't have a willie between their legs," Casey said. He thought Tommy was just pulling his leg. What else would they have? But Casey had never seen a girl's willy, or lack thereof, so who was he to say?

"Wrong." His father sneered. "Tommy is a stupid child and so are his parents. Being a man has nothing to do with his prick."

"Then what, sir?"

"Being a man is about how you act. Men are beings of power, of strength. We take what we want, because the world is ours. We run the world, not with our pricks, but with our minds and our words and our fists. Some people, Tommy's father perhaps, would like to think men and woman are equal. Those are the words of a sodomite."

Casey's father grabbed a book and removed it from the shelf. It was a thick book, one with no recognizable words, not even a *the* on the cover. His father flipped through the pages and opened the book to the middle. He laid it open on his desk and pointed to it. "There are some very smart men that I respect highly. They study the way the world works and they teach our purpose on earth. Philosophy, it is called. This book is *natural philosophy*: how we men fit in the natural world.

"The man who wrote this book believes that God created nature for men, gave us dominion over the creatures and resources of the world. He says that our role, as men, is to extend our power over the natural world as far as possible. I'm not so inclined to believe it was God's doing, but I understand the sentiment.

"The opposite belief also exists. They think men are a fraction of nature, instead of superior to. They would want us to live in harmony with nature, to work with it, to be fair. Your mother thinks this way, boy, but that philosophy has yet to keep her face from the back of my hand, isn't that right?"

"Yes, sir." Casey said. He knew the back of his father's hand well enough to know that was the truth.

"I'm telling you this because you need to learn what makes you a man. You need to know what makes you strong so that you can succeed over all others. A true man gets what he wants. He does not waver from his goals. When you put your mind to a thing, you must achieve it, or you may as well call yourself a woman."

Casey understood few of the words his father had spoken. He didn't know what *fi-lah-suh-fee* was, but he knew *take*, *want*, and *strength*. The message was clear enough. He feigned a smile and said, "Thank you, Father. You are a good teacher."

His father smiled back. He picked up the philosophy book, folded it closed, then swung and brought it hard across Casey's face. "Stand up straight, boy!" He shouted, his eyes sharp and crazed.

Casey straightened, pulling his shoulders back and turning his chin up. He ran his hand through his hair, combing it back into place. "Sorry, sir. Thank you for reminding me."

"You are welcome," his father said as he sat down at his desk again. "Now go and clean your room."

"Yes, sir." Casey turned and walked out, keeping his chin high. Tears swelled up his throat, but he held them back—like a *man*.

Casey's father yelled from the study. "And throw out the rest of those marbles."

No. The marbles are mine, Casey thought. *The* world *is mine.*

He felt the strength his father had spoken of. On the floor before him, the dust shimmered, probably from the tears in his eyes. He drew them back in, did not let them fall, and the dust settled again.

The world is mine, along with every speck of sand and every mote of dust. It is all mine.

***

Casey's crew came upon the storage pit late in the night, the moon peaking in the sky. Waiting for them was a hundred thousand pounds of dynamite.

And several dozen men, armed, in ranks. At their lead, a state marshal sat atop his horse with his arms crossed. Casey and his gang had not gotten off as easily as they had thought.

"We had our suspicions!" The marshal shouted from the edge of the pit. "We'd heard from Bluff's Reach, and it sounds like there was quite a commotion up there recently. Figured we'd come through, though something told us to stop here first. What would someone be planning, causing such trouble in a town like Bluff's Reach? What's so important to kill the owner of a random pit mine?" The marshal gestured behind himself at the stacks of explosives. "That, for one."

Casey looked up and down the ranks. Here were state police, soldiers, mine workers. There was no use in lying. "You've made a mistake," he said.

"A mistake? You're *here*, aren't you?"

"The mistake is that *you are*, too."

The marshal strode forward, getting a closer look at the men he had apprehended. "Ah. Casey Calhoun. A shame to see *you*, though I'm not surprised you're one to get your hands dirty."

"Quite dirty, indeed," Casey said, chuckling to himself at the implication.

He had hoped to avoid this sort of confrontation. Though taking care of the marshal and his men would be easy, hauling the load with less of his own men would not be. He needed to be careful. Back-and-forth gunfire would be the worst outcome.

Casey stepped off his horse.

The marshal and his men raised their weapons. A chorus of clicks sounded as they pulled back their triggers.

Casey's gang did the same.

"Whoa!" Casey raised his hands. "I want no shooting. May I remove my pistol?"

"Put it on the ground." The marshal tilted his own in a dropping motion.

Such a shame, Casey thought. *To set aside such a fine piece of iron...* While he loved the warm intimacy of ending life with lead, this was not the time.

"I'll say..." Casey grunted, bending to the ground. "I was hoping to get away with this undetected." He set his pistol in the dirt, then put his palm flat on the ground. "Now, I'm going to have such a mess on my hands."

Casey pushed into the ground with his strength. An invisible wave of energy spread from his palm, through the dirt, out into a wide radius.

"I—" the marshal started, but cut off as the earth tremored beneath him.

The ground quaked, and all the men before Casey wobbled uneasily. Several went to their knees for balance, where the sand sprang up and snared them in place.

The marshal struggled to lift his feet from the ground. The earth had folded over the man's boots, sucking down harder than he could pull away. "What is this?" He shouted.

"Your mistake," Casey said, his voice pleasantly straightforward. He held no hatred for the marshal. The man was only doing his job. Yet, unfortunately for him, he had gotten in the way.

Casey took a heaped handful of dirt and stood again. Power surged through him, exhilarating and arousing. He held his palm out and blew at the dirt. From this, a cloud tumbled onto the opposing men, covering them in dirt and filth. It stuck to them like tar, creeping over their chests, their arms, covering their hands and guns. The men panicked, taking aim at Casey and firing all at once. Only, their pistols did not fire. Instead, Casey heard dozens of dull clicks—triggers being pulled, hammers falling into jammed chambers. He had clogged all their weapons. The men, stuck in their stance, furiously swiped at the dirt, as if they had been attacked by a swarm of bees.

Slowly, Casey picked his own pistol back up from the ground. He thought of using it. He desperately wanted to. But this was not a time for sportsmanship. He need not intimidate these men. No, they would die simply, efficiently. Though a little flair *would* be fun.

Casey holstered his pistol, then bent once again to the ground. He pushed both hands in the dirt, digging them as deep as possible. He thought of the men, their lives, their place in the world, and imagined all that in his hands. He had more than just their lives in his grasp. Like a web, shattering its way through broken glass, their deaths would spread throughout the world, changing the course of history. Casey was an agent of change. He was a prime mover. In his mind, he was God.

Howling, Casey pushed with all his might. All that strength channeled through the earth.

The dirt around Casey's opponents erupted, sending several hardened spikes of rock and sand up through each man's body, piercing them from every direction. It all happened in an instant, followed by a horrible crunching, cracking sound.

Buck gasped from Casey's side. "Oh my..."

Casey strode forward to where the marshal's body stood, suspended over several earthen spikes. Blood drained from each puncture and saturated the ground. The mine pit grew dark, as if being shadowed from the moonlight.

Casey heard his men whispering. Someone vomited into the sand.

Buck came to Casey's side, his breath shaky. "Sir, that was... impressive."

"Yes," Casey said. He realized he was flexing his forearms and hands in a tight grip. He relaxed. His shoulders slumped. Exhaustion filled every muscle.

The sand spikes fell apart, and with them fell the dozens of corpses.

"Leave them," Casey said. "We keep going."

"Of course." Busk hesitated. "But, uh, sir—"

"You'd better not be going sissy on me." Casey growled.

"No, no! I'm not. I just—"

"I said keep moving!" Casey shouted. He felt dizzy, slightly faint, though he did not show it.

Buck looked Casey up and down, then made the smart decision. "Yes, sir." He took off to guide the caravan.

After this was all over, Casey was going to have to teach that boy a lesson in following orders. He was growing too sure of himself, too wise. He was starting to question Casey's methods. That would not be allowed.

Later, Casey thought. For now, the dynamite was the primary concern.

Casey returned to his horse and caught back up to Buck at the front of the caravan.

27

Kootala was having dinner with Missy: beef steaks, boiled carrots, and fresh rolls. They sat at her dinner table, which was covered with a light checkered tablecloth. Kootala pulled open a dinner roll and spread a slab of butter over its steaming surface. Missy sipped on a glass of thick red wine. It was a fine dinner, yet Kootala sat slumped in his chair, pouting.

"I think it's time you spend the night in your own home," Missy said. "I've got business to conduct, and as much as I enjoy your company, I need my house to myself."

"Alright, I'm sorry," Kootala said. "It's just hard to be home without... him."

"I know. I can't say I know how you feel, but I can understand anyway. You know I will always help you in any way you need. During the day, of course." Missy gave Kootala a playful punch on the arm.

"Whose business are you enjoying this evening, if I might ask?" Kootala teased.

"Don't you know it's impolite to kiss and tell?" she said with fake offense. She whispered, "Mr. Deetman has been awfully sore from rebuilding that barn, and Vanessa doesn't have the touch to relieve his tension."

"Oh, Missy!" Kootala exclaimed. "I aught to arrest you both!"

"You wouldn't dare lay a hand on me, Sheriff. I bite."

They both burst into laughter.

When they caught their breath, Missy spoke again. "And what about your business, Kootala? Anyone round here catch your eye? I heard rumors that the Barlow boy hasn't ever gone with a lady. He's close to your age, and almost as handsome."

Kootala turned his face down. "I don't want to think about those things right now. It's only been a few days, and I don't really know what to make of it all yet."

"Oh, come on now." Missy puffed. "Every time we talk about something serious, you get all sad and shut me out."

"Well, you can be rather insensitive." Kootala pouted. He rested his cheek on one hand and rolled a carrot around his plate with the other.

"Excuse me for trying to keep it light," Missy said as she chewed a chunk of steak.

"There's nothing light about my situation."

"I guess you're right, I'm sorry. But know that I'll be happy to talk about those things when you're ready, if ever," Missy said.

"During the day, right?" Kootala said with a light smile.

"That's right." Missy smiled back, pointing her fork at Kootala.

They finished their dinner, and Kootala helped Missy clean up after.

Kootala gave Missy a big, tight hug, then he left into the night.

Outside was dark and the air felt colder than usual, like an energy had been sapped out of the world. Faint light from oil lamps behind windows cast gangling shadows across the ground; black phantoms dancing in the night.

Kootala walked slowly through town, making the time stretch out as long as possible. It was a grim night, but he would rather be out with the phantoms than in his empty home. In fact, it wasn't much of a home anymore. A home isn't the bricks and mud and wood it's made with. That's just a house. Without cattle, a pasture is just a field. Kootala didn't want to return to just a house.

He walked down Main Street alone in the dark. The businesses were closed, shades drawn, and empty like his heart. A lone rectangle of light shone across the street, coming from the saloon. There was a light bustle of voices and music coming from inside, where LeAnn Cheek played the piano and people danced and sang along. Outside, the tune was hollow and flat like the shadows.

The gravel crunched in the darkness up Jointer Street. Kootala looked up and saw two figures standing in the dark. He couldn't make out their details, but he didn't have to.

"I told you not to return here," Kootala said to them.

"You know I'm not a good listener," Luke replied.

"What do you want? If you've come to make amends, you've wasted your time. And what is *she* doing here? I should shoot her where she stands."

"No shooting, no violence," Cassidy said. "Not here, anyway."

Kootala faked a laugh. "That's rich, coming from you."

"We found Katie Lybuck," Luke said. "She is with Doctor Barker and her father."

Kootala started. "Is she safe? Will she survive? If that is why you are here, then you have done your duty and can leave."

Luke responded. "Katie will be fine, but that's not why we're here. This town is in danger, Kootala. You are in danger. We need your help."

Kootala shouted suddenly. "And who put us in danger? People died at your hands! You two *are* the danger." Kootala spoke quietly again. "Get the hell out of my town."

"Wait, just listen," Luke said. "Our boss, Casey Calhoun, means to destroy this town and kill the people in it. We're going to stop him, but we need your help."

"And then I'm supposed to forgive you, is that it? You'll be the big hero, and that will make up for everything you've done?"

"No, Kootala. I'm not looking for forgiveness. Cassidy certainly isn't."

"You're the sheriff of this town," Cassidy said. "Are you going to protect it?"

Kootala was silent for a moment before responding. "How serious is it?" he asked.

Cassidy took a step forward. "If Casey gets his way, Bluff's Reach won't exist by this time tomorrow."

"Why would you two care? What changed? What is your purpose in this, if not for redemption?"

"The reasons hardly matter now," Cassidy said. "We can worry about our purposes later."

"What would we do?"

"Round up anyone who can help," Luke said. "Have them meet at our house in an hour. We can explain the situation to everyone and come up with a plan."

"There are many in this town that would see you both hang," Kootala said.

"And they will seek justice, but only after we save this town," Cassidy said.

"Alright then. One hour."

They split up. Cassidy followed Luke to his house, and Kootala went to gather help.

***

Kootala went to the saloon first, and gathered anyone who was sober. That was only LeAnn Cheek and Bill Williams. He also interrupted Missy, recruiting her and Mark Deetman. The five of them went out and gathered more. They interrupted dinners, sex, and good sleep. An hour later, just over twenty people were crowded around Luke and Kootala's front yard. Kootala stepped out onto his porch and greeted the small crowd.

"Evening, everyone. I'm glad you were able to join us on such short notice. I'm sure you have all been given a brief explanation. I expect you to keep the peace and hold your questions until we are done."

Someone interrupted immediately. "Where's Cassidy?"

"She's not here. We thought it best if she was not involved in this meeting." Kootala lied, and Cassidy watched from the darkness. "However, that does not mean she is absent from our plans. If that remains a problem for anyone after this meeting, we can discuss it then. For now, please hold your voices and keep an open mind."

Luke stepped out onto the porch, joining Kootala. "Casey Calhoun is currently enacting a plan to destroy this town and the people who live here. Many of you may know his name, some may even know him well, and you'd likely know how he operates. You folks will not let him harm the people of this town."

Kootala took over again. "Missy will lead an evacuation of the town, and the rest of you will assist her. Go and notify everyone. Have them pack only the essential items tonight. Gather your assets, your family items, and whatever else you deem most necessary. In the morning, leave the town and set up a temporary camp several miles to the west. We have some time, but not much. Try to keep calm and orderly, be straightforward with everyone and avoid causing a panic. Order and cooperation are imperative."

Again, Luke spoke. "Kootala will help you all tonight. In the morning, we will ride off to apprehend Casey and put an end to his plans."

Kootala continued. "Casey has a secret base of operations west of Lonely. He will be passing through Lonely around noon tomorrow. We will cut him off and, if necessary—"

Luke finished Kootala's sentence. "End his life."

"Right." Kootala agreed, though he was suddenly uncertain if he *could* do it. "We cannot let Casey reach Graben. We will need someone to set up on the edge of the bluff and watch the route into Graben. You should easily see his caravan from up here. If you see him, assume we have failed and do not return to Bluff's Reach. Should we succeed, we will return within a day or two. Any questions?"

A man from the back spoke up. "How can we trust Cassidy? And Luke, too. They've stolen and murdered in this town. You'd just as soon have us hand deliver all our valuables to them in the desert."

Luke responded. "Casey Calhoun wants nothing more in life than total and absolute power. No matter how much value you have in this town and in your pockets, it is nothing compared to what he will have if he succeeds. Cassidy and I are criminals, that is true. She has even taken lives in this town. I will not try to justify our crimes, but we have had our reasons, neither of which were for greed. Neither are we ruthless and without some sense of morality, however twisted that might be. But Casey has neither mercy nor morality. He is a man who takes what he wants without question. He is a man who bends the world to his whim, a god in his own mind. You may not like us or trust us, but you must trust that Casey needs to be stopped. If not now, then never."

Another person shouted, "If not for money or praise, then what reason do you have in this fight?"

Kootala thought about it, and saw Luke doing the same. They had no reason to hide their honesty.

Kootala answered first. "Peace."

"Love," Luke said next.

"Vengeance," Cassidy growled from the shadows, just loud enough for Kootala to hear.

The crowd murmured.

Kootala spoke again. "Does anyone object?"

They whispered among themselves, then Missy answered. "We're with you all the way."

"Then it is settled," Kootala announced with a passion. "Nobody will ever bring down the town of Bluff's Reach! Tonight we prepare; tomorrow we stand tall against evil! Tomorrow, we live on as stewards of good and righteousness!"

The crowd muttered in agreement. They did not cheer, as they were certainly unsure of this plan. Yet they would go with it. Better safe than sorry. They dispersed into the town to inform the others and prepare for evacuation. Kootala, Luke, and Cassidy remained.

"Thank you, Kootala," Luke said.

"This is just a job, no more," Kootala said. "Cassidy, you may shelter in my house tonight, but that is all. The day after tomorrow, you will be an outlaw again. You will be treated accordingly, should you remain in this county."

"That is fair," she said.

"And Lucas, you are a criminal, but you have not committed violence on the people of this town; those actions belong to Cassidy alone. Should you decide to remain here, no harm will come to you. Your punishment will be a debt to the people, equal to what you have stolen. These are my terms. Do we have an understanding?"

Luke and Cassidy both agreed.

"Fine. You two make our preparations for tomorrow. I will go out and help around town," Kootala said, then left into the night.

Once Luke and Cassidy were alone, Cassidy spoke again. "When it comes to it, I'll be the one to kill Casey Calhoun."

28

Bluff's Reach was alive with energy. Townsfolk loaded their last important belongings into carts and onto horses. The children rubbed the night from their tired eyes. Soon, the sun would emerge from the horizon and bring with it the chaos of the day. Most families would leave town as soon as light hit the ground. Others would stay longer with lingering doubts, but would eventually leave just in case. Nobody knew how the day would play out, but they felt it would be known before the afternoon came to a close.

Missy acted as the de facto commander of the evacuation. She made several rounds through town, checking people's progress and helping where she could. She kept things moving and reignited urgency when others began to slow. Being a leader proved to be a fitting and easy job for Missy. She had come to know the townsfolk intimately over the years, and knew exactly how to manage them now. With her hand, the evacuation was going well.

Katie's fever had broken in the night, and she awoke with the commotion that morning. She was panicked at first, and severely confused. The last few days had been a fog. But her father was by her side, and she knew she would be alright. Doctor Barker had splinted her leg, and the pain was bearable.

Luke, Kootala, and Cassidy mounted their horses and rode out across the plateau. They planned to be a quarter of the way to Lonely as the sun came up. They all carried iron, although they each had different apprehensions about their uses. Kootala feared he might have to use his. Cassidy feared she might not get the opportunity.

They rode hard and fast, stopping as little as possible; twice to pee, twice to water the horses and let the blood dry in their nostrils. Cassidy's stallion was happy to be worked hard again. Luke had returned Kootala's brown and retrieved his own spotted appaloosa. Sam Clangour's persona and horse were left dead in the desert, the buzzards picking at its bones.

They reached the end of the plateau at eight in the morning, then began their descent along the meandering switchbacks down into the valley. Riding slowed to a canter, as they were constantly turning and avoiding rocks and rills along the road. At their current gait, they would make Lonely around noon. Coming from the high road, they would be able to see Casey's caravan below. Importantly, they would know if they were too late to stop him.

By ten, they could see Lonely in the distance and the faint glimmer of Graben to the southeast. Between the towns, the land was still and quiet. Casey had not yet gone through Lonely.

On the southern horizon, a long train billowed a thin stream of black smoke into the air. It was bringing passengers or cargo into Graben, they thought. An engineer in Bluff's Reach saw the smoke too, and knew differently. The smoke was dark black, the result of inefficient burning, the engine being pushed to its limit. The train was racing toward Graben at an alarming pace.

They continued, and approached Lonely just before noon. They had seen no signs of activity from the west, and began to worry that Casey might not be coming at all. Or that he had already been through. Now, as they rode into the pissant little outpost, they began to feel the tines of deception and the dread of failure. It was dead quiet. The air was still, and they could hear their heartbeat in their ears. Gravel crunched under their horses' hooves.

A crack of gunfire broke the quiet, still air. A bullet whizzed off to the side of Luke's head.

"It's an ambush!" Cassidy yelled.

Four men appeared from behind an outcropping to the northwest, with Buck in the lead. Two more bullets fired, one spraying soil in front of Cassidy's horse.

Luke, Kootala, and Cassidy broke into a gallop and rode into Lonely. The ambushers were distant enough, and didn't have a good shot. They were smart, and held their fire.

With Cassidy in the lead, the three rode to the Lonely hotel and hid around its southern side. They were out of sight for the minute.

"What do we do?" Kootala asked.

"You won't shoot?" Luke asked back.

"I... I can't."

"Fine," Cassidy said, "Then you ride out and draw them along. Luke and I will ride around the back of the hotel and come out behind them when they pass. You need to ride fast, Kootala. These men will kill you without mercy."

"Ride to the stable and hide inside. Stand your ground, Kootala. Please," Luke said.

Kootala gave them an unsure look, then dashed out into the road. He turned south and headed for the stable.

The ambush rode into Lonely. They followed Kootala with the one-minded stupidity of adrenaline. They rode past the hotel with nothing on their mind but the death of the Indian man in front of them. Luke and Cassidy rode out from behind.

"Shoot the horses," Cassidy said.

They fired. A shot hit one of the men in the back and he toppled to the ground, dead. Two horses were hit and went down, their riders going down with them. One of the men shouted as his horse came down on his lower half. The other man rolled into the dirt, then sprung up onto his feet. He turned and aimed his gun, but Cassidy put a bullet through his chest before he could fire his own.

A single rider—Buck—rode on after Kootala.

Another bullet ripped through the air and sailed through Cassidy's shoulder, knocking her off her horse, too. The man with his legs under his horse aimed again. Luke finished him off with a shot to the throat. He clutched his neck and blood cascaded through his fingers like crimson nectar. Luke ran to Cassidy.

"No, go to Kootala!" She yelled. "Buck will kill him!"

Luke turned and raced toward the stable. His temples pounded with anger and his heart shuttered with fear.

***

Kootala was in the stable, hiding behind a pile of hay. He had drawn his gun, though it rattled in his unsteady hand.

Stacks of hay and straw bales lined the walls, almost to the ceiling. Most of the windows had been covered, so the only light came in through the open barn door. An illuminated rectangle lit the gravel and loose straw on the floor.

A horse stopped at the stable entrance, and a pair of boots stomped to the ground as the rider dismounted. The man spoke softly into the stable, his voice artificial, hiding a lightness underneath. "I ain't never heard of a queer sheriff," he said. His shadow crept across the dusty floor toward Kootala. He walked into view, facing the opposite side of the barn.

Kootala stood hidden in the shadows with his gun aimed at the man. His hands trembled. The man was young, too young to be caught up in this sort of business. Young and dumb and misguided, Kootala thought, but ambitious and dangerous too.

The young man spoke again. "I'd put this bullet right up your ass, but you'd like that, wouldn't you?" He laughed, like a schoolhouse bully.

Kootala's hand tightened with anger, but he could not pull the trigger. His gun trembled.

Use your Dust! Kootala shouted in his head. *Make an illusion, influence the man, cause a distraction. Something!*

The young man sensed him. He turned to the shadows and aimed at Kootala. "I can see the light reflecting off your iron," he said, smiling wickedly.

A gunshot echoed through the stable.

Kootala jumped, thinking he was dead. But he was not. He looked at his own hands, thinking he must have pulled the trigger, but his gun remained cold.

The man screamed and clenched his right wrist, now a mangled and bloody stump. His gun was on the ground, laying in the dirt next to a mass of tangled fingers and flesh. Kootala kicked the man's gun into the hay.

Luke's silhouette stood in the open barn door. He aimed at the man again.

"Luke, no!" Kootala yelled and stepped between them.

"Kootala, move. He would kill you without hesitation."

"And you would do the same? He is not a threat anymore."

"He is a murderer!"

"You would be a murderer, too. The others, that was self-defense. This man is unarmed."

"Literally," Cassidy said. She walked in with her hand clutching her bleeding shoulder. "You should have stayed home, Buck." She told the man.

"They're right," Buck cried to Kootala, still clutching his wrist stump. "You'd be wise to end me."

"No," Kootala said. "That is not how this works. And Luke, you aren't the law around here, I am. Holster your weapons and help this man tend his wound."

"But, Kootala—"

"Do it!" Kootala demanded. He felt an anger fill his eyes, beaming out as it had never before, not even when Kootala had discovered Luke's secret. It was new, and scary, and compelling.

Luke saw this change in Kootala, and did as he was told.

They cut Buck's shirt off, then wrapped it around his wrist. Kootala led him down the road.

Howard came out from the hotel, shouting and waving his hands in the air. "What the hell was that all about! You've all made quite a mess of my place here, and I have half the mind to—"

"Shut your mouth," Cassidy yelled back. "Don't act so surprised, Howard. You're lucky I don't shoot you in the head, too."

Howard's face turned down. "Cass, you know how it is." He began to shake with fear. "What are you going to do with me?" he asked.

"Nothing," Kootala answered. "Not yet anyway. You are going to tend to this man. Keep him well. And Cassidy, too."

"I'm fine," Cassidy said. "It hurts like hell, but I'll live."

"Fine, but at least get it cleaned up. We still need your help," Kootala said. He turned back to Buck and Howard. "You two are going to stay here. I will deal with you both lawfully in the coming days. You will keep your lives, however pitiful they may be. Luke will let loose your horses, and I wouldn't suggest you try to escape on foot. In the meantime, as payment for your lives, you tell us where Casey Calhoun is."

Kootala nodded to Luke, who left to the stable once again. Howard and Kootala cleaned and wrapped Buck's wrist and Cassidy's shoulder, and Kootala used some simple Dust to help dull the pain. Buck took a shot of morphine, anyway. Cassidy refused.

"Now speak," Kootala said. "Tell us where he is."

"Fuck you," Buck spat.

"I'll remind you that your life is in my hands. Be smart and cooperate."

"Alright." Buck began. "Casey called it off. He went east to play patty-cake with the yuppies."

Kootala grew dangerously angry. "Keep him here," he said to Cassidy, then strode outside. He came back a moment later with a handful of sand.

What would he do with that? Kootala's hand trembled. What could his Dust do to make Buck talk? Tickle him into submission? This was silly.

Buck's eyes grew wide. "What are you doing with that?" he asked.

Kootala looked down at his hand, and felt suddenly that he had nothing more than a useless pile of sand. Yet Buck was scared. *Interesting*, Kootala thought.

"Squeal." Cassidy commanded.

Buck's nervous face vanished, and then he smiled. "You thought I would fall for that?"

Anger came back to Kootala, boiling in his chest. For a brief moment, he felt that urge that he had avoided for so long. He wanted to desperately hurt Buck. Then, as soon as it had come, Kootala pushed the feeling away. Sure, Buck was a bad person, probably deserved whatever came to him, but it would not be Kootala who did *that*. If anything, Kootala pitied the boy. He followed a false idol. He was merely a shadow of Casey Calhoun.

Kootala focused on the sand, imagining what it could become, what it might take to make Buck talk. Could he compel the man, same as he soothed pain or emotions? Perhaps, if Kootala shifted his perspective. If he imagined Buck's reluctance as an injury of sorts, could he heal that, could he *fix* that break?

Dammit, Kootala cursed under his breath. What had that figure been trying to tell him during his hallucination? There was some-thing... else.

Buck was speaking again, goading Kootala, teasing.

Kootala ignored him.

From where do you draw your powers? Kongwuti's words.

Strength?

Wrong. Your strength, be it Grit or Dust, comes from your belief in yourself. Your power to alter the world is not a factor of values, nor of skill.

"Then what?" Kootala shouted aloud.

Cassidy and Buck looked at him like he was crazy.

"It's a tool," Kootala said. "What makes a tool?"

He shifted his perspective, desperately, imagining the Dust to be a tool. In Kootala's hand, the dirt coalesced into a hammer. A solid, physical hammer.

Buck screamed. "No! Please, no! I'll talk!"

Kootala startled, and the hammer dissolved away, scattering to the floor. Had he just...

No time to think on it.

"Speak," Kootala said.

Buck conceded, crying. "Casey lied to you, Cassidy. He didn't trust you to kill Luke and Kootala, so he lied about the caravan. He would've told you the truth, had you returned to Devil's Gulch in time. When he heard what you did to his quarters, he knew you had defected."

"Get to the important stuff." Cassidy demanded.

"Fine. He never received the dynamite in Devil's Gulch. Instead, he dropped *us* off, then *he* continued down the river and unloaded in Marble Springs. They loaded it up on a train that was scheduled to run to Graben today. Casey rode ahead and switched the track to an old one that runs into the mouth of the mine under the bluff. That train is on its way right now. Casey is down in Graben, waiting and watching the bluff."

Cassidy grabbed Buck's collar with her good arm and shook him furiously. "Where does that old track run?"

"It cuts around Graben to the north!" Buck sobbed. "You cross the track on the road into town. That little bridge a mile out of town doesn't go over an old riverbed. *That's* the old track."

"Dammit!" She yelled and shoved him free. "Kootala, we need to leave, now!"

"Alright, let's go get Luke," Kootala said.

They went out and helped Luke with the horses. They removed the saddles and bags from Buck's, Howard's, and the other men's horses, threw them to the dirt, and smacked the horses on the rump. The creatures took off running into the desert. Then Kootala, Luke, and Cassidy mounted their own and ran out toward Graben.

29

The column of smoke in the distance had grown, and Kootala could now see the thin line of a train pushing silently through the valley. It was much farther from Graben than they were, but it cut across the land at many times their speed.

They cantered down through the switchbacks as quickly as possible, jumping over the edges where the road was wide and shallow. The further they descended into the valley, the more gradual its slope became; they eventually increased to a full gallop.

Kootala wondered if everyone had made it out of Bluff's Reach. He hoped they had, and he hoped they had gone far enough away. Failure was materializing. The likelihood that the bluff would exist tomorrow was slipping away.

The sun had passed its peak in the afternoon sky, and its heat baked down with hatred.

As the trio approached Graben, the valley became the wide, flat escarpments that so resembled a giant staircase. Graben sat comfortably at the bottom along the river. From the southeast, the train grew larger as they all converged.

"There's the bridge." Cassidy pointed to it in the distance.

The bridge was small, only wide enough for a single wagon passing in either direction, but they were close enough to see it clearly.

A dull rumble had grown around them as the train got closer. It barreled toward the bridge, throwing a wave of fresh dirt and sand into the air as it uncovered ancient tracks.

"We won't catch the train from the road." Luke said.

"Turn east and follow the high ground." Cassidy pointed to one of the escarpments. "The train is going to have to follow the flats along the river. You should be able to cut it off as it follows the river to the north. I'll ride to Graben and find Casey."

"You can't do anything with that shoulder," Luke said. "He will kill you."

"Don't worry about me. You two focus on stopping that train!"

"Fine. Good luck, Cass," Luke said.

Cassidy smiled at them. "However this goes, I won't see you boys after. Be well. Be happy."

"Cassidy." Kootala gave her a stern look. "Good luck."

"And you. I'll be watching from Graben. For whatever happens." Cassidy tipped her hat.

They split; Cassidy continuing south toward Graben, Luke and Kootala turning east along the escarpments.

In the distance, the train plowed through the bridge and sent wood flying into the air. It continued fast, turning southeast as it detoured around Graben and headed for the Colorado River. Luke and Kootala raced across the ridges to the northeast, where the river drained from the mouth of Lake Powell.

***

Cassidy rode into Graben from the west. The smoke of the train crawled across the land to the left, and loomed over rooftops as she passed through the city's streets. She did not know for sure where to find Casey, but she had a pretty good idea. He would be watching the bluff, his lips pulled back in a snarl, his teeth dripping saliva, ready to gobble up the entire county. Cassidy supposed he could be watching from the north docks, where he would have the best view upriver. If all went Casey's way, he could fish Bluff's Reach right out of the river as it floated by.

Keeping calm as to not draw unwanted attention, Cassidy trotted slowly into town. She was in no hurry now. Luke and Kootala would either succeed or fail, and she had no part in that any longer. Her part in this was not a timely matter. Casey could die slowly, for all she cared.

He would be waiting for her, Cassidy figured. She was the deadliest woman in Arizona, and Casey would know those assholes in Lonely would only slow her down. They had merely been a distraction. Perhaps he wanted her to watch the destruction before he killed her. Either way, he would be prepared to end her on the docks of his new city. And, Cassidy knew, he would want to do it with his gun.

His mistake.

As Cassidy rode through Graben, she realized her worries of drawing attention had been unfounded. People had noticed the train smoke, and had likely congregated on the northwest side of the city to watch the horizon with curiosity. She rode through the main avenues without worry. If anyone had recognized her face—the few people left about their regular business—they didn't seem to care.

Cassidy stopped at the harbor and tied her horse to one of the posts, then walked along the boardwalk to the north. As she had expected, Casey was there, waiting.

The two were alone on the docks, save for the moored barges and ships.

It should have ended there, that very moment. Cassidy should have shot Casey on the spot. She *could have*, too. She had the quicker draw. Yet when it came down to it, Cassidy wanted more. She knew death came for everybody eventually, but most never saw it coming. If death was quick enough, its victims would pass, none the wiser.

Cassidy wanted Casey Calhoun to know.

She held her shotgun at her side and approached.

***

Luke and Kootala had ridden far northeast, and had almost converged with the train. They rode as fast as their horses could manage.

The train approached quickly from behind.

Kootala led, racing fast along the edge of a ridge with the sand-covered tracks running below and to his right.

Far ahead, Kootala saw another escarpment that stood blocking their path.

The train caught up and began drifting past the men.

Dust spewed out from the under the train, and a deafening roar echoed all around them.

Kootala shouted over the train. "Luke! The tracks get closest to the ridge just up ahead. We have to jump onto the train from there. It's our one shot!"

Luke nodded, and they rode to the cliff, where the end of the train quickly approached.

Doubt filled Kootala's heart. Uncertainty. *Fear*. He couldn't do this. *They* couldn't do this.

"I don't know about this!" Luke shouted. He clearly felt the same way.

Fine, Kootala thought. *Put away the feelings.*

The air was filled with dust all around them, and Kootala took in a gasping breath, focused his emotions, and blew out. Cinnamon wafted. Apples. Wet wood.

His heart calmed. His fear shrunk away. Not totally, but enough.

Kootala turned to Luke, saw his face resolve.

"Now!" Kootala yelled.

They jumped from their mounts and onto the top of the moving train.

Kootala overestimated his leap and nearly stumbled off the other side.

He caught himself and managed to steady.

Luke grabbed Kootala by the arm and pulled him forward. "We need to get to the front and pull the brakes."

They ran across the top of the train as best they could without falling. Luke in the lead now, they climbed through cargo flats and scampered over coal cars. The wind blew, and Kootala held his hat down with one hand. Their shirts rippled in the wind like trembling ghosts. As they continued to the front of the train, the bluff grew higher into the sky.

Finally, the men came upon the front of the train. What they saw left them in shock for a moment. The three cars behind the engine had been emptied and refilled with crates of dynamite. Too many to count. *Enough*, Kootala thought, *to reduce Bluff's Reach to nothing but dust.*

"Oh, Lord." Luke groaned over the wind. "This could level the plateau halfway to Lonely."

"And it *will* if we don't act fast," Kootala said. "Go on."

Luke led the way over the crates. Kootala's heart pounded in sync with the locomotive engine. He knew that one spark could set the entire train off.

Kootala dropped into the cab of the engine, leaving Luke topside to watch the approaching bluff.

An automatic feeder was funneling coal into the furnace hatch. Embers spewed out, roaring like hell, and...

Kootala's stomach sank.

The brake lever had been removed.

"The brakes are out!" He yelled up to Luke. "Everything is tampered with. I can't do anything to slow us down."

"Detach the cars!" Luke yelled back. "The engine will crash, but the rest should slow to a stop!"

Kootala slipped out the side door and carefully pulled himself around the side of the engine and to the back platform. He looked down at the coupler.

It was welded solid.

The train lurched, following the tracks as they turned toward the river. Its wheels screeched, howling and they rubbed against the curved rails.

***

"So, I guess you know about your parents?" Casey said, turning to face Cassidy as she approached.

"I was a fool for not realizing sooner," she replied.

"And you came for revenge."

"Have I ever been for anything else?"

"I guess not," Casey said sadly. "But you could have been. There is so much opportunity in this world, and I gave you every path to achieve greatness. I'm a smart man, but you are one thing I misjudged.

You've only ever seen what was right in front of you. That's how your kind always is."

"And what do you see, Casey, besides the barrel of a gun?" Cassidy raised her shotgun.

A reflection glistened to her left, and a pipe swung around, hitting her squarely on her bad shoulder. She howled in pain, spun round from the blow, and pulled the trigger. The man that had hit her burst open at the chest and flew backward off his feet. Cassidy's gun recoiled free from her grasp and fell to the ground. She, in turn, fell on her butt.

"Like I said..." Casey smiled. "You only see what's in front of you. Like a horse with blinders."

Casey removed his revolver and ran his thumb up and down the handle. He spun the chamber, then licked the barrel and smiled with sick arousal. He strode to Cassidy, grabbed her by the dreadlocks, and forced her to look north. "Let's watch," he said.

***

No brakes. A welded coupler. Little time.

"Kongwuti, guide me," Kootala said quietly.

"What are you doing down there?" Luke shouted from above. His silhouette flickered against the passing earth, standing tall above the train.

He knows who he is, Kootala thought. *Who am I?*

A groan echoed through the train. It raced furiously forward, not waiting for anyone. Time was running out.

What makes a man? What makes a hero? Missy's voice.

Where does a man get his Grit? Kongwuti.

Strength.

Wrong...belief in yourself... power to alter the world...

What are you?

Man, woman, Dust, Grit. It is all the same when broken down to the most basic grains.

"Perception," Kootala said aloud.

He had manifested a hammer, back in Lonely. He *had* Grit. The only difference, Kootala now realized, was his perception. Dust and Grit—they were never gained through your grasp on the world. Every man had Grit, regardless of his strength. Regardless of his power. It was how that man saw *himself* that mattered.

What makes a hero?

A hero is sure of themselves, to do what they know is right, when all the world is against them. A hero has Grit.

Kootala focused on the roiling spray of dirt and sand being kicked up as the train plowed over the tracks. In the past, Kootala would have imagined the dust behaving in tender manners, as seemed *natural*. He would have done only as he *thought* was naturally possible. Now, he knew different. He *was* nature.

The flying sand coalesced in the air, forming a tight stone, hovering just out of Kootala's reach. The rock spun, collecting more mass, and though Kootala held it with only his focus, it became heavy.

Kootala let go.

The stone fell, slamming into the coupler below.

The weld cracked.

The train jolted, turning. Metal screeched.

And the weld snapped.

"I did it!" Kootala shouted, then scrambled back up to the top of the engine as it decoupled from its cars.

Luke pulled Kootala up.

The two men stood on the top of the locomotive with wind blowing through their hair. Luke's hat blew off his head, tumbling into the spray of dust. Kootala held his own hat on with one hand.

The bluff loomed above them to the left. The river lay ahead of them, running perpendicular to the train. Minutes, maybe less, and they would turn along the river, head north, and crash into the massive wall of stone.

Luke had been smiling, but now it dropped away to horror. His face paled. "We're too late," Luke said. "Those cars won't slow down in time."

Kootala watched as they pulled ahead of the rest of the train. Though the cars slowed, they were heavy, and wouldn't slow *enough*. This train was still going to crash into the bluff, and the engine, speeding up, was going to hit it first.

The river approached.

"What are we doing?" Kootala asked.

The entrance to the bluff mine came into view: a gaping hole of rock and timbers in the wall of the bluff. It was just large enough to swallow the height and width of a train car.

They were so close to the bluff now that Kootala could not see the homes of Bluff's Reach over its edge.

The minutes had ran out. They had seconds.

"Luke! What are we doing?" Kootala yelled.

Luke raised his gun and aimed high above the train cars with the dynamite. He emptied his entire cylinder.

The train continued, unbothered.

Luke ejected his drum and dumped out the spent casings. He dug his hand in his pocket, then pulled out only dirt.

He had used the rest of his ammo in Lonely.

"Give me your gun," Luke said.

Kootala handed his pistol over, and Luke emptied that one as well.

"Come on, give me your ammo!" Luke shouted.

Kootala panicked. He pulled the remaining bullets from his shirt pocket and held them out to Luke.

The locomotive bounced.

Kootala dropped the ammo. The bullets bounced off metal and rolled over the edge into the cloud of dust.

"I'm sorry!" Kootala howled over the wind. "Luke, that is all we had left!"

Now what?

They were seconds from turning along the river. Seconds from the bluff.

"Jump?" Kootala asked.

Luke reached over and plucked the bullet from Kootala's hat band. He chambered the bullet and aimed.

Kootala hugged Luke from behind. He drew up a wave of Dust, let it envelop them, and steadied Luke's trembling hands.

Luke fired.

And Abner Brooks' final bullet ripped across the desert.

***

"I should have killed you instead of your mother." Casey whispered into Cassidy's ear.

"You're a coward," Cassidy said. "Hurting women while they're down. It's... weak."

"*WEAK!*" Casey shouted, shoving away.

Cassidy fell again to the hard dock planks.

"I am anything but weak!" Casey's eyes were crazed. His hair fell, unkempt, wild. "Is *this* weakness?"

Casey howled, arms stretched out to his sides. Bits of dirt and sand began climbing up from between dock planks, tumbling out of nearby barrels, rising in bubbles from below the water's surface.

Cassidy had thought the pier would be safe from Casey's Grit. She had been mistaken.

The flow of sand covered Cassidy up to the shoulders, encasing her, only her head exposed. Even her dreadlocks had been snared by the sand, pulling painfully at her scalp. Her shoulder exploded in pain, and she cried out.

"Weak!" Casey's mouth splattered spit. He had gone rabid. He began to ramble, some nonsense about business, capitalism, nature.

All bullshit, Cassidy thought.

"You've no power," Cassidy interrupted. She spoke as a matter of fact.

"What?"

Cassidy smiled. She had never been a liar, she was brutally honest, and so Casey always believed her every word. Hopefully she could deceive him now, as he had done to her all along. "Your power," she said. "It's gone. All your assets. Your stocks. Your bonds. Every slip of paper that gives you power, control over this city, is stuffed inside that mine."

"You—" Casey looked to the north. "No, you couldn't have. When would you have found the time…" He trailed off.

"Your shares in the East-West Excavation and Rail Company, sold off. The industry in Graben, consolidated *away* from shareholders in Bluff's Reach. The people evacuated. When that town sinks into the earth, the only thing going with it is *your* power."

Casey laughed, though it was not convincing.

Would he believe it? Would this work?

Cassidy laughed back, and *she* was genuine. "Casey, you lose. Your strength in the west is gone. You are *weak*."

"No!" Casey shouted, then recoiled as if he had been slapped.

The cocoon of sand around Cassidy crumbled away and slipped through the cracks between dock panels. She fell forward, onto her knees. Her lie had worked! She hadn't destroyed any of Casey's wealth, but it did not matter. It was his perception of his self-worth that gave him strength. In that, he crumbled, too.

Casey bent forward, heaving, as if simply breathing was a terrible chore. He stood upright, growling. "You Black bitch! I *should* have kept your mother instead, after all. She was from a better time, back when you did as you were told." He raised his pistol at Cassidy's head. "Such a shame. Now I have a whole mess to clean up, and I have to go kill those fags myself. But first..." he laughed. "I'm going to enjoy killing one more ni—"

The earth shook with a mighty roar, and the air crashed through Casey's chest, cutting his words short. He looked to the north with pure ecstasy. In his brief moment of distraction, Cassidy grabbed her shotgun.

She fired.

Another explosion ripped through the air and blew Casey's arm off at the shoulder. He flew to his back, screaming, rolling, clutching at his shoulder with his other hand.

"Sit up!" Cassidy barked.

Casey quieted, then rose.

The two sat across from each other, both with ruined shoulders.

Except now Cassidy held all the power.

She leveled her shotgun at her former boss.

Casey laughed again, blood gurgling in his throat. "You wouldn't execute a helpless old man, would you?"

"I'm not a good person," Cassidy said. "But I always keep my promise, and I hold one hell of a grudge."

She shot again.

Casey's head exploded, mirroring the mushroom cloud growing behind him in the distance.

***

Kootala had hardly registered Luke's gun going off before the chasing train cars vaporized into a spray of molten steel. A wave of heat slammed against his skin.

The rails buckled, and the locomotive shook under their feet. It began to topple as they rounded the corner along the river.

Kootala clutched Luke even closer, pulling him tightly against himself. He sucked in a lung-bursting breath of hot dust.

Waasam, judge me.

Kootala focused his Grit, then leaped away from the train. Around them, he spun a protective shell, as the Spider Grandmother might have done. He only hoped it would be enough.

Hot channels seared Kootala's back as molten shrapnel sliced through his Grit.

They plunged into the river.

And Kootala held Luke tighter than ever before.

END OF PART TWO

Intermission

Charlie Rose walked carefully among the wreckage, being mindful to avoid sharp juts of shredded metal. A large portion of Graben's population was out there, too, stumbling among the remains of the train. They would almost certainly be searching for valuables to scavenge. Charlie, however, was just curious. He recognized his lumber, of course. That, he would never admit. The wreck was still fresh, the details of how and why it happened were only speculation, but he knew he had some hand in it.

Fortunately, he had already been paid.

And thank God nobody had been hurt. Right?

Charlie looked down the rails to the east, where a mile of cars had tipped onto their side, spilling coal into the desert. The closest of those piles was still smoking.

The locomotive was nowhere to be found. Presumably, it had exploded, taking out the front several cars with it. Amazing that it had happened just before crashing into the bluff.

Where did those tracks lead, anyway?

A man was digging, elbow deep, in a pile of rubble. From it he pulled out a busted revolver. He noticed Charlie watching, held the gun up, said, "You believe this mess?"

"It's astounding," Charlie said, going to the man.

The man extended a hand.

Charlie took it and helped the man to his feet.

"Thank you," the man said, smiling.

Good Lord, he was handsome. Charlie's heart skipped.

"I, uh, was going to see where this track led," Charlie said, flustered. "Join me?"

The man considered this for a moment, then clapped his hand on Charlie's back. "Sure thing, bud."

They walked along the old, sand-covered tracks, exchanging pleasantries. The man, Calvin, was a ship-hand, and told stories of his adventures along the Colorado, hauling lumber and steel back and forth from California. Charlie told Calvin of his lumber mill. All the while, Charlie kept one eye on Calvin's jeans. They fit him well, that was for sure.

Eventually, they came upon an opening in the wall. The entrance to an old mine.

"Did you know this was here?" Calvin asked.

"Surely not!" Charlie laughed. "I think you'd have a hard time finding anyone who did."

"Amazing," Calvin said, stepping through the opening's shadow. "Come on in."

In, in, his voice echoed.

"I'm not sure..." Charlie stood at the very edge of the shadow, trying to see into the chamber.

Calvin's hand came out, grabbed Charlie by the buttons of shirt, and pulled him in. The man towed Charlie to the side and pushed him up against a wall, leaning into him. Charlie's heart ponded furiously, and he could feel Calvin's doing the same.

"What say you?" Calvin asked. "Care to... explore?"

"Yes, please." Charlie begged, then grabbed Calvin back and pulled him further into the mine.

PART THREE

PEACE

30

A day had passed on the bluff, and most of the residents of Bluff's Reach had settled back into their homes. It would be some time before *daily life* returned to normal, but they were safe for now, all thanks to Kootala and Luke Morgan, and yes, even Cassidy Reeve.

They day previous, many people had scrambled to the edge of the bluff to get a good look at the wreckage below. Laying there in the sand, not more than a mile from the wall of the bluff, lay a charred scrap heap. There it would stay, for years, they thought. It was not worth cleaning up. Though perhaps they might find the remains of the heroes who had stopped it.

They assumed the worst for Sheriff Morgan. He had died a hero, they said. And for that, they could wait a few days before finding a new sheriff.

A few days, but not much more than that. They still feared another attack by Casey Calhoun and his gang.

***

Missy sat in the dirt at the edge of town, looking west as the sun sank lower in the sky. Katie Lybuck sat at her side, her leg extended in a ridged cast.

"Is there any good left out here?" Missy asked.

Katie remained silent. She hadn't spoken since coming back to town.

Missy cried. She cried because her best friend was gone, and because she was scared about the future. She wept with her head hung down in her lap.

Katie rested her head on Missy's shoulder. Wordless though she was, that gesture was enough.

A pair of boots walked in front of the women, and a voice spoke softly.

"Don't cry, cowgirl," Kootala said.

Missy jumped up and hugged Kootala, nearly tackling him to the ground. Kootala broke free, wincing. He was in serious pain, but not enough, apparently, to keep him down. Missy giggled happily. "We thought the worst! You're a day late!" She scolded.

"Yeah, well, we had other business to take care of along the way." Kootala gestured to his wagon.

Missy helped Katie stand up and handed her a crutch. They looked out at Kootala's wagon.

Howard and Buck were sitting in the wagon. Howard's hands were bound in his lap. Buck's legs were bound at the ankle and he was missing a hand. A sock was tied over his good hand so he couldn't untie his legs. Luke sat beside them, wrapped from hips to shoulders in medical cloth. He waved at them and smiled through obvious pain.

"Those men are in my custody," Kootala said. "We had to patch Luke up at the doctor in Graben. Though *I* got shrapnel in my back, *he* got serious burns on his face and chest. Poor guy. If I hadn't tackled him..." Kootala trailed off.

Missy hugged Kootala again, gently this time, then asked him, "What now?"

"Well, these men will get booked in my jail and stand trial for their crimes. All three of them."

"Luke?" Missy questioned.

"Yes, Luke too. He broke the law, and he is going to pay back everything he stole."

"Kootala, you ass!" Missy punched him on the arm. Katie giggled. "He has more than paid us back. He saved the whole town. He should be free and absolved of his past."

Kootala smiled knowingly. "Well, if that is what the town wants, I guess I'd have to go along with it."

"And what about you?" Katie asked.

"I keep going on. I've got a duty here, and I won't abandon my town. If Casey is gone, another will fill the space he left behind. I've got to protect us from that. And maybe I'll have some help, too." Kootala looked at Luke and smiled. "As soon as he's healed up."

"Well, I guess we won't keep you any longer, Sheriff Kootala," Missy said. "But maybe we can all get a drink at the saloon later?"

"Sure, that sounds nice," Kootala said.

***

A Black woman with a constellation of freckles under her eyes entered the post office in Marble Springs, Arizona. She grabbed a piece of paper and a pen and wrote a brief letter:

Dear Luke and Kootala,

Cassidy Reeve, for all intents and good will, is dead.

Casey Calhoun is dead as well. His body will find no mercy, just another piece of litter among the wolves and howling winds. His soul will be judged by whoever guards the gate to hell. His legacy, the truly final

piece left of a dead man, will blow away to nothing in the dusts of the
desert.

   For you both,
   Be well.

   —C

She put the letter in an envelope and addressed it to Luke Morgan, Bluff's Reach. She gave the letter to the teller and paid the postage.

   The woman left and rode west toward California. What she would find out there was unknown. She had lived life with a single purpose, and that was now fulfilled. Maybe, she hoped, she could find another.

***

Kootala booked Howard and Buck, and set them up in their cells. He told them that they would be treated well, and would have a fair trial. He gave them a hot meal, locked up the office, and went home. He figured that Howard would get off easily enough. He had really only been an accomplice to Casey's gang. Buck, on the other hand... Well, justice would see about him.

   At home, Kootala made up another hot meal of beef stew, Luke's favorite, and brought a steaming bowl of it to Luke in their bedroom. Luke sat up with difficulty and took the bowl of stew.

   "Kootala, can we try again?" Luke said between bites. "Can we start over?"

   Kootala sat on the bed next to him. "You deceived me and put me in danger. That is not something I will likely forget. But you did what you did out of love. That doesn't make it right, but it proves that you will never compromise your love for me. Maybe I can learn to do the same for you."

"Then let's do it all again, this time on honesty, understanding..."

"Forgiveness,"

"...and compassion."

"I think that would be perfect," Kootala said.

"We can do good by each other and by this town. Be stewards of this land, right?" Luke asked.

"Right."

Luke smiled mischievously. "Hey, Kootala, go open the top drawer of the dresser over there." He pointed with a nod of his head. "There's a little leather pouch under the shirts. Grab it for me."

Kootala gave him a curious look, then went to the dresser. He opened the drawer and found the pouch. It was small, roughly the size of his palm, and made of deep black cowhide leather. There was something hard and heavy inside.

"I hid that before we left. Open it," Luke said.

Kootala pulled the drawstring and turned it upside down. A jagged, shimmering green chunk of glassy mineral fell out into his palm.

"This is beautiful, Luke. What is it?" he asked.

"Lightning glass. I found it in the sand and saved it for you. Do you like it?"

"Yes. I like it very much," Kootala said, examining the beauty in its fractal reflections. He returned to the bed and sat with Luke.

They sat in silence for a while. Luke finished his stew and Kootala ran his fingers through Luke's hair.

They were good. They were at peace.

Luke had found his honesty. Kootala, his Grit. Together, they had re-found their love, and that was worth more to them than anything else in the world.

Out in the wicked and wild frontier, every day was a mystery and survival was undecided. And though Kootala couldn't know what came next for them, he knew two things were certain. That their love was true, and that one day they would go together before Waasam and see only jewels.

Acknowledgements

Luke and Kootala's story is one that has been dear to my heart for many years, and I am so proud to finally share it with my readers.

It started with two sentences: *What makes a man? What makes a hero?*

The rest I wrote by hand, in a notebook, at a desk in my little office—part of an old trailer house that had been *frankenstiened* on to our kitchen. I scribbled it out in a month. And it was shit. So I let it sit, wrote something else, and came back. Again and again, for years, until the story was good enough to share.

I want to thank those that took this book one step further, from *shareable* to *publishable*. To my critique partners and beta readers. My editor. To Jordan Lewerissa for the stunning cover art and design. To my supportive family. And to my husband Cody, for he is the sole reason I wanted to tell this story in the first place.

Also, thank you to my readers. All the Grit in the world wouldn't make this possible without you.

About the author

Drew Baker is a science fiction, fantasy, and horror author with a passion for pushing the boundaries of creative storytelling. Whether exploring bizarre and outlandish fantasy worlds, or mind-bendingly complicated science fiction, Drew vows to *always* deliver interesting stories.

Visit Drew's website for more books, free reads, and to join his email list for updates about future publications.

http://drewbakerauthor.com